Shadeland

Book One of The Ethereal Crossings

D.L. Miles

CONTENTS

ACKNOWLEDGMENTS

I'd like to thank my parents for always being supportive of my writing, and listening to me constantly talk about plots and characters. Special thanks to JoAnn, for encouraging me to put my writing into the world.

And an extra special thanks to all the readers that took a chance on my ebooks! I wouldn't be anywhere without you!

i

Prologue

"You'll regret this!" she screamed. "I swear I'll make you regret this bounty hunter!"

The bounty hunter smashed the door shut after shoving the blue-haired creature inside. The house creaked in protest and a vine fell down over his arm. He brushed it off with a gruff movement, wincing as he reopened a wound the witch had given him.

"You're trapped, witch," he shouted inside. "You won't be making any more deals now."

He had expected her to cry out again, to scream and thrash against the door but she didn't. She only laughed, "You think you can hold me here? You may be spell-marked, hunter, but I will learn every inch of this hole. There is nowhere anyone can hide from me!"

He spun on his heel, knowing how right she was. The stars sparkled overhead, not giving away how screwed up the world had become.

Ever since the freaks came out of hiding his business had been busier than ever. Though he liked to be busy with work, it was getting out of hand with all the vampires,

werewolves and every other…*Eidolon* he had never heard
of. The bounty hunter stretched his leg before jumping
into his car, feeling the sting of a new tattoo; it might be
sore now, but it had saved him from getting his ass kicked
by that witch again. Being spell-marked would only
protect him for so long from her power.

His eyes fell over the house, the boarded up windows
and the shingles falling off made it look haunted. *Well, now
it officially is*, he thought. It was broken down and the yard
was overrun with weeds, the only thing in the garden that
looked like they may bloom was the roses set along the
fence. He grunted, feeling an open slice on his back as he
leaned further into the leather seat. His hand moved to
turn the radio on, a voice buzzing into his ear.

"This so called 'revolution'," came a male's voice, "is
really over, isn't it Jill? I mean, what did they really want?
And how can we give it to them? If it means they'll leave
us alone, I'm all for it!"

"Joe," said his female companion, Jill, "these
creatures, these Eidolon's, are not monsters. This isn't
some 'revolution' in the traditional sense, they aren't here
to…to take over, they're just making their presence known
to us. What's wrong with that?"

"That sounds like sympathizer talk!" Joe laughed.
"But seriously, look what they've done to the world! New
York City has had record lootings, Toronto has reported
hundreds dead from the stadium fire…and right here in
town we've had a few fires and even some assaults! If you
ask me, they should have stayed in their little island in
Bermuda."

"The humans are the ones looting," Jill shouted.
"You are the ones attacking us, attacking each other! And
this isn't a 'revolution', it's…more of a coming out party.
We are citizens too, and it's time all you humans know
about it! I'm sick of hiding! We outnumber you, yet you
make all the decisions!"

"Jill…" Joe said, obviously taken aback by his coworkers outburst. The bounty hunter clicked the radio off, hearing enough.

"A coming out party, eh?" he pondered.

With a turn of the key, the car roared to a start, and he looked ahead at the darkened road, only hearing a residual banging from the witches door. The bounty hunter shook his head and brushed his hair back with one hand as he pulled away from the house, wondering when he would have to come back here. He had a feeling he would be coming back to Ellengale very soon.

Chapter 1

One year after the "revolution"…

"I'm so glad your dad is letting you come with me," he said, "we'll get to learn so much. You'll love it." Luke clapped his hands together in the passenger seat, clearly excited about the coming lecture. I rolled my eyes and kept driving, I had come this far, I wasn't about to snake my way out now. He patted my leg and said, "Liv, you'll see."

"Do you remember when we were eight," I started, "and you told me your biggest secret ever?"

"Yes…" He had no idea where I was going with this.

"And do you remember how I didn't care? I still don't care. I will never care." It was Luke's turn to roll his eyes at me. When would he learn that I was just too indifferent to what had happened in the past year?

"Turn left up here," he instructed with a smile. He was starting to act like a child. Wait, no, he wasn't just starting; he had always acted like a child.

I pulled into the Ellengale Community College

4

student parking lot and waited behind two other cars to get past the guard. Luke flashed a parking permit at a lanky man, he didn't even look old enough to be called a man in fact. His name tag read "Johnson" and he nodded us through, his finger slamming down on a button to allow us passage.

Stopping in the first spot I found we stepped out of the car.

"Did you have to park so far away?" Luke questioned as he shut the door. He gestured to the guard's tiny hut twenty feet from where we had parked and the furthest point from the B Hall entrance. I shrugged.

"Easier this way."

Soon, Luke and I glided through the glass doors of B Hall. The entrance was nearly empty and I glanced at a large printed clock hanging on the beige wall. 5:05 PM; we were late. My eyes shifted toward Luke in time to see him give me a dirty look, most likely thinking about how far away I had parked. Without a word I nodded my head towards two women seated in front of a set of large wooden doors. Obviously the school went all out on making this place feel non-threatening. I felt conflicted as to whether or not it was working.

I walked up to the women and took a brief moment to consider where we were, after all this time. Hands in my sweater pockets, I stared down at the blonde woman. She seemed normal enough; humming a small tune beneath her breath while she scribbled something down on paper. Brown roots showed through under the bleached strands with eyebrows matching neither of the colours on her head. Her nametag read "Heather".

Luke cleared his throat beside me, drawing everyone's attention. The blonde woman and her petite partner smiled at him, their thoughts written cleanly on their faces. Luke was a reasonably attractive man; sandy brown hair, big blue eyes with a lean figure. I was often told by others that he was every girls dream. I didn't see it; he was just Luke to me, the boy that I had grown up with. Lucky me. At least according to the girls at school that never talked to me unless Luke was picking me up.

"What can I help you with?" the blonde asked, completely ignoring me. She set her pen down and folded her hands in front of her, focusing all of her attention on Luke. This much, I was used to.

"We're here for Dr. Wineman's lecture," Luke replied, "we're uh, we're a little late." He gave a small, innocent shrug.

"Names?" She lifted her pen and flipped through some papers.

"Lucan Harroway," he said. When the woman gave me an observant look he added, "Plus one." He held up one finger before quickly putting it back in his pocket. The receptionist looked down her list and checked off the name. Next to her, the small one handed Luke two stickers saying "Hi, my name is" and a blank space.

"Write your names and stick it to your chest," she instructed, "humans on the left, everyone else on the right." She patted her own nametag, sitting over her heart.

"Oh, um, all right," Luke said nervously as he picked up a pen. Elegantly, he wrote his name in cursive and peeled the back off. He was about to stick it over his heart but quickly rethought and patted it down on the right side of his chest. I tried not to give him a pitying look; poor Luke had never wanted to broadcast the fact that he wasn't human, even after the "revolution" last year. Without looking me in the eye he handed the second sticker to me with a pen.

Unlike my friend, I didn't have to think about what to write, or where to place the sticker. I quickly wrote "+1" in the empty space and stuck it over my heart. Nobody seemed to notice what I had written though. I felt more amused than insulted by their lack of observation.

"Walk on in," Heather said, that same secretive smile on her lips, "the doctor is just getting started." I held my

6

arm out to gesture for Luke to go first. He followed my order and carefully touched the door handle. Pushing the entry open, he peeked his head in first before stepping inside. I followed behind him, not nearly as nervous as he was, but then again, I had no reason to be.

"Welcome to New History!" The man at the front of the lecture hall looked at us with open arms. I glanced around at the rows of chairs, the five dozen other people were looking at us too. "Please, take a seat. I was just getting the introduction finished."

"Sorry," Luke said, holding his hands up.

"Not to worry," the man said, "everyone is wel—" he stopped talking when he saw me. Or saw my badge to be more accurate. His already bright eyes lit up even more. "A human!" I gave a small, panicked look towards Luke, who was already at the first step up the chairs. The number one reason I didn't want to come was about to happen. Humans almost never showed up to these things, so they stood out when they did; and not everyone was so welcoming either.

"Uh, she's not—" Luke tried to stop him, but the kind Dr. Wineman was already in front of me with three long strides.

"We never get human's here," he exclaimed and wrapped me in a warm hug. I couldn't help but notice he smelled like a mix of vanilla and cinnamon as my face pressed into his chest. My arms stayed at my sides as my fingers grew tense, not knowing what to do. "I knew the human's would come around, it was only a matter of time."

His head rested on mine and he sighed happily. With one free eye, I surveyed the room; nobody else had the nametags over their heart, which meant I was the only human. Great.

The doctor continued, "Now tell me, darling, what made you decide to come and learn about New History? And so young! How old are you?"

"Seventeen," I said quietly, hoping he would be the only one to hear me. I was often told how mature I looked, at least compared to others my age. Luke was the opposite; always being mistaken for younger when in reality he had just turned twenty.

He pushed me back and held onto my shoulders as I blinked at him. My pause didn't seem to bother him though, a large smile still plastered on his face when he released me from his grip. He kept his hands firmly on my shoulders, not letting go until I answered why I was there, so instead of saying the reason I merely pointed at Luke. If I was going to suffer through this, so was he.

As my one, plain finger rose, Luke flinched at the stairs. I hated to be singled out in a crowd but Luke hated it just a little bit more than me.

"I just thought it would be good for her to learn," he explained, "with everything that has happened." The doctor took a quick look at Luke's nametag and gave a knowing nod before patting me once on the back. I wondered if he knew Luke had lied; we were here for his benefit, not mine.

"Well, take a seat," he said, "you'll be learning a lot." Luke let out a small sigh of relief as I walked over to him. I resisted the urge to wipe away at my arms, feeling as if the doctor was still hugging me. It felt strange to hug someone I didn't know, or to even shake hands with them. Luke said that made me weird.

We found the last two seats together at the very back of the room, allowing us to easily see over everyone else. The seats rested on the end of the row, so I only had to sit next to Luke and the aisle. Thank God for tiny favours.

"Thank you all for coming," Dr. Wineman said, "and welcome to New History. Here you will learn all about what the humans never knew about the past. You will find out what started the revolution and what ended it a year ago. You will learn who and what the players really were and maybe learn a little bit about yourself. Your true self."

"Sounds like a lot of information for one class," I mumbled to Luke without taking my gaze off the speaker. I saw he began to play with his hands from the corner of my eye.

"Did I say one class?" He laughed cautiously. "Because it's actually a six week course. Guess I forgot to mention that?"

"Hmm," was all I managed to say.

"I'm sure you all know what happened last year," the doctor said, he seemed to enjoy talking with his hands, "the revolution started for those of us with... for those of us who aren't human. And within a week, it had ended."

But what a week it had been. My hometown didn't have much happen, a few fires and looters, but the rest of the world lost their minds on a whole new scale. What did the non-humans expect though, coming out all of a sudden like that? One day demons, vampires and the occult were just stories; the next, they were real. They went from haunting children's nightmares to haunting everyone and the humans didn't really like that. I was lucky, I already knew because of Luke.

Luke had told me when I was eight years old that he wasn't exactly normal. He wasn't a demon either, but not fully human. At eight I was amazed; he told me that everything from my nightmares and my dreams were real, that about half of the people I saw everyday weren't what they appeared. He thought I would hate him though, call him a monster and run away. I didn't, I swore to keep his secret and I did just that. I smiled to myself, remembering how Luke's parents reacted when they found out I knew. What seemed to annoy them the most was that he only told me because I swore not to tell; that that was all it took for him to confess it to me.

When the humans discovered who their neighbours were, who their friends were, they sort of freaked out. Very few of them accepted it, most feel that the Eidolon, those that aren't human, should be tagged, like animals;

they're still petitioning to have it done. I try to ignore what people say about Eidolon's, I try to stay out of the battle altogether. It annoyed me how they felt my closest friend should be treated, but I wasn't welcome to fight on the side of Eidolon's, since I was a human.

Luke elbowed me in the ribs to draw my attention back to the doctor. I hadn't noticed I had begun staring at the ceiling, lost in thought.

"Now how many of you," Dr. Wineman said, "know exactly where you come from." People glanced around the room as a few raised their hands in the air. I counted about fifteen. "And how many of you have absolutely no clue as to what you are; you just woke up and started having abilities." Almost everyone else in the room raised their hands, most being very careful not to be the first. Most Eidolon's that didn't know who they were and were still nervous to identify themselves in public. There are a lot of humans out there that are ready to kill if necessary. Actually, there are a lot of humans out there ready to kill if not necessary. I noticed Luke never raised his hand; which made sense; he didn't fit into either category.

"Don't be ashamed," the doctor said, "it's perfectly normal. After all, Cleopatra may have had no idea of her true nature." The crowd began to murmur amongst themselves at the mention of the Egyptian queen. I had to admit, my interest was piqued.

"Yes that's right," Dr. Wineman smiled, his lesson going as planned, "Cleopatra was not human. Can anyone guess what she was?" Nobody said a word and I spotted a few shrugs across the room.

"Succubus," I mumbled under my breath, quiet enough so that even Luke couldn't hear.

"What was that?" Dr. Wineman was watching me now and he pointed to me, excited. Damn, how did he hear? Whatever he was, it gave him good hearing. "Ms...plus one," he said after looking at my nametag, "cute. So, what did you say?" I saw Luke cover his eyes in embarrassment over what I had written. Made us even, he tricked me into a six week course, I embarrassed him.

Everyone was looking at me now, some with curiosity as to how I knew the answer and some with annoyance that a human knew more than them. It's not like I actually knew though, I had just guessed.

"Succubus," I said again, barely any louder than before. I kept my eyes down, not wanting to make eye contact with anyone in the room. It was a little strange that I was right, I supposed.

"Please, louder so everyone can hear," the doctor's smile grew wider. Was he enjoying my discomfort or the fact that a human was right about something for once? I guessed it was the latter. I didn't like talking loudly, or even talking much at all so I looked to Luke and he knew what to do.

"Succubus," he said loudly, "Cleopatra was a succubus." The fact that Luke answered for me seemed to throw the doctor, whose endless smile finally faltered.

"Uh, correct," he beamed, "Cleopatra was indeed a succubus. Ms... plus one, would you mind telling us how you knew and perhaps your real name?" He chuckled to himself, amused.

"Just guessed," I said, "it seemed obvious." Luke repeated my answer but never said what my name was, probably because I didn't tell him to.

"You just guessed?" Dr. Wineman seemed surprised, enough so that he forgot to ask for my name. I nodded at him, confirming the truth. "Well, an excellent guess it was! But how did you arrive at the answer? There are a lot of creatures out there to choose from, why succubus? Most people don't even know what a succubus is. And to know at your age..." Why did the doctor want me to explain so much? I inhaled deeply through my nose.

"Cleopatra was known for her beauty and seducing men at a young age," I explained, not trying to be heard, "she was also ruthless when it came to killing and backstabbing. Seemed obvious." Luke didn't repeat anything this time and the doctor seemed happy with the answer. Then again, he seemed happy all the time; it seemed out of place with his greying hair and distinguished reputation.

"Very good!" he clapped his hands and began to wander around the room again. "Cleopatra is only one of many famous, or infamous I should say, people in history that were not actually human. How about you all shout out some names and I'll tell you if they were human or not." He stuck both hands towards the crowd and flicked his fingers towards himself. For a moment everyone was silent but it quickly changed.

The crowd began shouting names, most of them celebrities; the doctor ignored them.

"Nixon!" One man yelled from the center row and Dr. Wineman pointed at him, a large grin on his face.

"Excellent choice young man," he said to quiet the others down, "Nixon was in fact human." Some people laughed, while others were surprised.

"Hitler!" Another man said from the other side of the room. Not an imaginative bunch here, they were just going for the obvious. The doctor laughed, most likely thinking what I was. It made me wonder how many times he had to go through the same people in this class.

"Adolph Hitler was human," he said and some people groaned, "but he did know of demons. He summoned one and sold his soul. Can anyone guess what for?"

"Power?" the same man who suggested Hitler said. Dr. Wineman shook his head. Other people began suggesting money, world domination, an army. No imagination what so ever.

"Probably charisma," I breathed quietly, not thinking the doctor would hear me again. I thought wrong.

"Correct!" He shouted and pointed once more at me. Suddenly all eyes were on me again. I shrunk a little in my seat, making a mental note not to say anything else.

"Hitler had summoned a demon and sold his soul for charisma. Another guess?" I gave a weak smile and shrugged. He eyed me a moment before moving on. "Two more and then we'll continue!"

"Elvis!" The woman in the front row said.

"Yes!" Dr. Wineman said, "Elvis was in fact not human. He was a Satyr. Some of you may be thinking that doesn't make sense, but it does." He tilted his head, thoughtful. "Satyr's are most known for being half man, half goat. I'm sure most you of are aware that Elvis was not this. Over time the Satyr's evolved, shedding their half goat appearance and Elvis was the one Satyr in a million that didn't party like his kind or lust after women. One more and then we move on!" I was a little surprised the doctor didn't elaborate on what had happened after Elvis died.

I began to contemplate over Elvis the Satyr. Satyrs were immortal beings weren't they? So then he really didn't die, he was still alive, somewhere; which would explain all the supposed sightings of him, or at least most of them. Crazy would have explained them better pre-revolution. My eyes began to drift upwards again as I became lost in thought, thinking about immortality. Luke gave me another elbow to the ribs to pay attention.

"Amelia Earhart," said the girl in front of me. She didn't shout like the others, in fact, she was rather quiet. That didn't stop Dr. Wineman from hearing her though.

"Ah, Ms. Earhart," he said, "she is a mystery, even to us." By "us" he must have meant Eidolon's. I found it interesting that even they didn't know what had happened to her. Unless they did know, and they just didn't want anyone else to figure it out. I wasn't going to be surprised if it turned out she wasn't human, or her disappearance had anything to do with Eidolon's.

"Let's continue on then," the doctor said as he walked over to the projector. He began to fumble with it, confused as to how it worked; like all teachers were. Next to me Luke pulled out a small note pad, ready to take down anything he thought should be remembered. Apparently the fact that Cleopatra and Elvis weren't human was not note-worthy to him.

"Do you have a pen?" he asked me, not as prepared as I had given him credit for. I reached into my handbag and handed him a purple gel pen. He grimaced and I gave a small smirk to myself, still watching Dr. Wineman work on the projector. "Thanks."

I had a feeling this was going to be a long three hours and an even longer six weeks.

Chapter 2

Time was relevant, I told myself. Just because it ticked slowly by for me, didn't mean it was the same for Luke, who at the moment was furiously writing down everything Dr. Wineman said. This was what every day in class felt like to me. I glanced at the large white clock above the emergency exit that matched the one in the hall entrance. 7:55 PM.

"And that concludes New History to the year sixteen-hundred," the doctor said, "I look forward to seeing you all this Friday." The crowd began to shuffle but I stayed still until Luke nudged me to get up. I stood and walked to the back to the aisle stairs, letting people walk down before me. Luke leaned on the wall behind us and we watched as the Eidolon's trailed down towards the exit.

"This Friday, huh," I prodded Luke. He knew what I was thinking.

"I forgot to mention," he said disarmingly, "it's twice a week. Isn't that great? It won't interfere with your exams though, I swear." Great; that's one word for it. Why would he think I even cared about my exams? I looked at him from the corner of my eye. "I know you don't want to be here, but it's important to me. I need to know this stuff Liv, and I want to share it with you." I looked back to the flood of people, almost all of them were already out the door and gone.

"Whatever," I sighed as I took a step down. Luke perked up.

"Thank you," he said. Anyone else would have been insulted by my reaction, but he knew me too well. He knew exactly what I meant by "whatever". I would suffer through the next classes for him; he had done enough suffering for me after all.

The doctor had begun to fiddle with the projector again as everyone left. The second my foot hit the last step he looked up at me and then to Luke.

"Wait a moment, please," he said, and I looked back to Luke, who had only shrugged, "I just want to ask you something." He straightened his back and took a step towards us, only to pull the projector down off its pedestal. Dr. Wineman caught it before it hit the floor with an unusual speed and grace and carefully placed it back. His coat stuck out on the left, caught on something on the projector. He unhooked it and took a careful step forward, watching the projector to make sure it wasn't going to fall again. If I was about his age I would find him adorable, but right now I found it a little sad.

"Yes, doctor?" Luke asked, more curious about why the doctor had stopped us than I was.

"I just wanted to ask your friend a question," he said looking at me, "Liv, did you really just guess at those answers?" My first thought was "how did he know my name?" until I remembered he had advanced hearing and Luke had said my name at the top of the stairs.

I shrugged and said, "It just seemed obvious." Dr. Wineman gently touched his chin, considering my answer.

"You keep saying that." He reached his hand out to me and I stared at it. Luke swatted my hand upwards, forcing it closer to the doctors and we shook hands. "You're a bright young girl, very little humans would be able to guess those answers. I look forward to seeing you Friday." He smiled at me, but it felt different, like he was too busy thinking of something else to make it genuine.

"We look forward to it too," Luke said with a grin. "Let's go Liv, or we'll miss our show!" He led me out the door and waved goodbye to the doctor. We were the last ones to leave the B Hall, and as the wooden doors shut behind us I felt as if Dr. Wineman had never stopped watching me.

Was it really so odd for me to guess those answers? Besides, it's not like I knew what Elvis was, or even Amelia Earhart; I only knew Cleopatra and Hitler, both of which I had guessed on instinct. I merely put two and two together, was it so odd?

"Weird," I whispered to myself as Luke opened the glass door for me.

"Oh, I'm weird, am I?" he questioned while we walked. "You write plus one as your name, answer questions you shouldn't know the answer to, but I'm weird for opening the door for you." I looked down at the nametag over my heart and ripped it off, throwing it in the first trash bin I found. I held a hand out to Luke but he just said, "What?"

"I was going to throw out your nametag…" I explained, as if it really needed to do that.

"No way," he refused, "I'm keeping this; it's going to be going in my post-revolution scrapbook to commemorate our first class." He smiled proudly and patted his chest. Luke was the only man I knew that would be proud of having a scrapbook.

"Hmm," I said and we continued walking to the car.

The parking lot was almost completely empty by the time we had returned. It seemed that no one had wasted any time getting home. What was so important on a Tuesday night? I looked up at the sky and counted what few stars were there; seven dim lights shone down through the clouds.

A soft breeze chilled me through my sweater and I noticed it did the same to Luke. It was strangely cold at night for late June and I hoped it would get warmer soon. But then again, the smell of summer always reminded me of fire after the revolution.

I unlocked the car from a few feet away and Luke quickened his pace to get ahead of me. He opened my door, as he always did; ever the gentleman. I rolled my eyes and got in, turning on the heater while he ran around the front and jumped into the passenger seat.

Checking the rear view mirror I caught a glimpse of my eyes. Normally my hazel eyes looked weary and tired from either not enough sleep or too much, but tonight they didn't look so bad. Not great, but not bad. I adjusted the mirror properly and pulled out of the parking lot, ready for the half hour drive home.

Sitting down on the couch next to Luke seemed a larger relief than it should've been. It was nine o'clock at night and I was going to have to prepare myself for the coming weeks of New History, and in two days, an exam. Or should I say, prepare myself for the coming lessons with Dr. Wineman. He had seemed nice enough, but I didn't like how much attention he had given me.

"It's cool that your dad is letting you stay here," Luke said, flipping on the television and starting his routine of changing channels between the news and what he had deemed "our show". I didn't like watching either, but I wasn't about to burst his bubble when he finally settled on the news for a moment.

"Earlier today a woman was found dead in her apartment," said the overly cheerful reporter, "it is still unknown as to how she died but police say it does appear to involve some sort of non-human." Luke changed the channel with "tch" noise, angry that the blame was on an

Eidolon already.

"It really could have been one," I told him, "you changed the channel too soon to know anything else." I understood his pain over the subject, but like the humans, he also tended to assume too much as well. It made sense, Luke's parents knew what he was but they were human, so he was raised like a human. He rolled his eyes at me and changed the channel back to the news.

"Rosa Navarro was last seen leaving work at The Corner to get to her car." A reporter's high pitched voice was heard while they showed a screen-shot of a small dark-skinned woman with blue eyes. She was pretty. The screen flashed back to the same reporter from before. "We have just received this video tape," she said, holding a finger to her ear, "of a man throwing Rosa into her car."

A dark parking lot came onto the screen as Luke and I watched. I saw Rosa walk onto the screen, barely visible with whatever kind of security camera was viewing her. She reached into her small clutch and pulled out what I assumed to be a set of keys. Her fingers flipped through them, one by one, trying to find the one for her car.

The reporter whispered something, almost sounding like a gasp, just before a hooded person stepped into view. They hit Rosa over the head with some sort of long, blunt object and carefully carried her further from the camera. Just as they were about to go out of view, the person looked up at the security camera and the tape buzzed out in a flash of black and white. The cheery eyed reporter came back on screen, less cheery now, and told the world to call the police tip line with any possible information on the man they had now identified as John Walker.

"That's stupid," I said.

"What?" Luke asked. "Because it's so obviously human?"

"Hmm, partly. But I was talking about how they think it's a man and an Eidolon." Luke turned to me as he changed back to "our" show.

"What do you mean?"

"Nothing," I said, it was going to be too tiresome to explain, and I didn't want to make Luke go on one of his humans-blame-Eidolon's-for-everything-now   rants. "Night."

"Come on!" he called to me as I stepped over his legs and headed to the bathroom. "Keeping secrets isn't nice!" I couldn't help but smile at that. Just as I was about to close the door to the bathroom, there was a knock on the apartments front door.

"Liv it's me," came Charlie's voice, "Luke told me you're staying over and I need your help!" I sighed and rested my head a moment on my door. So close, yet so, so far. Slowly, I made my way to the front door, Luke ignoring both me and Charlie to watch his show. She called again, "Liv!"

"I'm here," I said, opening the door to find Charlie in nothing but a towel holding up two shirts. She really wasn't the shy type, that much I knew; the rest of her however, was a total mystery. "What is it?"

"I'm going out tonight with some friends," she explained, "and I don't know what to wear!" She thrust the two shirts forward, if they could even be called shirts. I didn't take them from her and merely pointed at the pink one.

"That one," I said, "goodnight." I tried to shut the door, but Charlie stopped me and swung it back open.

"Wait," she said, "you should come out with us! We're all going to The Corner, it'll be fun." She shuffled in her towel to show me, I assumed, how much fun dancing would be. Why would she want to go to the club when another woman had just been kidnapped from and then murdered in her home? Maybe because they knew who her assailant was? I didn't react so Luke did it for me.

"She'd love to," he said with a pat on my shoulder and then whispered in my ear, "go out, have fun." He shoved me out the door before I had a chance to flee.

"Great!" Charlie said, brown hair bouncing on her bare shoulders. "Let's go do your hair!" She grabbed my wrist and pulled me into her apartment next to mine. I groaned and knew there was no escape for me.

I guessed I was going dancing tonight.

Chapter 3

Charlie and her friends walked two feet ahead of me as we entered the club; partly because her friends didn't like me much and partly because I felt like a fool dressed the way I was. Although it probably helped me get into the club faster, allowing me to blend in with those that were legally allowed inside. Dressed in the tightest possible jeans anyone could imagine with a crimson halter top I was completely exposed, the only positive thought I had was that I liked the French braid Charlie had given me. I missed my sweater, my nice, loose, covers everything sweater. Luke was going to die when I got home.

Not only was I tired, I was about to go deaf too from the volume of the music. The bass and drums vibrated through my chest as we got closer to the dance floor. Looking around, I could already see the men eyeing up Charlie and her gang of harpies. The second they reached the glowing dance pad, they were approached by a few guys. I, on the other hand, headed straight for the bar, hopeful that I wouldn't see anyone from school.

The bar was off to the side, with a basic rectangular

shape to it. There were less people than usual there, maybe because of the murder. When I spotted a vacant stool near the bathroom doors I dashed for it, just barely beating a blonde woman as she headed to refresh her drink. As I sat down I noticed she looked familiar, but quickly looked away from her as she sent me a glower. The harpies had deemed me the designated driver the second they saw me, probably as a sort of payback for existing, though I didn't care; I didn't drink, even if I was old enough. I would be relatively happy if nobody talked to me tonight.

I had considered leaving them here, just taking Charlie's car and heading back home. But then I remembered about Rosa Navarro. Kidnapped here, taken to her own apartment and killed in some way unknown to the police. I glanced around the room; how could nobody care? Murderers didn't usually kill one person and move on with their life, did they? Well, unless it was personal.

"Getcha anythin'?" the bartender asked me. She smiled at me with unusually white teeth but I thought she seemed nice as she leaned on the counter towards me.

"Bottled water?" I asked, not really sure if clubs served such a thing. She nodded and pulled one from under the counter. When she passed it to me she asked for $3.50.

I reached into my pocket to pull out some change when a five slapped down next to me. I felt a large hand on my right shoulder and turned my head to look at it. The fingernails were clean cut and smooth, like out of a magazine.

"I got this," a man said as he pulled me closer to his chest, "can't have a pretty girl like her paying for her own drinks." He had some sort of southern accent and a strangely off-putting voice. I couldn't smell any liquor on his breath and the bartender just took the money and left. Turning I found Luke smiling at me. "You should see the look on your face right now," he said in his fake voice.

23

"I hate you," was all I could manage to say. Normally I wouldn't say something like that to him, but I was tired and irritated. He took the seat next to mine and opened the water for a drink. "That's mine."

"Hey, I paid for it," he smirked at me and I stole the bottle from him just before it touched his lips. "Your hair looks nice."

"What are you doing here?"

"You didn't actually think I would leave you here alone did you?" He took the water back from me and took a drink.

"Maybe," I said, thinking he would have. He was always trying to get me out of the apartment, meeting new people. "What now?"

I could've been happily sleeping right now, but instead I was stuck at some club, watching people dance and molest each other. Not exactly my idea of a good time. I was amazed more people didn't get kidnapped and killed at places like this. Maybe they did though, and the cops just never put two and two together.

"We could dance," he suggested with a shrug. His eyes drifted out over the dance floor and stopped when they found Charlie. Luke sighed.

"Just dance with her," I said. Luke had had a crush on Charlie ever since he had moved into the apartment next to hers. When he had first arrived she had shown a very clear interest in him, but he would never make a move and she quickly moved on.

"She's human," he said, "I can't."

"Sure," I replied, not bothering to go into the same conversation again and again. We sat in silence and watched the people in the room; or at least I watched the other people, Luke watched Charlie.

After two hours of dancing and drinking, Charlie and her band of harpies decided it was time to head home. Two of them decided it wasn't their home they wanted though and left with men they had just met. The others stumbled through the crowd with the help of Luke and me. Making it out into the cool night air seemed like a blessing in comparison to the sweltering heat of the club. That place had so many people in it; it had to be a fire hazard.

"I parked behind you guys," Luke said, trying to keep one of the harpies from falling over, "are they staying with you for the night Charlie?"

"No," she slurred, her friends arm around her neck, "Alysha is, but Alice is going back to her boyfriends." Luke nodded and we made it to the cars. I helped Charlie get Alysha into her car when Luke made a suggestion.

"Where does Alice's boyfriend live?" he asked. "I can drop her off and you guys can just head home; it'll be faster."

"Are you sure?" I asked, wondering if Alice's boyfriend was the jealous type. I couldn't imagine any man being too pleased to find his girlfriend being brought home by a stranger, especially one that's a man.

"Yeah, it's fine," he said and I opened the passenger door of his car. He set Alice inside and Charlie told him the address. We quickly said our goodbyes and went our separate ways.

I helped Charlie get her friend into her apartment, laying her down on the couch. Charlie's apartment was like a mirror version of Luke's, like all the others in the building. Whenever I visited her I would pretend I was stepping into a parallel universe, like this was the soon-to-be apartment of a different Liv. Maybe that Liv liked to go out and dance and drink.

"Thanks," Charlie said as I made a quick escape to the door, "we're going out next Friday, wanna come?"

"Sorry, can't," I didn't even have to lie this time, "got a thing with Luke."

"Okay, if you change your mind you're always welcome!" She smiled, truly meaning it. I wished more people in the world could be like her; I wished *I* could be more like her. Charlie was happy just because the sun rose every day. She trusted people easily and nothing could get her down.

"Kay, 'night," I said. Right, like I would ever be welcome into her group. Charlie was nice; she was a genuine person, her friends? Not so much.

As I stepped out into the yellowed hallway I saw Luke was just coming around the corner. The incandescent lighting made the bags under his eyes appear much larger than they probably were and I was afraid to ask how I looked. Although, I didn't really care.

We walked into our apartment and went to our rooms. When I finally managed to lie down in bed, the clock read 1:19 AM. I sighed and closed my eyes, forgetting to even change into different clothes or take my hair down.

Chapter 4

I awoke only a few hours later to a pounding on the front door. Stumbling through the hallway, I noticed that Luke's door was just opening; he came out weary eyed and confused.

"What's going on?" he asked me, as if I would really know. I ignored his question and continued to the door. When I opened it I was greeted by two policemen, neither of them looking too happy. Luke came up next to me, hand leaning on the open passage.

"Lucan Harroway?" the taller cop asked, hands at his sides, with elbows slightly bent. I found it curious, even at such a time, that they were not in his pockets, or on his hips.

"Yes?" Luke said, panic starting to show in his voice. "Is something wrong?"

"You're under arrest for the suspected murder of Alice Harper, Alex Stafoff and Rosa Navarro." The officer grabbed Luke by the wrist and pulled him into the hallway, shoving him against the wall. He grabbed the handcuffs from his waist and strapped them to Luke's wrists.

"What?" Luke shouted. "What are you talking about? Murder?" The tall cop began walking him down the hall, leaving me with his partner, dumbfounded. I tried taking a few steps out of my doorway, hand reaching for Luke but was stopped.

"I need to ask you a few questions," the policeman said, "it shouldn't take too long. Can I come in?" He gestured towards the living room, completely accustomed to the situation. I was not as used to it as he was.

"No," I said, "what are your questions?" He gave me a long look, not pleased that I wasn't letting him inside. I disregarded the way his lips pursed under his mustache, watching the hallway as Luke was taken away.

"All right miss," he said, "what's your name?" I looked down at his badge and saw his name was Harley. His eyes seemed to run down my outfit, probably seeing me as some party girl; I didn't blame him, not with what I was wearing then.

"Liv," I said. He took out a notepad and scribbled something down on it then looked up at me, not even bothering to move his head up. "Burnett."

"And can you tell me what happened last night? Were you at The Corner?" His eyes drifted down my outfit and back up again. He already knew the answer; he was just fishing for something. I told him everything that had happened that night without further prodding; including every insignificant detail right down to what we said, how Luke had done a fake accent and the exact time I had gone to bed. By the time I was done telling him, Harley was staring at me, a blank look in his eyes.

"That's…everything?" he said, no longer taking notes. Was that not what he wanted? I didn't think I had missed anything and right now every detail mattered.

"Yes."

"All right, thank you," he put his notepad away and tucked the pen in his breast pocket. "We'll contact you if we need anything else." Harley turned to leave and I just watched him go, like I had Luke.

Walking into the police station my legs felt weak. Staying up half the night and then being woken up by police for the second half didn't sit well with my body. I couldn't even be sure I was wearing suitable outdoor clothes. After Officer Harley left, I had dashed into my room thrown on the first thing I saw; loose blue jeans and a flimsy sweater. I probably looked like a crack addict with my matching bedhead and bloodshot eyes; it would explain some of the looks I was getting.

I set my hands on the receptionist's desk and she glanced up at me. The woman before me looked nice, but…naïve, like you could tell her you were royalty and she would believe you.

"What can I help you with?" she asked, not caring about my appearance. That was a plus at least, until I remembered she probably saw people like me every day.

"I need to see Luke Harroway, please," I requested, not really knowing how this worked. There were most likely specific hours I was supposed to be there and even then I might not be able to talk with a murder suspect alone.

"I'm sorry," she said, the kindness in her eyes was gone as soon as she heard his name, "but you won't be able to see him." She glanced to the stairs on her left quickly but went back to stapling papers and typing on her keyboard, no longer interested in helping me. Guilty until proven innocent seemed to be her thought.

"Then is Officer Harley here?" I asked, needing to know what was going on. The receptionist, Bunny her nameplate read, sighed and folded her hands before looking at me.

"Look, honey," she started, "this is a very delicate case. Whatever your boyfriend did, you probably don't wanna know."

"Where's Officer Harley?" I repeated.

"He's at a crime scene," Bunny said, "but he won't be back till nine!" She had to yell the last part to me as I walked out the door. I was going to get answers if it killed me. Turning left outside I fast walked my way past an alley when a thought occurred to me.

I glanced around to make sure nobody was watching me, specifically officers. When I saw it was safe I ducked into the alleyway.

Thinking back to when we were younger, I tried to remember how Luke had told me to reach out to him. If I wanted it bad enough, he would be able to hear my thoughts, at least the ones I wanted him to hear. Somebody walked by the mouth of the alleyway so I kneeled behind a dumpster, hopefully nobody would notice me there. Doing this in my car would be easier but it was too far away, limiting the chances of Luke hearing me. Holding the sides of my head I reached out to Luke.

Luke, I thought, *Luke, are you there?* Pain shot between my temples as Luke found his way to me. I could feel that he wasn't pleased with what I was doing.

Don't hurt yourself, he warned, *this situation sucks enough as it is.*

Hearing his voice in my head made me feel a little better but I still wished I could've seen him.

"Are you okay?" I asked aloud, knowing how stupid the question was.

I've been better, he laughed, *they think I murdered Alice last night, and the other girl, Rosa something.*

"Navarro." I had started talking out loud rather than think my thoughts to him. It made the pain a little more bearable for our communication. It also helped me look insane to anyone around me; something I had realized the hard way as a child.

What?

"Never mind," I said, looking around the dumpster again. "What evidence do they have?"

Just the fact that I was last seen coming out of Alice's boyfriend's house, he told me, *and that Alice and her boyfriend are dead. I was the last person to see them alive!* I didn't speak as I thought about everything. They could only hold onto Luke for 48 hours with no real evidence.

"Okay," I said, "I'm going to figure out what's going on." I stepped out from behind the dumpster before Luke could try and stop me. I was about to block him out when he reached to me again, forcing me to hold my head and lean forward to stop the pain; it didn't work.

Wait he called. *Just...be careful! Don't do anything stupid!* Walking out of the alleyway rubbing my temples I noticed a man standing there. He was just standing there, watching me.

His hair was shaggy but blown back; I would bet he had just woken up like that, but it suited him with a matching pair of aviator's over his eyes. His leather jacket hung loose on his hips but tight on his shoulders and was open to reveal a plain white tee-shirt over grey jeans and large black boots. He was watching me, hands in his pockets; casual.

What was I supposed to do? He had obviously seen me talking with...well myself. I figured I could go one of two ways; I could keep walking and completely ignore him or I could threaten him into submission. I chose to ignore him.

With as much strength as possible, I strode past him, only briefly looking at his sunglasses. My legs felt wobbly as I turned away from the stranger, being suddenly aware that I was being watched made it hard to walk properly. It took a lot to not look back at him.

Once I was safely in my car, I pulled out my phone. Bunny had said that Officer Harley was at a crime scene, and since he had asked me questions, it was safe to assume said crime scene was Alice's boyfriend's house. Searching through my contacts I found Charlie's number and dialled.

"Hello?" she answered after two rings. There was

nothing in her voice to say she had heard about Alice's death. I wasn't about to tell her, not over the phone at least.

"Hey, it's Liv," I started. How would this conversation go?

"Hey! What's up? Change your mind about Friday?"

"Not exactly," I said. "Can you tell me what Alice's boyfriend's house address? And his name? Luke uh...forgot something there last night."

"Oh, uh, sure. His name is Alex something. He lives down Cherryhill Boulevard, he throws wicked parties. Why?"

"I'll tell you later, thanks," I hung up without another word. Charlie wasn't going to take the news of her friends' death well, the least I could do was tell her in person; or let the police talk to her first. We weren't close but I had talked to her a lot and I knew mid-twenties party girls didn't come much nicer than her.

I put the car in drive and headed towards Cherryhill Boulevard.

Chapter 5

I parked around the corner from Cherryhill Boulevard after seeing a number of police vehicles there; it wasn't hard to guess which one belonged to Alex. As I turned my car off I heard an engine roar up behind me, my mirror showing me a reflection of a Dodge Charger pull up against my bumper. I began walking to the house Luke had been at hours earlier, dismissing the idling engine behind me.

When I arrived at the appropriate house I scanned the area for Officer Harley, or even his partner that had arrested Luke. I couldn't see either of them through the number of people blocking the way but I saw two body bags being loaded into a coroner's van. A woman near me gasped when she saw them but I remained motionless. Was I supposed to react like that? Probably. Maybe I was even supposed to be more distraught since I saw one of them only a few hours ago.

I moved through the crowd to get a closer look but was stopped by yellow tape. One small policeman stood on the other side of the barrier, making sure to keep people out. I wondered, would they answer any questions?

"What happened?" a man asked coming up next to me, as if reading my mind and helping me find out the answer. The officer's walkie-talkie buzzed before he could answer. He held up a hand to the man.

"We're all done back here," the voice said, "we're heading back."

"Copy," said the officer. I backed away just as he began telling the man what was going on. I had considered listening in on his story, but it's not like he would give any real detail, not to a civilian. Walking back to my car I spotted a blonde television reporter, the same one that had told the world about Rosa's tragic kidnapping and death. She didn't have any cameras with her but she did have a small recording device and was talking with an elderly couple.

Trying to appear casual, I wandered past them at a slow pace.

"Can you tell me what you saw?" the reporter asked, the same gleam in her eyes as before.

"We saw the killer leave," said the man, "a young boy, no older than my son." The man described Luke perfectly, for what he must have seen in the dark at least. They were awfully sure he was the killer.

"He was just a boy," his wife commented, "why would he do such a thing? He must be one of those…*things*." The disgust in her voice was apparent but I was too far away to hear the reporters reply.

Anger burned through my body at her comment about the Eidolon's. Typical humans. So they were the ones that had seen Luke, but how did the cops find him so fast? It wasn't like they knew exactly who he was, it just wasn't possible in such a short time frame. I needed to see this crime scene for myself, and I knew just the way.

The officers said that they were done in the back and headed somewhere else; that must have meant they were done checking the backyard and the house. I passed my car and the Charger, engine still running, trying to see if anyone was inside. The windows were tinted too much though and all I could make out was a figure; I couldn't even tell if it was male or female. Continuing past, I rounded the block till I found the bike path that would lead back to Alex's house. Checking behind me to make sure nobody was really watching, I kept going, thinking about what a stupid idea this was.

I was lucky Alex lived where he did. Cherryhill Boulevard was on the edge of a minuscule conservation area, filled with pathways and trees. The dirt road was empty since everyone was out in front of house forty-five, giving me the perfect opportunity to get in on my own.

It wasn't hard to tell which house was which. The noise alone told me which one belonged to Alex; I could hear the people out front talking and the loud buzzing from walkie-talkies. The house itself was obscured by trees and bushes so I stepped a few feet in just to get a look. If any cops saw me I could simply lie and say I was curious. No strict repercussions until they found out I was Luke's roommate, which probably wouldn't take too long. Staying behind a tree I scanned the backyard.

It was simple, no flowers, just trees and leafy green plants that wouldn't need much attention. There was a large patio just in front of sliding glass doors where a man and woman in suits stood. I could see the shiny golden badge on the woman's belt, declaring her a detective but the man didn't display his; I assumed he was her partner. An officer walked out the patio doors to meet them.

"There's nothing here," said the woman, "he left through the front after bringing her home from the club." Officer Harley came out from the open patio door.

"Did you want us to check the rest of the back again?" the police officer asked, making a small hand motion to the back yard and I hunkered down lower behind a bush. I didn't risk peeking out for another look, only then realising how stupid an idea this was. But what other way did I have?

"No," said the male detective, "there's no point, we have the killer in custody and we've found all we can here." Poking my head just over the top of the bush I saw them walk towards the side of the house. "Let's head back with the others and get the kid into interrogation."

Kid, I scoffed. Luke was twenty and being called a kid by a thirty-something cop. It was a little stereotypical really. The three disappeared into the front yard but I remained motionless for a few more minutes. I heard cars drive away and the crowd sounded like it was dispersing. Once it was quiet I stood up and rubbed my legs, hoping to get the feeling back. Squatting like that felt worse than the jeans Charlie had made me wear.

There was no yellow tape in the backyard to keep people out. Not exactly on the ball here; they were putting all their hopes on Luke. Wouldn't they feel foolish when the next murder happened. Very carefully I walked up to the glass doors.

"Tch," I accidentally said when I noticed the door was still opened. Assuming someone was still inside I listened for any movement. Even though there were no sounds coming from inside the house my heart was beating quite loudly. Peering around the corner I saw an empty room and felt it was safe enough to pass through the threshold, careful to avoid the drops of blood.

I had entered into a basic living room and if it wasn't for the very obvious murder that occurred here, it would look quite welcoming. The white couch had red splattered over it and when I moved closer I saw there was a drying pool on the floor. The glass table could have been where someone had hit their head, the corner was coated in a dark liquid I assumed was more blood.

The loveseat that sat kitty-corner to the couch was pristine, not a mark on it. I walked over to observe it, why was there nothing there? In the back of the cushion I saw something tucked away, almost completely out of sight.

Taking a quick look over my shoulder I pulled at the string between the cushions to reveal a green stone necklace. I didn't recognize it from the previous night, but it could still belong to Alice. I took a picture of it with my cell phone and placed it back where I had found it, moving on.

Across the room was a yellow sign with the number one on it sitting atop a cabinet. I saw a small white card in front of it and I had a feeling I knew what it was. As I got closer I could clearly see Luke's face on it; his college ID card.

"Idiot," I mumbled to myself. That was how they had found Luke so easily; his ID had been left with his name and student number on it. I didn't have time to think about anything else, there were footsteps coming towards me. Just before I saw someone turn down the hall I dashed inside the closet next to the cabinet.

"Get the card," a man said in a voice obviously used to mock his superior, "how could you forget the card?" I pushed myself against the right of the closet; if I stood anywhere else he could have seen me. He grumbled, "I already filmed everything, not my job to do this." I waited until I heard the front door shut and checked if it was clear.

Seeing the living room empty again made me feel a little better. As I got out of the closet I noticed a tiny yellow butterfly sitting on the drops of blood by the back doors. The temperature seemed to drop as I watched it flutter its wings before taking off down the opposite hallway, following the blood trail.

I followed after it, avoiding stepping on any evidence, or anything that looked like it could be evidence. Each drop of blood had a yellow sign and a number to go with it, making it a little difficult to navigate the thin hall. I watched my feet as I walked. The signs ended when they reached the next room.

What first caught my attention was the black tape outline of a person. They were small and I knew

37

immediately that it was Alice, not her boyfriend. There was no blood in this room, it was completely clean. The white carpeting was freshly cleaned and the bed was made. Matching lamps sat on either side of it atop mahogany nightstands. Taking another step inside my eye caught some movement.

At my feet was the butterfly, small and shimmering, flapping its wings as it sat on a television remote, just out of reach of Alice's outlines hand. I looked around but didn't see a TV, so was the remote for the one in the living room? Why would it be all the way over here, unless Alice carried it with her in a panic?

The butterfly flew into the air again, this time it floated over the bed, landing on the tall bookshelf. Below it I noticed some fallen books. They didn't fit with the rest of the room; no blood whatsoever, everything else was in its place, but not these books.

I bent down next to them, reaching a hand out to touch them but quickly drawing back. I didn't want to leave any evidence. The books weren't familiar to me; all of them lying open to be read. They were paperback, so to get them to stay open on their own meant they had to be crushed down, the spine almost broken. All of them appeared to be different genre's, different writers.

The only thing they had in common was they were open to page four and five. Was Alice or her boyfriend trying to tell the world something with this? I took a photo with my phone, making sure to get one of the outline and remote as well. I watched as the butterfly flew back into the living room. Taking one last look around I decided it was time for me to go as well.

Safely exiting the crime scene and finding my way to the bike path my heart finally calmed down enough for me to breathe properly and comb through the photos on my phone; Luke really was in trouble. Not only was he seen entering and leaving the house, he had somehow left his ID there. I was hoping that the fact he wasn't coated in blood would help, but after seeing where Alice had died and how clean it was that hope was gone. I stopped at the end of the bike path as I came to the picture of the necklace.

It was out of place. If it was on a table, or even the bed, I would have brushed it off as nothing. But it was hidden in the back of the loveseat; placed there by someone. It was a clue; I just didn't know what kind of clue it was.

I shoved my phone back in my pocket, anger and a touch of despair starting to take over. For now, the cops had nothing but Luke's ID and a couple of witnesses. Soon they would find time of death, maybe that would save him; I told them everything, being very specific about times and places. Maybe Alice and Alex died after we had gotten home, after Luke had gone to bed. Somehow I knew that wasn't going to be the case.

As I pulled my keys out of my pocket I heard a shuffling behind me. I spun around quickly, but there was nobody there. I stared around; nothing out of the ordinary. Turning back to my car I unlocked it and hopped inside, locking the doors behind me as fast as I could

I took a deep breath and weighed my options. There was no way I would be able to visit Luke in jail, so what should I do? Charlie was the first thing that came to my mind. She deserved to know about Alice and the cops probably hadn't talked to her just yet. I dialled her number and she picked up right away.

"Hey," I said, "are you busy?" I knew since she had answered instantly that she wasn't and the tone of her voice said she still hadn't heard the news.

"Nah," she answered, "I've got the day off. What's up?"

"I'm coming over; I should be there in about fifteen minutes. We need to talk."

"About what?" Her voice was filled with concern

now, as it should be. Someone saying "we need to talk" never ended with good news.

"I'll tell you when I get there," I said and hung up. It wasn't going to be easy telling her, and it didn't help that I had zero experience with delivering bad news. As I drove back to Luke's I tried to think of the right words to use, but I just couldn't find them.

Chapter 6

I sat in front of the apartment building and stared up at it, taking in its concrete exterior coated in windows and balconies. Charlie was about to have her day ruined and she was probably going to ask why I didn't tell her sooner that her friend was dead; like say, when I asked her for the address. Would she really understand why I did it? Doubtful, but a possibility at the very least.

With a heavy sigh I opened my door and headed inside. As I climbed into the elevator I swore I saw the same black Charger that had parked behind me earlier pass by but it quickly disappeared as the doors closed. The ride upstairs went far too fast and before I knew it I was knocking on Charlie's door. There was no answer.

I knocked again, this time calling out.

"Hey," I said, "Charlie, it's me." Nothing. It wasn't like her not to answer the door so I tried turning the knob. The door swung open and displayed a dark, empty hallway. "Charlie?" Fear rose in my stomach; something was wrong.

I walked down towards her living room after shutting

the front door, the temperature so low I could see my breath come out in white puffs. I expected to see her sitting on her couch, headphones in and bouncing to the beat. Instead I found her lying on the floor, motionless. Running to her side I touched her neck, she was cold, eyes wide open. I couldn't feel a pulse. Unsure of what to do, all I managed to say was a weak, "Charlie?"

I knew she was dead, but some part of me just told me she would wake up soon. The hopeful part of me that said I wasn't seeing one of the nicest girls I had ever met on the floor, breathless and frozen. I had only talked to her twenty minutes ago, the familiar fear in my stomach giving me a flashback to my childhood; a different body suddenly in front of me. I heard a siren in the close distance and I noticed the phone in her hand; the number on the screen read 911. I reached for the phone but then heard movement behind me.

Spinning around I came face to face with a cloaked figure. They moved like fog towards me, fading into the air almost, like smoke. They made no noise, so what had I heard? The edges of the figure dissipated into the air just like my breath. They weren't human, that much I knew. I stood up to face them, or at least defend myself; not like I knew how to protect myself against what looked like smoke. As they approached me we were both startled by the front door being kicked open.

"Down!" a man yelled and I ducked just after seeing him raise a gun. He fired at the smoke, the shot so loud I had to cover my ears. I opened my eyes and looked up to see the figure was gone, leaving me alone with the man with the gun. My eyes couldn't focus on what was in front of me and I fell backwards next to Charlie. When the ringing in my ears stopped I could tell the sirens were just outside the building. He said a gruff, "Come here."

The man ran to me and grabbed my arm, dragging me to my front door. I was too surprised and tired to react.

"Keys," he said, setting a pair of aviator sunglasses on

his head.

"What?" I asked. I had never been so lost in my life, never so…disoriented.

"Keys," he yelled and turned his head as footsteps were heard in the staircase. "Unless you want the cops to think you killed her."

I thought for a moment and quickly shoved him aside to open my door. The second it unlocked he pushed me inside and slammed it shut. His back was against the door and he pulled me into his chest, covering my mouth. I tried to tell him to get off, but it was useless. He pressed my head into his chest; I only came up to his shoulder.

"Shut up," he warned, tightening his grip on my mouth as he locked my arms down with his other, gun toting arm.

Just outside my doorway I could hear police thundering through to Charlie's apartment. My heart was racing, just like it had when I had broken into the crime scene. I wasn't sure if I should be afraid of the man though he had technically saved me from whatever killed Charlie, and then he helped me not get arrested. But he was now trapping me in what was soon to be my own apartment.

I could smell the leather of his jacket just underneath the smell of his skin; which was a little like dirt and steel blended together. I thought of his sunglasses and it made me feel like I knew him. I just had no idea from where.

I don't know how long we stood there, listening to the commotion outside as police searched Charlie's apartment for the killer. Finally, there was a knock at the door. The man released me from his arms and turned me to face him.

"Don't make a sound, okay?" he said and I simply nodded, only then realising who he was. He was the man that had watched me talk with Luke, or from his point of view, myself, in the alleyway next to the police station. He had a gun, so did that mean he was a cop? Because he sure didn't dress like one. Detective would be more likely, but then again, we wouldn't be in this situation, hiding from the police.

The man opened the door once his gun was tucked into the back of his pants. I was about to come around to face the officer with him but he shoved his hand in my face, pushing me backwards. I took that as a "stay-back-and-leave-this-to-me" message. Not knowing what else to do, I let him take the lead.

"Do you live here?" the officer asked. They were not the ones from earlier.

"No," the man replied, "just visiting my girlfriend. Is something going on?" How did he manage to sound so innocent? I was a fairly good liar when the need arose, but he was spectacular. He had just shot off a gun in my direction and even I found myself believing his act.

"There's been an incident next door," the officer said, "did you hear anything? See anyone go in or out of the apartment?"

"Incident? No, nothing." I was a little jealous at how well he could do this. "We've been in bed all morning; I was just on my way out. Was it…was it Charlie?" My eyes widened a little; he knew Charlie?

"I'm sorry," the officer said, "we can't say anything at this time."

"Oh…all right," the man looked down the hallway to the bathroom, "I don't think she'll take this very well." The officer said goodbye and left without further prodding. The man shut my door and turned to face me.

Instinctively, I took a step back, only to remember there was a wall there. My eyes glanced at the kitchen where a set of knives sat neatly on the countertop and then back to him.

"You'd never make it," he said, blue eyes piercing into me, apparently reading my every thought. I didn't say anything and he crossed his arms at me. Now what? I stared into his eyes and he stared right back, unblinking.

For some reason he looked away first, into the kitchen. "We need to stay here for a bit." He turned and went into the living room.

Instead of following him, I walked right out the front door. Bet he wasn't expecting that. I shut and locked the deadbolt behind me, making sure that he wouldn't be able to get out without a key. It crossed my mind that he would kick the door down, like he had Charlie's, but there were cops just next door; he couldn't do it without raising suspicion.

The doorknob rattled and he banged on the door, frustrated. Trying not to look out of place I glanced into Charlie's apartment, already bordered off by yellow tape; all the officers inside. The door sat on the floor, the man had completely broken it down, right off its hinges. I raised my eyebrows at that; it was impressive.

As I walked down the hallway to the elevator I kept my head down, it wouldn't go well if anyone recognized me. I pretended to check my phone for messages when I spotted the two detectives from the first crime scene.

"Another one? Already?" the female detective asked.

"Yep," the male said, "that means the kid didn't do it." He pointed at the uniformed officer behind her. "Radio the station to let the kid go, but make sure he knows he's still a suspect. They could be working together." The officer nodded and did as he was told. *They?*

When the elevator doors closed I smiled wide. Luke was going free, so I wouldn't have to do anything else to try and help him. Soon it was going to be behind us and we could return to a nice, semi-normal life where smoke didn't try to kill me, Luke wasn't in jail and crazed gunmen didn't try to lock me in my apartment. Yet he *was* locked in my apartment and it was only a matter of time till he found his way to the fire escape. With that thought in mind, I ran to my car the second the doors reopened, bumping into a woman on the way.

My heart sank in my chest when I saw my car. I had parked in the far corner of the lot, next to a line of trees on the passenger side and nothing else on the left. Unfortunately behind it was sitting a black Charger, just an inch away from my trunk; I had no way of getting out, completely blocked in.

So it seemed the black Charger belonged to the man currently in the apartment. Perfect. Rather than waiting around for him to get me, I started towards the police station. It was within walking distance anyway, I would get Luke and then figure out what to do then.

"Hey!"

I turned to see the man in the leather jacket pointing at me. I started running in the opposite direction without another thought, hoping he wouldn't chase after me. I hoped wrong. He began to run towards me as he yelled, "Stop!"

I ran down an alley, trying to lose the man using a shortcut only locals knew about. Hopping the three foot fence with a little help from a box it wasn't long before I made it to the police station.

Out of breath I checked behind me. He was there; he was actually there just behind me. The man was coming up fast but stopped as a cop car drove by; a dead stop in fact. I watched as he eyed the police cruiser passing by. He put his hands on his hips and shook his head towards the ground; he didn't want to confront me so close the police station. The man looked back up at me and I shrugged at him, my lips twitching to hold back a superior smile. I turned and walked into the station, knowing I would most likely regret this sooner or later. Most likely sooner, if I knew any better.

Just as I opened the door Luke was standing at the receptionist's desk asking to get something else to wear.

"So what," he said, "I just have to walk back in my boxers?"

I hadn't thought about that. He was arrested

wearing only stripped blue boxers and a white tank top; but I thought they would have given him something to wear at least. Officer Bunny was going to answer him when she saw me and pointed.

"Look, you're girlfriends here," she said, not impressed that he was being released so soon, "she can drive you home."

"Girlfri—" he started and turned to see me. He seemed incredibly relieved and I felt it in his hug. I lightly hugged him back. "I've never been so happy to see you in my life."

"Yeah," I said, "me to. I've got some…news." He let me go and looked into my eyes.

"Bad news?"

I nodded and the grateful sparkle in his eye disappeared.

I sat with Luke on the front steps of the police station and explained what had happened, speaking quietly so nobody overheard about finding Charlie and seeing the smoke figure. We were waiting for a taxi to arrive; I didn't want to risk running into the gunman on our way home. Luke had asked why I didn't drive down but I only told him I had felt like the walk. He wasn't impressed, most likely resisting the urge to ask me why I didn't anticipate his need for pants.

"So the only reason I've been released is because Charlie's dead?" he asked eventually, pain making his voice crack.

"It's not your fault," I said.

"I should've seen it," he said, "I should've seen it with Alice and with Charlie and even Alex!"

"It's not your fault," I repeated.

"No, but I should've…seen it,"—he waved his hands by his head—"I'm an Eidolon, this is what I'm supposed to do Liv."

"Do they have any real evidence that you did it?"

"No, nothing. But they think I'm partners with that guy that took Rosa…so I just…I don't know."

That was a blessing at least; them not having any real evidence. A taxi pulled up to the curb and we climbed in. Luke told the driver our address and he started driving, not seeming to care that Luke had no pants on. At first I was going to tell him to go somewhere else, the gunman knew where we lived, but he wouldn't risk anything with the cops patrolling the area.

That raised another question though; did the detectives know that Charlie lived right next door to their original suspect? They must know by now, but if they didn't, they were about to find out.

The taxi pulled up in front of our place. I paid him with the money I thankfully had in my pocket, forgotten from another time. Luke quickly went into the building and pressed the elevator button. I checked the area around and didn't see a Charger anywhere, or any sign of the gunman. That was either a good thing, because he was gone, or a bad thing because he was waiting upstairs. I guessed I was going to find out soon enough.

The elevator doors opened and we found we were facing the two detectives. They didn't seem surprised to see Luke standing in front of them though. Without a word they walked past us, the male detective moved two fingers to point at his eyes before shoving them in Luke's direction. Luke swallowed loud enough for me to hear and we went up without a word.

My heart was pumping when we came to our door. Was he in there, waiting? I opened it to find an empty apartment, quiet and dark, it felt it was safe to go in. Luke immediately went to his room for a change of clothes and I went to mine. I checked my closet first to make sure nobody was there, and then moved on to Luke's.

"What are you doing?" he asked as he put on a fresh shirt.

"Nothing," I said. I was going to keep the gunman to

myself, along with breaking into a crime scene. Luke didn't need to know any of it, not if I wanted our lives to go back to how they were. This would remain a secret, for him. I smiled at him. "Nothing at all."

"I've been awake all night," Luke said, "I'm going to lay down for a bit." I nodded and left his room, shutting the door behind me. Peeling my sweater off, I tossed it into my room before walking into the bathroom. I flipped the light on and splashed my face with some cool water. As I looked into the mirror I felt a primal fear squeeze my stomach.

The shower curtain was all the way across; I always made sure to keep it open, and I made sure Luke did too. It was a pet peeve, or paranoia as Luke would say, of mine from years of being scared by my brothers; a closed curtain was easy to hide behind. That way, when it was closed, like now, I knew somebody was hiding behind it. Slowly, I reached for the door.

"Please, don't do that," came a voice as the curtains swung open, revealing the man in the leather jacket bearing his silver pistol. He stepped out of the shower and wiggled his finger. "Come here." I sighed and did as I was told. I would have been much more comfortable locked in a tiny room with a possible killer if I had my sweater on and not just a far too tight halter top. Maybe.

He took a pair of handcuffs out of his back pocket and locked my left hand to the fake, center drawer on the counter. Obviously I was not a threat to him, otherwise he would have cuffed me to something a little sturdier.

"I have to say," he started as I tugged on my restraints, noticing the wood was beginning to chip around the handle, "I wasn't expecting you to run." I shrugged at him, looking into the mirror rather than making eye contact again. He suddenly grabbed my face and forced me to look into his eyes. "You're welcome, by the way, for saving you earlier. You were about to join your neighbour on the floor if it wasn't for me." He had me there.

"Thanks," I said looking back down as he released me, "I guess. Who are you?"

"No no no," he said, waving his gun back and forth, "I'll ask the questions first. What were you doing in the Stafoff house? Your boyfriend forget something after he killed the lovers?" He leaned against the far wall and I followed him with my eyes. He must have felt my anger at his comment.

Instead of answering, I yanked on the cuffs with one hand, wincing as they slid on my wrist. The weak handle ripped right off of the wood. The man looked surprised but didn't rush to stop me. I moved to the door, not really running; I knew he wasn't going to hurt me, not now anyway. He was investigating just like I was, in a strange and illegal way.

"What are you doing?" he said, grabbing my wrist and spinning me around. He pressed the gun to my head but it didn't scare me and he seemed to notice that. He put it away, glancing away from me every so often. "Look, I'm trying to find the killer and everything points to your boyfriend."

"No it doesn't," I said looking down. "Just…go away. Luke just wants a normal life."

As much as I would like to help the man catch a killer, I needed to think of Luke. He didn't need this right now, not after everything that had happened with the revolution. Luke had always wanted a normal, human life and I was going to make sure that's what he got.

The man took off the handcuffs and leaned in close to my face, forcing me to back up against the door. I did give myself credit for not looking away this time though.

"Too bad," he whispered, "because you're already involved." He set my cellphone onto the bathroom counter and moved me out of the way to open the door. "I'll be in touch soon." He walked to the front door and left me in my bathroom, wondering what to do.

Chapter 7

"I can't believe you agreed so easily to this," Luke said, unaware of what I was actually thinking, "what's the deal?"

I shrugged and kept walking towards B Hall. We were early this time, and ever since the gunman had been in our bathroom I had been glued to Luke's side. Partly because I didn't want to be alone when my stalker showed up and partly because I didn't want him to be alone should anything else happen. I had already spotted the Charger when I went in to take my final exam yesterday, and then again later that night when Luke and I were celebrating my graduation. I was finally free from high school but it wasn't quite the glorious feeling I had imagined it would be.

I stopped in the parking lot and stared forward. Turning my head slowly to the right, I looked at the car there, parked innocently in the corner spot. A black Dodge Charger, thankfully empty...well, maybe that *wasn't* a good thing. Circling around, the lot was void of people, only Luke and I there.

"What is it?" Luke asked.

"Nothing," I said, "let's hurry up." I pushed him towards the hall and we made it safely inside.

I didn't like this. I didn't like how that man made me feel so uneasy, so out of control. One day I was going about my own way, enjoying a relatively normal life with Luke, the next I was stuck panicking over some stranger in an old car. It wasn't like me to panic so easily. Was this how most humans felt after the revolution? And a better question, did Luke notice how I was feeling? He tended to pick up on those things quickly, whether he used his abilities or not.

We sat down in the same two seats as before, the hall not as full. It was no coincidence that the gunman's car was there, and I couldn't imagine that there was an identical car rolling around town. He must be here to see me; after all, he did say he would be "in touch". My fingers brushed against the phone in my pocket.

He had programmed his number into it and how he had gotten it, I'll never know. I must have dropped it while running to the police station. It was simple enough to find the new entry since I only had seven other contacts, none of them named Jared. I furrowed my brow, wondering if it was his real name. I found it unlikely, but stranger things have happened.

"Who's Jared?" Luke asked next to me. I shuffled my feet back as a person slid by and sat next to Luke.

"Nobody," I replied. Part of me felt bad for lying to him, but he wanted a normal life and this was the only way to do it. I wasn't about to let some guy named Jared destroy all my hard work at giving Luke his normal life.

Luke's eyes bore down on me as I tried to ignore him. I tried thinking random thoughts to throw him off, to not let him see Jared or the fact that I had broken into a crime scene. Unfortunately, trying not to think of those things made me think of them. That had never happened to me before either; usually I was the master at manipulating

Luke's abilities.

"He broke into our apartment?" His tone was soft but assertive. "And you broke into a crime scene? What part of 'be careful' do you not understand?"

"It's not that big a deal," I said, attempting to save myself and pretend nothing had happened. I shrugged, trying to wave him off. "I just wanted to see everything for myself."

He stared at me and I allowed him to see everything I had seen. A shiver ran up and then down my spine with an uncomfortably familiar gnawing sensation at my temples. I rubbed at them, trying to make it go away.

"Sorry," he said, eyes finally looking away. "I know you don't like when I...do that."

"It's okay." We had bigger things to think about now anyway; things like Jared. I rubbed my eyes, needing more sleep than I had gotten in the past two days. Every time I went to bed all I could think about was what if he was right around the corner? I couldn't even count how many times I had walked into the bathroom just to make sure it was empty, or opened my closet door to remind myself he wasn't there. This wasn't fair, Jared was ruining my calm state of mind and he didn't even have to lift a finger.

When I opened my eyes Dr. Wineman had just walked into the room. He looked like a completely different person; he was no longer full of energy and his eyes didn't seem to have the same brightness as before. He set his briefcase down on the table next to the projector and stood for one second too long. It was apparent something was on his mind.

A few minutes later the room was once again filled with Eidolons. From the looks of it everyone had taken the same seat they had days earlier. The fact that they weren't human didn't make them any less predictable. Dr. Wineman let his eyes roll over the room, counting each student. Something flashed over his face when he came to me and Luke; for a moment, I thought it almost looked like relief. But there was no reason he should feel relieved after seeing us, right?

My next thoughts questioned whether or not if the doctor knew about Luke's arrest. There was nothing in the newspapers; I had made sure to check. It just said that there was suspect in custody and the next day it said that Charlie was dead and their "suspect" was released. As glad as I was that nobody was named in the article, it didn't stop people from talking.

The murders were just about what everyone was talking about. Most said that the unnamed suspect had committed the crimes, perhaps with a partner. I imagined even the cops were suspicious that Luke had a partner; that was why they told him not to leave town. I didn't even seem to come up as a possible killer since nobody had bothered talking to me since the night Alice died.

"Welcome back to New History," Dr. Wineman said with a feeble smile. "Today we are going to talk about the revolution. I was going to save this for a later class, but many of you have approached me asking about it." He shuffled through his bag and pulled out a computer. Holding up one finger he asked for the class to wait while he set up the projector.

"I wonder what he'll tell us that we don't already know," Luke whispered to me. I raised one eyebrow, waiting for the doctor find the files he was looking for. I didn't think Luke was going to talk to me for the rest of the lecture, not after using his...abilities on me. He was still afraid it would hurt me like before; he should've known better that it never hurt as much anymore, at least not as much as the first time.

"Guess we'll find out," I said, a little curious too. Last year when the Eidolon's came out of the closet a lot of people asked "why now" or "why not sooner". The media answered the questions, but everyone was different. Some newspapers said that they chose now because they felt it would be simple with the popularity of fantasy stories, others said it was because it was a now or never sort of thing. The television told us that the Eidolon's were accidentally exposed to the government and some said they were trying to eradicate the human race. Most people believed it was because the Eidolon's were planning on enslaving humanity, which caused uproar. I had my own theories on the subject but neither I nor Luke knew the truth.

"This area was not as affected as others," Dr. Wineman said, pulling me back to reality, "that much you know. But the real reason was never reported as to why we chose now to reveal ourselves to the world. Many of us still believe it to be a mistake."

"So do the humans," I mumbled accidentally, forgetting for a brief moment that the doctor had excellent hearing. It must've sounded bitter, as if I didn't think it was a good idea, but the doctor didn't react to it too much. He paused for a moment, eyes keeping to the floor, and continued.

"Human's call us monsters, like we're not people, because they don't understand us," the he said, "but we have a word for ourselves; the Etheric Shade. The term comes from our origins in the Shadeland Islands, nestled deep within the Bermuda Triangle, hidden on another plane of existence; the latest generations abbreviating it to either Etheric's or recently, the Eidolon's. Please, use these terms rather than non-humans, or...monsters." He made a face when he used the human phrase and I realised that even he wasn't above feeling insulted by the humans. Guess the doctor wasn't as happy as he seemed.

"What really caused us to reveal ourselves to the world is simply that our population was growing too large," Dr. Wineman said, crossing his arms behind his back as he began to pace. "A hundred years ago only about fifteen per cent of the world was part of the Etheric's, then there was a count ten years ago that raised that number the forty-five per cent, and now we're almost at sixty-three per cent. Over half of the world is not fully human and this is what made them think we're trying to enslave them." He rolled his eyes and came to a stop. So that was it? The only reason we know about the Eidolon's is because of a population spike? It seemed oddly simple. I peeked at Luke next to me, taking small notes on the topic.

"Our population grew fast because we began to make families with humans," the doctor said. He looked down at his left hand and played with what looked like a wedding ring. If he was thinking about his wife, shouldn't he look happier? Instead he just looked...lost. "Hundreds of years ago it was tradition to marry into the same...species so to speak. But slowly we lost that tradition and began to love humans. Though some families"—he paused and twirled his ring again—"still feel being with a human is wrong." Dr. Wineman stopped.

"Is it just me or does he look kind of sad?" Luke whispered. It wasn't just him, but I only shrugged in reply.

"Last class I had mentioned the Shadeland council," the doctor said, almost jolting out of his daze, "they are the leaders of the Etheric Shade. Last year they concluded that it was only a matter of time before the humans somehow discovered our existence, and they decided that if we were going to come out, it would be on our terms." He began pacing again. "So the council went to the world leaders and told them everything. I'm sure you remember the announcements made by the countries; they were played on loop for days on end. But unfortunately shortly after that the riots started."

I flinched at the thought of the riots. Other places just had thefts and beatings, we had fires and lots of them. I glanced at Luke, hoping he didn't see my movement but he had. He reached out to touch my hand but I tucked it safely in my pocket, out of his reach. I was careful not to look at him again.

"Thankfully it was not long till they ended," Dr.

Wineman continued, "and though there is still much violence going on, it is no comparison to Revolution Week." I wondered if it was going to get better, if the humans would ever stop their violence against the Eidolon's and vice versa. It did occur to me though, that things could be a lot worse. My thoughts drifted to different "what ifs" as the doctor told the class about the revolution. Luke gave me a gentle tap to my arm with his elbow. He was awfully pushy about my paying attention to the lecture, which when considering what happened two nights ago was a little unfair.

"Doctor," a woman said from the back of the class, "can you tell us more about Shadeland? I don't know about anyone else, but I've never heard much about it…" She slouched in her seat a bit, embarrassed by her lack of knowledge. Around us others nodded their heads, feeling the same. Dr. Wineman grimaced, maybe concerned with how he should answer.

"I'm sorry," he replied, "but Shadeland is a place that only the purebloods and elders may go. I can't tell you anything about it that you don't already know." Interesting. So if Shadeland was in the Bermuda Triangle, and Amelia Earhart disappeared there, then does that mean she went to Shadeland because she was a pureblood? I contemplated that thought; but why would the doctor lie about it? I couldn't think of a real reason.

"What exactly is a pureblood?" Luke asked, raising his hand halfway. I was surprised he asked, but after seeing the look on his face he clearly hadn't meant to ask it out loud. Nobody shot him any accusing looks, most people seemed to nod their head in agreement. Dr. Wineman gave him a quizzical look. I was about ready to give him the same look; "pureblood" sounded a little self-explanatory.

"A pureblood is an Eidolon that has no human blood within them," the doctor explained slowly, "they're very rare these days, almost all of the Etheric Shade's are mixed with humans." He touched his chin lightly before moving on with his lecture.

Two and a half hours later the class finished early. Like the previous lecture, Luke and I stood to let people pass by before walking down ourselves. Once we got to the bottom the doctor asked to talk to us again, this time he was watching Luke rather than me.

"Yes?" Luke asked, sounding more worried than anything. After the week he had had, I didn't blame him.

"I would just like to talk to you about your earlier question," Dr. Wineman said, "alone if you don't mind." Luke looked at me and shrugged his shoulders, giving me the okay to leave. I waved at the doctor and stepped outside, shutting the door behind me.

I checked the time, wondering how long Luke was going to be with the doctor. A noise caught my attention and I turned just in time to see the blonde receptionist with the mismatched roots and eyebrows walking down a hall towards the washroom…her name had been Heather? Dismissing her I pulled out my phone and began playing solitaire.

Moments later Luke stepped out of the classroom with a hardened look on his face.

"You okay?" I asked, only ever seeing that look on his face twice before.

"Yeah," he said with a wave of his hand, as if to wave away the problem, "I just need to use the washroom." I nodded and he walked down the same hall the mismatched blonde had gone down.

It was only a few minutes before I could see my breath. Slowly, I let out a puff of crisp, white air to be sure I wasn't seeing things. I looked around me, but I was alone. I let out another breath and my mind went immediately to Charlie's apartment.

The temperature dropped and my phone fell to the floor. Everything was moving in slow-motion now as I rushed to the bathroom door. My legs couldn't move fast enough, as if I was in a nightmare that I couldn't control. I had no idea why I went there, but something was wrong. There was something dangerous just around the corner, that was the only thing I was sure of as I rushed into the women's washroom.

I threw the door open, the first thing I saw was the mismatched blonde lying on the floor, skin a frozen blue; above her stood the smoke, wavering in the air. It almost looked as if it was struggling to stay still, like it couldn't focus on being in the room.

When it noticed me it appeared to shift in my direction, I couldn't tell what it was trying to do as it stayed floating above the woman. I opened my mouth to say something, to scream, to make any noise possible but nothing came out. The edges of the smoke began to move faster then, and when I blinked it was gone, dissipated into the air.

I took a shaky step forward, the door swinging shut behind me. A few more steps in and I was at the foot of the woman on the floor. I waved my hands where the smoke had been and decided that it was safe…ish. There was nothing there, at least nothing I could see or feel. I noticed that I could no longer see my breath either. From the open window I could hear a strange clicking close by, as if someone was just outside tapping on the wall.

Kneeling down I touched the woman's neck to feel for a pulse; nothing. Her skin was cold, just like Charlie's had been, her eyes glazed over with a white film as she stared at the ceiling, or more likely at her attacker.

Air brushed across my face, shifting my hair in front of my eyes. I didn't care; I just stared down at the blonde woman's eyes. After a while I finally looked up at the open window, is that how it had gotten in? Was there an open window at Charlie's or Alex's? I didn't know.

On unsteady legs I lifted myself. Moving as quickly as I could I walked out of the bathroom and picked up my phone and dialled for help. Regret filled my heart knowing

Luke was in the other room.

"Nine-one-one, what is your emergency?" the operator said calmly. Luke stepped out of the hallway and walked up next to me.

"Was it just me or did it get really cold for a minute there?" he asked, pointing his thumb towards the bathroom. I just looked into his eyes, seeing nothing but innocence. He did not need this again. Luke held up his hands to apologize once he saw the phone in my hand.

"Yes," I said into the phone, "I need to report a…murder, I think." Luke's eyes widened.

"What?" he said and looked around as if he would see a body. I gave the operator the address and was told to wait. It took only five minutes for the first siren to be heard and six minutes till there were flashing lights outside of B Hall.

chapter 8

I sat out front of the B Hall entrance next to Luke and Dr. Wineman. None of us spoke; we just sat there and watched as the emergency vehicles were replaced by squad cars. I could feel a headache beginning in the back of my head and it only got worse when I saw the two detectives pull up. Luke and I had lied about my age, ensuring my father never found out about this; if he did, he might not let me leave the house again, let alone move in with Luke.

The detectives didn't talk to any of the uniformed officers, when they spotted Luke it was almost like they knew exactly what had happened. But what had happened? What was I going to tell them?

The childish side of my brain told me to tell the truth, word for word just like before. But the reality-stricken side told me to lie for Luke. The truth would only make him look guilty, or at least more suspect. I was torn between the right thing to do and helping my life-long friend.

"Why am I not surprised?" the male detective said as

he walked up to us. His eyes darted over me and Dr. Wineman as he reached into his jacket and pulled out a badge. "I'm Detective Young and this is Detective Miller. Mind telling us what happened?" The woman flicked her eyes, resisting a roll as if to say she already knew. They hadn't even looked at the crime scene and already had Luke convicted.

"Saw her walk into the bathroom," I said, "then when I went in I found her, with the smoke."

"Smoke?" the detectives said at once.

"Smoke?" Dr. Wineman questioned me now, sounding more surprised than anyone should.

"Smoke," I repeated, "then it disappeared and I called for help."

"And where were you with all of this happening?" Det. Young crossed his arms at Luke, daring him to answer. Here was the moment of truth, or it would be the moment of non-truth.

"He was with me," Dr. Wineman chimed in, drawing all of our attention, "he had some questions about the lecture and wanted to ask them privately." Well, I wasn't expecting the good doctor to lie for me. "We had stepped out just when Liv called for help."

Det. Young gave a long look to Dr. Wineman before uncrossing his arms and softening his features.

"All right," he said, "the officer will take your statements now." With a wave of his hand Officer Harley hustled over to us. I wasn't sure what the expression on his face meant, but I had guessed it was a mixture of surprise and disappointment directed, oddly enough, at me rather than Luke.

"You've got terrible luck, kid," he said to me. I blinked up at him, unsure of what to say. Neither of the men by my side spoke for me thankfully.

"Why?" I asked. I didn't think my luck was so bad to be pitied by a stranger.

"Well... never mind," he pulled out the same notepad

as before and flipped to an empty page. "So what exactly,"—he made eye contact with me and corrected himself—"what happened here?"

I told him everything that had happened, including times and where I had stood. The only thing I didn't mention was the temperature drop. If I had noticed it, and Luke had noticed it, then Dr. Wineman definitely noticed it. He seemed to know something we didn't, why else would he lie and say Luke was with him the whole time?

By the time I had finished Officer Harley was just watching me again and so was Dr. Wineman.

"Thank you," Harley said as he set his notepad and pen away, "I think the detectives want to talk to you again." He looked over to the glass doors and my eyes followed with his. Det. Miller came through and charged towards us, plastic bag in hand.

"Do you know what this is?" She practically demanded us to know as she held up the plastic evidence bag. Inside were small bullets, eight by my count. I knew nothing about guns but they looked like they would fit into a handgun easily.

"Bullets?" Luke said, asking more than telling.

"Care to explain?" she yelled as her partner came out of building and pulled her away, scolding her about showing evidence to us. "We'll get you for this! I know it was you, you damn monster!" Det. Young yanked on her arm and dragged her inside. Around us some of the officers gave nervous looks to each other, while others just looked angry. I took that as a sign that they weren't human; they clearly didn't approve of Det. Miller's behaviour. Officer Harley didn't seem too impressed with his superior either. Luke was speechless.

"It's okay," Dr. Wineman said, reaching behind me to rest his hand on Luke's shoulder, "I know it wasn't you." I found that strangely comforting, knowing I wasn't the only one that believed in Luke's innocence.

"Thanks doctor," Luke said, his mind further gone

than I had originally thought, "I think I need to go home now." He stood up when Officer Harley stopped him.

"Do you need me to get someone to take you home?" he asked, concerned with Luke's expression. So he didn't think Luke was guilty either? Interesting, considering he had been one of the original officers to arrest him.

"I don't...I don't know." Luke looked at me and I shook my head, standing.

"No," I said, "I'm okay to drive." The officer looked to Dr. Wineman who raised his hand in response. As we walked back towards the car I held onto Luke's arm and carefully looked back at the doctor. I mouthed "thank you" but he only gave me a concerned look in return.

Pushing Luke towards the other end of the parking area was a lot harder than I had wanted it to be. As we walked I noticed that the dark Charger was gone from its spot. Suddenly, I remembered the other problem I had besides Luke being blamed for the murders; I had Jared to contend with. I quickly scanned the area around me but didn't see any sign of him. Breathing a small sigh of relief I hurried Luke to the car and shoved him in the passenger seat.

"He lied for me," Luke said as we drove away, "why would he do that?"

"Because he knows it wasn't you," I said, trying to focus on the road rather than the situation.

"No he doesn't, he really doesn't."

"Are you trying to say that you did it then?"

"No!" Luke turned to me. "I just, I don't want him to get in trouble, if it's found out."

"Somehow I think that's the least of his concerns." I tucked a stray hair behind my ear while Luke eyed me.

"What do you mean?" he asked.

"I mean, there's something he isn't telling us," I said, not explaining any more than I had to. Luke seemed to take the hint that I didn't want to talk and stayed quiet for the rest of the drive.

As soon as we arrived home Luke all but dove into his room; it didn't help either of us to see the yellow tape across Charlie's door. I walked into the bathroom and shut the door behind me, taking a second to lean on it and breathe, eyes closed.

I opened one eye and saw that the shower curtain was open, just as I had left it. Jared wasn't there...unless he was in my closet. I groaned, cursing myself for having the thought and walked over to the sink to splash water on my face. When I looked into the mirror I heard a faint ringing coming from my pocket.

"What is that?" I whispered to my reflection. I reached inside my sweater and pulled out my phone; I got so few phone calls I didn't recognize my own ring tone. Perfect.

The caller ID read "unknown caller" and I debated for two rings if I should answer or not. I decided it was better to answer, since my phone said everyone was an "unknown caller". It could be family calling to check in, and it might be better if they knew what was going on. Then again, maybe not.

"Hello?" I said, trying to stay quiet so Luke didn't hear.

"Come downstairs," said a male voice, "we need to have a chat." It took me two seconds to realize who was on the other end of the line; Jared.

"About what?" I asked. He really was a stalker.

"About how you manage to keep your hair *so* shiny." He sounded agitated. I touched my hair thinking, for a moment, that he was serious. "What do you think I want to talk about? The crime scene you were just at, so get down here now, or I'll come up. I'm at your car." The phone clicked and he was gone. The thought of having Jared come into my apartment didn't sit well, so I made my way back to the car.

I stepped out into the night air and inhaled, telling

65

myself that it would all be okay. I didn't believe myself for a second.

Across the lot stood Jared in what seemed to be his signature leather jacket and jeans. He was leaning against the back door of his charger as he watched me come out. I kept my left hand over my phone and my right one on my keys, hidden safely in my pockets.

"What is it?" I asked, stopping a few feet away from him. He observed the space between us unhappily.

"In the car," he said and he opened the passenger door for me. I didn't move.

"No," I said. Did he really think I was just going to get into a vehicle with a stalker that I knew had a gun? He gripped the door, grimacing.

"Get in, or I throw you in," he threatened. This, at least, I was prepared for. I pulled my car keys out of my pocket and set my thumb over the panic button.

"Not happening," I said with a wave of my hand. It was small neighbourhood, so when car alarms went off, people came outside, and they came fast. Thinking about it more though, I realized the fatal flaw; Jared could haul me into the car and drive off before anyone even peeked out the window. I had expected Jared to groan in frustration, or at least shut the door, but instead he took a step towards me, smiling.

I didn't move, trying to appear more confident than I felt on sore feet. Jared advanced forward till he was only a foot away, calling my bluff. His arm shot out and grabbed mine; by reaction I hit the panic button. Nothing happened.

"What?" I said aloud, more to myself than him. I struggled backwards but he was too strong and I was tossed into his car, door slamming shut beside me. Caught off guard, I continued to press the panic button, pointing it towards my car as if that would help. Jared climbed in and began to drive away. I pressed the button again, this time Jared swatted the keys from my hand.

"Give it up already," he told me, "I disabled your alarm." I picked my keys from the car floor.

"You knew I would bring it," I said, surprised he would think that far ahead. So much for my plan; I felt stupid not anticipating he would do something like this until it was too late. His engine roared as we drove down the street, turning every so often. If I didn't know any better I would say we were heading downtown.

"Of course I did." He smiled to himself. "You're not as smart as you think you are. But you are pretty crafty, I'll give you that."

"What do you mean?" I didn't think I had ever asked that question in my life. It felt thick across my tongue and I hoped I would never have to ask it again.

"You broke into the Stafoff crime scene," he said, "and you took some pictures." I decided that the best thing to do now was play stupid.

"What are you talking about?" I said and crossed my arms, looking out the window. My first assumption was right; we were now in the downtown area. Jared stopped the car in front of the diner and got out. My older brother had always taken me here when I was little and in some way I knew this wasn't going to be another happy memory to join the others. Jared walked around to the passenger side and opened my door, hauling me out of the seat. Keeping one hand on my elbow he walked me into the diner and sat me down at a booth by the window. "What are you doing?"

"Let's just call it insurance," he said, signalling the waitress for two coffees. Insurance for what? I was sure I was supposed to feel better having other people around me, but it didn't; I wasn't one hundred per cent sure Jared wouldn't kill them all if he wanted to hurt me. An older woman brought us the coffees and left when we said we didn't want to order anything else.

"What do you want?" I asked, wrapping my hands around the cup. He eyed my hands, knowing what I was thinking. I looked down, annoyed that he seemed to see through me as easily as Luke could. No throwing coffee in his face today while trying to escape, I supposed.

"I need to know what you saw,"—he took a sip of the coffee—"earlier, with the dead girl in the bathroom."

"Why?" I was getting annoyed with his secrecy. Why should I share with him when I only knew his name? A name which was most likely fake.

"Listen," he said leaning back in the booth, "I'm trying to find whoever did these people in, so why not try and help?"

"Then tell me who you are, if you really want me to help," I looked up at him as he ran a hand through his hair.

"You already know my name, I put it in your phone," he watched the people around us rather than me.

"You know what I mean." Besides, it's not like I believed that was his real name.

"I'm a bounty hunter," he said, finally breaking down, "and I've been hired to catch Rosa Navarro's killer." He took another drink. "So tell me what you saw."

"Why should I believe you?" I had to admit, he did have that movie-esque bounty hunter feel to him, and it would explain him being around so much, but I wasn't about to just believe him. "Do you have any proof?"

"I have a gun."

"That isn't proof." It was my turn to take a sip of coffee now. Somewhere inside me I knew he wasn't lying, but he had caused me to lose a lot of sleep and something about him just…bothered me. Maybe it was because he reminded me of a bully, the kind of person who applied pressure until you did what they wanted. The corner of his lip twitched, resisting a smile. I had to admit, this back and forth was a little fun; I had never had such a worthy opponent, especially one that looked like him.

"Do you want me to help or not?" he asked. He must've not had people resist him like this, because he wasn't very good at convincing me to help. "'Cause as I see it, you're boyfriend is guilty. So why don't you just drop the tough girl act and tell me what happened." I was acting like a "tough girl"? I watched him for a moment, considering my options. Was he testing me?

What did he want me to say? That I had seen Luke go into the bathroom and minutes later a woman was dead? As if I would ever tell him that; it would make Luke look like the killer.

"I saw the smoke," I said instead, he didn't need to know everything to find the true killer, "but it disappeared like before."

"It didn't attack you like last time?" I thought back to Charlie's apartment, the smoke coming towards me. It had just dissipated this time, leaving me alone, so why?

"No," I said, "it just left." Jared rubbed over his mouth, contemplating. "Do you know what's doing it?"

I stared down at the liquid in my cup and remembered the feel of Charlie's skin. We had never been close, but she was a good person; she didn't deserve to die. She didn't deserve to be *murdered*. Jared must have picked up on my thoughts as I looked up to see his eyes soften. So some part of him did have feelings or maybe he was just smart enough to fake it?

"Look," he told me, "whatever is doing this isn't human. So tell me what you saw at the crime scenes."

"Well," I began, wondering why he used the plural, "at Charlie's there was smoke, same with the bathroom. There wasn't any blood like at Alice's."

"What was at the Stafoff place?" Jared asked. "I couldn't get into that one." He gave me a look, telling me he was a little annoyed that I had managed to get in. He could've gotten in after me, but I guessed by then he was more interested in me. I felt a little stupid, remembering what I had done and knowing that things could have been a lot worse if it wasn't Jared that had seen me.

"Blood," I said, "a lot of it. I think it was just Alex's

though, the room they found Alice in was clean except…"
I thought of the books.

"Except…" he prodded.

"Well there were some books,"—I turned the cup around in my hands, knowing how stupid I was about to sound—"they were on the floor by the bookshelf. All of them were opened to the same pages."

"What books?" I couldn't hear anything in his voice, other than curiosity. It made me feel slightly better.

"I don't know; they were all different. The only thing they had in common was that they were opened to pages four and five." I didn't explain how the spines had been cracked so they could stay open; I thought that would be obvious.

"Anything else?" Jared asked, dismissing the books. It irked me a little, but I moved on and told him about the stone jammed between the cushions. He stared at me. "So what you're telling me is, you found some open books and a necklace in a house and you think they mean something?" Well, when he put it like that…

"I suppose," was all I said.

Chapter 9

When I got home I really didn't feel like sleeping. Jared had looked at the photo's I took of the crime scene and ignored what I thought were clues left behind by both the killer and the victims. After he told me I was a complete waste of his time he said he would "be in touch" again. I really hoped he wouldn't be.

He was so confusing. If I was a complete waste of time why would he be in touch? And did "being in touch" mean he would call me or kidnap me again? Maybe it meant both? I rubbed my eyes, drained and just a little bit lost. Flipping the television on, I flopped onto the couch as the news came up.

"Another body was found today at Ellengale Community College," said the same reporter as before, "police have released that witnesses say it was the work of an Eidolon"—I never said that—"and the deaths of Rosa Navarro, Charlotte Hill, Alice Harper and Alexi Stafoff are connected. The suspect that was in jail earlier this week had been released for insufficient evidence. The manhunt is still on for—" For a brief moment I thought they might actually name Luke, but the reported quickly switched the topic to world news, blaming more tragedies on the Eidolon's.

I began changing channels, never staying on one for more than a few minutes. There really wasn't much on in the middle of the night.

"Liv," came a voice, "hey Liv! Wake up!" I opened my eyes to find Luke looming over me, a toothbrush in his mouth. "Did you sleep on the couch all night?" His voice was muffled by the toothbrush but I still understood what he said. I looked around the apartment, everything the same including the reporter on the news. I read her name; Cindy. She seemed to work a lot. But then again, journalists never seemed to sleep; they probably couldn't afford it.

"I guess so," I said sitting up. It had been a while since I had fallen asleep on a couch, I couldn't even remember about what time I fell asleep.

"I got called into work," Luke said walking to the bathroom. I heard him rinse out his mouth before he stepped back into the living room. "So I gotta go in for the afternoon. What are you going to do today?"

"I don't know," maybe go visit Dr. Wineman to ask why he lied for you? "I'll figure something out."

He eyed me, suspicious. Luke knew me too well for his own good, but he ignored his feelings, like always. Living in denial as usual, I see.

"Well, I'll talk to you later then." I said goodbye and he headed out the door. I wondered if he would tell any of his coworkers about what had happened; then felt stupid for even considering the idea. Luke would never tell a soul about being arrested for murder and then being released, only to find another body days later at both his home and place of learning. He knew almost every victim in some way, maybe even Rosa. It's not like he would remember if he bumped into her on the street or passed her at The Corner.

But then again, I was connected to all the victims, too. I sat on the couch, television still on. Why were they all dying? What did they have in common? Charlie, Alice and Rosa were all at the club the day before they died, but what about Heather? It was never mentioned that she was at The Corner. In fact, she was at the lecture with Luke and me before she died.

And then there were the bullets found where she died. I hadn't noticed them when I was in there, but I was very focused on the smoke hanging over her body. What exactly did the bullets have to do with anything? It was never reported that any of them were shot, in fact, it didn't make sense if they were shot; there was no blood except for Alex's. At least…that's what I had assumed.

I laid back down and pulled my phone out of my pocket to go through the photos again. I stopped when I came to the stone necklace. Jared didn't see any significance in it, but something about it stuck with me. Nobody seemed to think twice about it in Alex's house, but why would it have been where it was?

Tucking my phone away I thought maybe it wasn't anything at all, maybe it was just a necklace Alice had lost down the cushion. But maybe it was something. I heard a shuffling outside of my apartment and a door shutting, shifting my train of thought. Was somebody in Charlie's place?

I walked on the balls of my feet to the front door and peeked through the peephole. In the hallway were two police officers, heading down the hall and away from Charlie's apartment. I figured they had been there to collect evidence or double check something and once they were out of sight I poked my head into the hallway.

Charlie's door was still taped side to side with yellow tape. The red tape that sealed the door was broken from the police before and it gave me an idea. I had been too surprised and terrified to see the room clearly, to look for any possible connections between there and Alice's place of death.

Gingerly, I twisted the cool knob and stepped under the yellow tape, noticing that the temperature this time was much warmer. Somehow I didn't find that comforting.

I walked down the hallway, suddenly having a flashback. Everything looked so different; it was brighter than I remembered but it was just as eerie. The photos that hung on the wall featuring my previous neighbour with family and friends made me feel a little sick; their smiles seemed mocking and empty. I stopped, bare foot and blank faced when I came across a picture of Charlie with Alice and two other familiar faces; Rosa and Heather.

Charlie sat at the bar with her arms around Alice and Heather while Rosa stood behind the bar, smiling. How had I missed this? They all knew each other, and they all hung out at The Corner. Now they were all dead; that couldn't have been a coincidence. Did the police find this connection yet? I tilted my head, observing the photograph. It was strange being in a dead woman's apartment, I felt like I had to keep checking over my shoulder to see if she would be there, but all I saw was empty space. I took a photo of the picture on the wall and walked into Charlie's living room.

I could still see the ghost of her bouncing around the room. I could see her on the sofa, watching television, see her vacuuming and dancing around on the carpet. If you had asked me a week ago if I would care if Charlie moved out, my answer probably would have been "no". But now, I realized how comfortingly normal she was; she didn't even care much about the Eidolon's. I wondered if that was why Luke liked her.

The room where Charlie had died looked exactly as before, plus two bullet holes in the far wall. They never came up in any news reports, and if they were never mentioned what else wasn't? I had always assumed police kept most details about active cases quiet, but I thought two bullet holes in the wall would be worth mentioning.

Tucking a stray hair behind my ear I debated where to start looking. Nothing seemed out of place like it had at Alice's crime scene. The stack of magazines still sat on the coffee table, the telephone still sat on the floor where Charlie had dialled and the decorative pillows were still disorganized on the couch. The pillows made me think of something.

I stepped over to the sofa and dug around in the cushions. Careful to remember where each one was supposed to be, I pulled up the pillows one by one until I came across a silver chain, hidden beneath them all. I pulled it out to reveal a green stone, exactly like at Alex's home. My phone clicked as I took a photo, this time I put the stone in my pocket, knowing that the cops weren't going to find it anytime soon. After all, they didn't seem to find the other one. I placed the pillows back where I had found them, best I could, smiling as I noticed all of them had teddy bears across their face.

I took one last look around the room, wanting to investigate more and find any other clues that could lead to the killer, but there was nothing. Nothing was out of place; it was as if Charlie just lied down and died after trying to call for help. Finally, I walked back to the photo of the four girls. Nobody would notice it missing, right?

Carefully, I lifted the frame from its hook and turned it over, taking the photo out. I set the frame back in its place and stared down at the picture, contemplating how they all knew each other. Studying the rest of the photo I couldn't see anything out of the ordinary, there was nobody in the background watching them, nothing on the counter to suggest something suspicious, the only thing— my thoughts were interrupted by a the floor creaking behind me.

"Who took the photo?" Jared said as I turned to find him leaning over me with a hand resting on the wall, his face mere inches from my own. I tried not to react but my eyes widened in surprise when I saw him; I hadn't even heard him come in, let alone walk right up behind me. What if he had been someone dangerous? Right...stupid question, considering past events.

"I'm getting to that," I said, hoping I didn't sound as flustered as I felt, noticing my face heat up. I turned the photo over to see if it was written on the back but it didn't say much. It listed the girls' names from left to right and after that it just said "Taken by B". This discovery wasn't spectacular, but it was a start. Jared grabbed the photo out of my hand and stuffed it in his pocket. "Hey!"

"What do you think you're going to do with it?" he asked, leaning against the wall and crossing his arms. "And what do you think you're doing in an active crime scene in your bare feet?" I looked down, suddenly realizing that I had never put shoes on, or even socks before I came in. He laughed, knowing I was beaten.

"Whatever," I said and left, avoiding the yellow tape still strapped to the doorway. Jared might have the photo, but I had something else; the stone necklace. I wasn't about to tell him about it, he would just laugh it off. I only made it to the entrance of my apartment before he caught up.

"Hold it, honey," he said as he grabbed my arm. I turned to face him but he was already pushing me into the apartment just like before. I was thankful he didn't have his gun pointed at me but I saw a flash of it underneath his jacket. He shut the door behind us, making sure to lock it. I didn't see how that would solve anything, nobody was here but us. *Oh no*, I thought, *nobody's here but us*. "What're you gonna do now?"

Taking a step back to leave a not-so-safe two feet between us I looked up at him.

"What do you care?" it sounded a lot more personal that it had in my head. Why was that? Okay, maybe I was a little insulted he had brushed off my thoughts so easily but that shouldn't have mattered to me. Nothing had ever mattered before, anyway.

"Because you're getting in the way," he said, "and when people get in the way, they get hurt."

"Is that a threat?" I eyed him, he seemed like the threatening type, but for some reason it almost sounded like he *didn't* want me to get hurt. I changed my mind when I remembered the gun and changed it back again when I remembered he had saved me with said gun. My brain was going to get whiplash being around Jared this much.

"No, it's more like…a friendly warning." Warnings could be friendly? "Whatever is doing the killings is targeting girls involved with your boyfriend. You tend to fit the type." I pursed my lips, not wanting to admit I had noticed the connection as well.

"Well they're all involved with me too," I said, "that doesn't mean anything." He stared down at me, something he did quite often I noticed. I hoped he was considering my words, mulling them over to try and figure out the meaning. I had done it often enough in the past hours; he could at least do the same.

"Why don't you quit with the doe-eyed Nancy Drew investigation here honey," I narrowed my eyes, he kept calling me that. "Because it isn't cute anymore."

"Doe-eyed?" I questioned. Why was that the part that bothered me most? "No," it was my turn to cross my arms at him. "I want to find out who killed them." We watched each other for a long moment before he looked away. For a bounty hunter with a gun he wasn't very good at standing up to people. *Or maybe it's just me*, a voice said in my head. I quickly shoved that thought aside with a blush.

"You're not going to leave it to the professionals, are you?" Jared asked, already foreseeing my answer.

"If you're such a professional why do you keep asking me for help?" He didn't have a reply for that one. Jared had never officially asked me for help, but he did ask what

I saw at the Alice crime scene. That was something I could hold over his head.

"Fine," he said uncrossing his arms and running a hand through his hair. It was only then that I understood his hair looked blown back because he was always brushing it back, stressed. "What did you take from the apartment?" He walked into the living room and sat down on the couch, where I normally sat. I followed him in but stayed standing.

"What?" I asked, confused. He wasn't there long enough to have seen me take the necklace; there was no way he could've known that.

"You've been keeping something in your pocket," he explained, stretching his arms over the back of the sofa. "You keep your phone in your left pocket because you're left handed, but you've been touching something in your right. I can see your hand moving." I blinked, wondering how he would know I was left-handed.

I looked down at my pockets, not even aware I was doing something. Most of the time we had been talking I was rubbing the stone between my fingers subconsciously. Wow, he actually was kind of like a professional. I tried to think of something to say, but there were no words for how stupid I felt. Tugging on the chain carefully the stone slid out of my pocket, allowing it to dangle in the air.

"I found it in the cushions," I said. He watched the stone wave back and forth until it came to a gentle stop.

"What is it with you and rocks?" he asked.

This was exactly why I didn't want to tell him; he would never see it as a clue. He extended his hand to me, palm up. Frowning, I reluctantly handed over the necklace, taking a quick step back to stay away from him. Jared held it up in the air to examine it before he sighed. "Well I guess it means something if it was at two crime scenes." He kept his gaze away from me.

I smirked at him, knowing why he wouldn't look me in the eyes. Jared was embarrassed for not recognizing a clue when someone shoved it in his face.

"What do you think it means?" I asked, hoping he would have an answer. This was new to me, asking someone else a question. Luke would say I was growing as a person.

"What do you mean?" he looked at me with an exhausted glance, as if my question wasn't justified. I shifted my weight, a little uncomfortable suddenly being under such scrutiny.

"Well," I started, "stones and crystals tend to have meanings. If they were at both crime scenes maybe someone put them there for a reason." Jared considered it over in his mind and appeared to come to the conclusion that I wasn't completely useless. That might have been a point in my favour, just maybe.

"See ya," he said and shot off the sofa, headed for the door. He still had the necklace in his hand and photograph in his pocket.

"Wait!" I said, reaching for him. "I'm coming too."

"No you're not."

"Yes, I am." He was already unlocking the door and I considered grabbing his arm like he often did to me. I decided against the idea, yanking my hand back to my side. "I found it, I get to go."

"You don't even know where I'm going," he said walking into the hallway and down to the elevator. I quickly slipped into a pair of moccasins and ran out the door.

"No," I said following him, "but you're going to find something out about the stone and I want to be there."

"You won't want to be there," he clicked the down button next to the doors and we waited.

"I'm going," I said and mimicked his crossed arms stance. He had kidnapped me more than once, mocked my ideas only to find out I was right; I wasn't about to just let him go without me. I wanted to know how this was connected and I wanted to find out who was behind everything.

"Fine," Jared conceded, "just let me do the talking."

I nodded, agreeing. It's not like I talked that much anyway.

I had to confess, I really loved Jared's car. Though, yes, it did give me nightmares for a while, it was *cool*. My father had always wanted me to bring home a boyfriend with a car like that; instead he got Luke, who I wasn't even dating despite everyone's accusations. I sat in the passenger seat beside Jared and gently touched the door. Observing the interior of it, I tried to guess what year it was made; my guess was a while ago. I knew nothing about cars.

"What year was this made?" I asked, the words coming out of my mouth before I could stop them. Jared gave me a sidelong glance, not expecting the question.

"Sixty-nine, why?"

"Just wondering," I looked in the back seat, assuming to see junk food wrappers or bottles of water, magazines even. Part of me expected to see a gun or two, but there was nothing; it was clean. Or at least it was clean on the surface; who knows what lay beneath its blank cover.

"Why did you make it so loud," I questioned, "wouldn't a bounty hunter need to stay under the radar?" Because his car was noticeable, so much so that while we drove I could see people turning their heads to find the source of the roar. Its sound was part of why I always noticed it in the first place. Jared just laughed.

"I drive everywhere," he said, "I may as well like the car I'm driving." It made sense, I couldn't imagine security would let him on an airplane with a gun...and whatever else he carried with him that was out of sight. My mind began to drift off, thinking of what other things Jared may have on him and the things he had seen over time. My thoughts told me I watched far too many movies.

"Do you only hunt Eidolon's?" I asked. The general

public only knew of Eidolon's for about a year, but was Jared one of the few that knew before then?

"I only started after the revolution," he explained, running his hand through his hair again, "I hunt whoever I'm paid to hunt. Business is booming since all the freaks came out of hiding."

"They aren't freaks," I said, annoyance clear in my voice, "they just aren't fully human. There's a difference."

"Right," he rolled his eyes. "I forgot, you're dating one." I shifted in my seat, my opinion of Jared changed every hour, no, every minute and it was getting on my nerves. I preferred hating, liking, or not giving a care about someone, no grey areas. Jared was *all* grey area.

The rest of the car ride remained silent, neither of us wanting to talk. Or perhaps it was just me that didn't want to talk; Jared seemed content with the silence anyway. I finally broke the tension when the car stopped in front of a broken down house.

"Where are we?" I asked, adrenaline starting to rise. I hadn't thought of how stupid it was to just go somewhere with Jared, a complete stranger.

"I know someone who'll know about the stone," he said, shifting into park. We climbed out of the car.

"Who is it?" I looked at the house, not understanding how anyone could call it home. The first two steps of the wooden porch were broken down, actually most of the porch was gone. The railings were coated in plant life and grim while the windows were decorated with bars and what appeared to be cardboard, blocking any view inside or out. The small red-brick exterior had vines growing up its sides and what had probably been a nice garden was overgrown with weeds, the only part that looked like it would bloom again were the roses aligned against the fence. Their thorns stuck out on the stems, as if to threaten anyone walking by.

"Human," he said hands in his pockets, "sort of, if you were wondering." I really wasn't, that hadn't even been on my list of questions for him. "She knows things about...well anything really."

"Clearly she knows nothing of gardening."

"Well, she doesn't get out much."

Jared made his way to the door and I followed a few feet back, careful to watch my surroundings. He knocked on the door but there was no reply.

"Not home?" I asked.

"She's here," he said with another knock. "Open up ya dumb witch!" I wasn't sure if he meant that literally or as an insult. In today's world it could go either way.

"Go away!" came a voice from inside the house.

"Open the door Yamuna," Jared said loudly, "or I'll kick it down." Silence bore down on us from all angles, and I took another glance around. Jared nudged me to the side and out of his way. As I took a step back the wood beneath my foot cracked and broke, causing me to fall. As the rest of my body made contact with the rotted wood it caved in and I fell through it completely, landing on the dirt below. Pain rang through my tail bone then vibrated throughout the rest of my body. As the dust settled back to the ground and I looked up, I found I had only fallen about two feet.

Jared looked down on me, an amused expression on his face. He reached his hand to me and I hesitated to take it but did. As I stood up in the hole a woman appeared next to him, hand touching her lips.

"You okay?" Jared asked as he kneeled down, not paying any attention to the woman next to him. He brushed dirt off of my shoulder while I slapped it off the rest of my body. He helped me climb out of the hole with a chuckle. Oh, look, he was good again... sort of.

"Yeah," I said with a cough. The woman never said a word, she walked back inside and was about to shut the door when Jared caught it with his foot.

"Go away," the woman said with only the slightest hint of an Indian accent, her blue hair falling in front of her face. Her hair colour struck me as odd, it was such a pale blue compared to her smooth, brown skin; she looked to be in her early thirties at the most.

"I need a favour," Jared said and he pushed his way inside. I noticed he had a habit of home invasions. The woman backed away and snapped her fingers but nothing happened. She continued to snap them until she gave us both a frightened look. "Can't do that anymore." Jared showed her something on his ankle with a lift to his pant leg. She sneered at him but stopped backing up. What did he just show her?

"Why should I help you?" she hugged herself, glaring at him as if it would make him disappear. It wouldn't, I'd tried. "You're the one who trapped me here after all."

"Like I said, I need a favour," he smiled at her. I wondered what he was playing at, since she didn't seem too inclined to help us out.

"I'm never helping you, bounty hunter," she walked into the room next to her. Jared followed her, and I after him, hesitantly. I stepped into a very new age kitchen and it was then that I noticed the interior of the house was nothing like outside. It was all shiny and clean, nothing broken, nothing…rotting. The woman sat down and watched Jared, her eyes darting to me for only a second. "Who are you?"

"That doesn't matter," Jared answered for me, "I just need you to identify something for me."

"Sorry you fell down," she said to me as she stood, "don't get out too much because of him." The woman walked over to a tea pot in the corner and poured herself a cup. She glanced up at me before getting a second cup out. Briskly, she walked over to me and shoved it into my hand, then gesturing for me to sit at the round table. I did so, mostly out of surprise, not because I wanted to. Jared sat down next to me, annoyed that I had done so. The witch said, "Name's Yamuna."

"Liv," I said, cautious of where Jared set his hands.

"Thank you." I held up the tea and took a sip, earl gray.

"You're not one of him are you? You don't look like one," Yamuna looked to Jared then back at me. Did she mean a bounty hunter? I could only assume so.

"No," I answered, "just working to catch my best friend's neighbour's killer." I didn't see the point in lying to her. She didn't seem interested in helping Jared, so maybe if she knew the truth she would at least help me. Jared's hand brushed back his hair as I broke the one rule he gave me. "Can you help?"

"With what? I'm under house arrest, I can't leave these walls," she opened her arms to display her prison.

"He seems to think you can help," I said with another sip of the tea. Yamuna looked at Jared expectantly, waiting for an explanation. He pulled the stone out of his pocket and set it on the table. Yamuna looked down at it.

"Please," she scoffed, "you're losing your touch bounty hunter. You want me to tell you what this is?" She picked the rock up and waved it in the air. Was it supposed to be obvious or did she just misunderstand the question?

"Please," I said, "they were found at two of the crime scenes, possibly more." Her grey eyes travelled between Jared and me, thoughtful. Yamuna sighed.

"It's agate," she told us, "it's used for a lot of things. Though it isn't very clean, I doubt it would have done any good." She eyed the stone in her fingers.

"What is it used for?" Jared asked. He really wasn't the patient type, especially with people.

"Well this particular colour of agate is used to promote good health," Yamuna set the stone down with a shrug, "most novices' buy it thinking it can be used for luck or protection."

"Protection?" I repeated. Yamuna nodded at me while Jared touched his hair again. So were Charlie and Alice using the stones thinking they would protect them? No, the stones were stuffed in the couches, so they had no idea they even existed. So somebody else planted them there, hoping to keep the girls safe. Judging by the look on Jared's face he came to the same conclusion I had.

That only brought up more questions. Who wanted to protect them so much that they would break into their homes and hide the stones? And more importantly, why did they need protection in the first place?

Chapter 10

It wasn't all that difficult to not do anything. After Jared and I discovered that the stones were placed in the houses for protection he decided it was time for me to go home. I didn't argue, he had said he needed to think about what to do next, and that his "process" did not involve me. Part of me knew that was a lie, but he was a bounty hunter and I...well, I wasn't. What point was there in arguing?

On the drive home I had tried asking him about Yamuna, and what she had meant when she said he had trapped her there. All he gave me was the fact that she was doing things she shouldn't have been doing and needed to be brought in last year during the revolution. His face was dark when he spoke and I knew there was more to it; I just didn't know how I would figure out what that was. There was something about Yamuna that kind of scared me, but was still intriguing. When I had asked him what had made the witches eyes go so wide he only brushed me off, mumbling something about being "spell-marked".

I had looked up what that meant, but it didn't make sense to me. I found a few forums asking about it, and only a few serious answers. From what I could tell, being spell-marked meant you were protected from most spells, but only the basic ones; any witch or Eidolon powerful enough could easily get through the mark. It was no wonder Yamuna reacted the way she had.

So while Jared was out doing…whatever it was Jared did, I was lying on my borrowed bed, staring at the ceiling. I tapped my fingers on my stomach, feeling a little useless. I had only felt this way once before I met Jared, and now there were murders all around me. Sure, I understood what it was like to feel useless, but not helpless at the same time. The detectives were hunting for evidence that pointed to Luke and I couldn't do anything to stop it; I was amazed they didn't keep him in lockup just because it looked like he'd committed the murders.

I rolled over in bed and sighed, watching my lifeless phone on the nightstand. For the first time in my life I was wishing for a guy to call me. Suddenly my phone rang.

Rushing to pick it up, I answered. "Hello?"

"Hey Liv," came Luke's voice on the other end, "I need a favour."

"What is it?" I sighed, heart pumping for nothing. I rubbed my eyes and checked the clock; it was only a little after three.

"We need some help at work, a few people called in sick," he explained, "do you think you could come help for a couple hours till the next shift comes on?" I weighed my options. I could stay at home, watching my phone not ring, or I could go into work and keep my mind off of everything that had happened. That was what Luke was doing; otherwise he never would have gone in today in the first place.

"Sure," I said, "I'll be there in a few minutes." Spending time with Luke may even lift my spirits too.

"Thanks! See you soon." I hung up the phone and leaned back on my pillow for a moment before getting up. I changed into a more suitable outfit for work other than jeans and a tee-shirt and headed out the door.

It was only about eight minutes before I was walking through the large glass doors of work. It was next to a few identical buildings, all filled with busy people on their phones and typing on their computers. People always asked me why I worked in such a tedious job; the simple answer was it paid a lot and was easier than anything else. For some reason, I knew if Jared saw me here I would be made fun of. I knew my office work was something he probably couldn't even comprehend doing and thinking that made me wonder how long he had been a bounty hunter.

Riding the elevator I tried to think of more work related things than murder. It wasn't working very well, so I just started to count with the floors.

Floor seven... has Jared found anything out? Floor eight... why would someone try and protect the girls without telling them they were in danger? Floor nine... did Luke have any idea how grave the situation was? Floor ten... what was going to happen if the killer was never caught?

The elevator dinged and I got out on the eleventh floor, grateful that I could start doing paperwork or filing or anything really. Counting the floors was just like counting the questions in my head, but worse because I had more questions than floors. Striding into the plain white office, I found Luke's cubicle next to mine and made my way there.

My job wasn't hard, it was really just filing. Take information from here, put it there then put it back here again. Simple, the only thing it involved was typing and occasionally calling people should something go missing. The worst part about the job was that people called in sick a lot; meaning Luke and I would get called in to come work just about every week, despite the fact that I told them I could only work weekends. It didn't matter much, since we never made too many plans anyway. Well, *I* never made plans.

As I walked through the office I noticed nobody was talking. Everyone in the room was hunched over their computers, doing their work. It was odd, since most of the time everyone worked as hard as possible to do nothing at all.

"Hey," I said as I rounded the corner to Luke's cubicle. He was surrounded by paperwork, files towering over him as he stared at his computer screen. The bags under his eyes were ridiculous, since he had seemed fine this morning, despite obvious setbacks. Was everything starting to hit him now? I knew it had taken a bit to really sink in for me.

"Hey," he said back, "thanks for coming in. It'll be so much easier with you here."

"Sure," I held out my arms, "what do you want me to do?"

"Do you remember how last week they had to hire the building owner's niece?" he asked, scrolling through the page on his screen. "Well she's a moron." I raised my eyebrows at that; Luke wasn't one to insult a person so lightly.

"What happened?" Luke set a few files in my hands, careful not to use too much force.

"She went through all of last year's files and changed the date to this year," he shook his head, "and then reorganized them with this year's files." Luke sounded like he might cry. He took this job too seriously, it's not like we filed anything really important.

"Why did she do that?"

"Because she thought that they were the wrong year. She actually thought they were wrong and changed them all." I resisted a smile, knowing Luke would be mad if I laughed. It was kind of funny though, there were thousands of files there, and it must have taken a while to change them.

"So we're changing them back?"

"Yeah," he said, "we need to go through the files up till June and figure out which ones are from last year and which ones from this year." He stopped for a moment to type something into the computer. "We've already got from June to December changed, we're letting tonight's group put it into the main system though."

"Okay then," I said and walked over to my own slice of mind numbing semi-privacy. As insane as it sounded, I didn't mind doing stuff like this. But then again, I wasn't what one would call a motivated worker. I did the work given to me, in a reasonable amount of time and then stopped. Luke was more of the get things done quickly kind of person and find the next duty to be done.

An hour of reading and typing went by without a single peep from my phone. I had to set it to silent in case it did ring though; nobody would have been impressed if I answered it with so much work to be done. As I leaned back in my chair I rolled my head back and forth, feeling the familiar pain in my neck. Standing I rested my arms on the wall between me and Luke.

"Wanna get a coffee?" I asked, needing a break and knowing Luke needed one even more. He sighed at his computer screen and lazily tapped the down key, debating.

"Yeah," he said, rubbing his face, "sure." As he pushed himself off of his chair two of our coworkers drifted by, deep in conversation.

"Did you hear about how they let the suspect go?" One of them said, Susie, I thought her name was.

"Yeah," the other one, Amber, said, "it's obviously not him. I mean, there was another killing while he was in custody." They turned a corner into the office kitchen and I didn't know what to say.

"I can get the coffee," I said, carefully choosing my words, "if you don't want to listen to them." Luke stared towards the kitchen, a lost and weary look on his face.

"No," he said, "I should get used to it. Let's go." He sighed again, about the fifteenth sigh I had heard that hour. We walked into the kitchen to find Susie and Amber sitting at the table, still gossiping about the murders. They looked far too interested for it to be considered a sane interest.

I poured two cups of coffee, the last of what was left. Glancing out into the office, I thought it would be best to make some more, so I rinsed out the container and threw out the old coffee grinds. Luke passed me a filter from the cupboard without a word, probably listening in on the girls' conversation. They were still debating as to whether the released suspect was guilty or not.

"I say he is," Susie said, getting a little upset that her co-worker didn't agree, "I mean, the papers said he was present at almost all the crime scenes. With witnesses I might add!" I turned and leaned on the counter next to Luke and watched them.

"I'm not sure," Amber said, twisting her cup on the table, "there was that one girl that died when he was in jail! How did he do that?" Susie thought.

"He has a partner," she said proudly, "that John guy. Plus he's not human, so he has superpowers that let him do it." Amber stared down her friend.

"Superpowers?" she said in a tone showing she wasn't impressed. If I didn't know any better, I'd say Amber was involved with the Eidolon's if she was that annoyed. Only an Eidolon that knew what they were before the revolution was annoyed when their abilities were referred to as "superpowers".

"Etheric's," I corrected them, hoping to make Amber maybe feel a bit better. The girls only gave me confused looks; they almost looked surprised that I could talk. "They prefer to be called Etheric's or Eidolon's."

"Where did you hear that?" It was Amber that asked, not Susie. I was a little surprised.

"We're taking a New History course at the college with Dr. Wineman," Luke said, "that was something the professor said." The girls nodded in agreement, not really bothering to correct themselves or ask more questions. I just hoped they didn't make the connection between the latest killing and the college.

"So have you guys heard anything weird about the killings?" I asked, wanting to seize the opportunity to find out more. Even rumours tended to have some sort of truth to them. Susie looked around the room before getting up to shut the door. She even went as far to close the blinds, giving us total privacy.

"I have heard one thing," she said sitting back down. Amber leaned in, excited with all the secrecy. "It's a hundred per cent true too."

"What is it?" Luke asked, suddenly as interested as Amber. I would be too, I supposed, if I was the number one suspect.

"My boyfriend's friend knew the first girl, Rosa," Susie said, the wide smile on her face making me uncomfortable, "and it turns out, she was pregnant!"

"No!" Amber gasped. Was the news really that interesting? Enough for her to smile about it? It just sounded tragic to me...

"Yes!" Susie confirmed. "She had just found out she was, like, three months pregnant! She was going to keep the baby by the way, at least that's what I'm told."

"That's so sad," Amber said, emotion clear on her face. I couldn't tell if she was actually feeling empathy or not.

"Yeah," Luke agreed, looking down at his coffee.

"Why wasn't that mentioned in the newspaper?" I questioned. It seemed like something worth mentioning. Susie shrugged.

"Don't know," she said, "I hear she didn't even have a boyfriend, and all her family is back in...wherever she's from." She waved her hand in the air.

"I'm going to get back to work," Luke said, rolling his

head as I had earlier. "There's so much to do." Susie and Amber agreed but as we walked out the door I heard them continue to gossip. Part of me wanted to stay and listen to what they had to say, but I doubted it would be very useful. I would have to make sure to ask Jared about the pregnancy thing, if he ever called that was.

Sitting down back at my desk I saw my phone sitting next to the mouse. Checking for any messages I was greeted with nothing; Jared still hadn't called. It hadn't been that long since he dropped me off at home but I was still irked at how long this was taking him. I wanted to help and he wasn't letting me, though it wasn't like there was much for me to do anyway. It just felt wrong to go about my everyday life when Luke was in trouble and there were murders all over town. What if Jared *never* called and he was only humouring me to get me to leave him alone? Having those thoughts put on top of my family constantly asking why I'm not going to college come September was making me stressed out more than I had ever been.

I went back to work, the numbers barely taking my mind off of everything. When the clock finally hit six we headed home, with a lot less conversation than usual. If Luke did talk to me, it was only about work, or something else that didn't mean anything. He was avoiding the topic like the plague and I let him.

As we pulled into our building's parking lot I saw Jared's car waiting there. My heart jumped into my throat for a second as I drove past, wondering if he was inside; it was too dark to see anything clearly though. Luke didn't seem to notice my interest in the car; after all, he only knew of Jared from my thoughts, he had never actually met him or noticed the Charger.

We stepped out of the car when suddenly Jared jumped from the back seat of his. He grabbed Luke and locked his arms behind his back, cuffing him with a little too much violence for my taste.

"What are you doing?" Luke shouted before I could.

"Arresting you," Jared said, far too calm, "you need to be in jail."

"But he didn't do anything!" I yelled. I had thought Jared knew that, why would he be arresting Luke? "You know he's innocent!"

Jared didn't say another word as he threw Luke into the back of his Charger, speeding off before I could even get around my car to stop him. I swore under my breath, confused and a little hurt. Jared was supposed to be on my side, he was supposed to be helping prove Luke's innocence, not arresting him. It was then that I had realized Jared was a bounty hunter. He didn't care about innocent or guilty, he cared about the money. My face burned with anger, the unfamiliar feeling of betrayal welling inside of me.

I only pouted in the parking lot for a few seconds before getting in my car and heading to the police station. Jared was arresting Luke, so he would be there. And if he was still there when I arrived I didn't know what I was going to do. I had never hit anyone before, but I was considering it now.

When I drove into the station Jared was just coming out the front doors, with Luke nowhere in sight. Parking crooked on the yellow line I dove out of my car and charged at him.

"Where's Luke?" I asked, fury clear in my voice. Jared shoved a piece of paper into his pocket and looked down at me.

"Inside," he said. I went to go around him, feeling Luke was more important than my anger at the moment when Jared grabbed my arm. "He's in questioning, you can't see him. And you won't see him for a while. They want him in jail, and it's better that way." He let go and walked towards his car.

"Why did you arrest him?" I asked, following his steps.

"Trust me, honey, it's for his own good."

"Why should I trust you?" I yelled at him now. "And

94

stop calling me that!" He opened his car door and leaned on it to face me.

"Well, for one I saved your life," he counted on his fingers, "and two, no, I won't stop." He got in and started the engine. I wasn't going to let him leave so easily. Moving as quickly as possible I got into the back seat, not wanting to risk trying for the passenger side door. "What are you doing?"

"Luke's innocent," I said, "you know that."

"I do," he told me, to my surprise, "but he's in the way."

"What are you talking about?" Jared turned the car off and turned to face me.

"He's the only suspect in four open murder cases," he explained, "the cops are so focused on him that they don't see anyone else. He's all they've got so they released a warrant for his arrest. Some higher up doesn't like non-humans, but it's only a matter of time before someone screams racist."

"So why arrest him? That doesn't make sense."

"Sooner or later there's going to be another murder," he said, sighing, "and if your boyfriend's in jail for two of those murders there isn't a jury out there that would convict him." Unless they're all Eidolon hating humans that is, which, if Luke went to trial, was very likely. I wondered what "higher up" Jared was referring to, imagining it might be one of the detectives.

"So what, either Luke goes to jail for crimes he didn't commit," I started, "or another girl dies to set him free?" Jared lowered his eyes, no happier with the outcome than I was.

"It sucks but that's how it is." Angered with how easily he was taking this I stepped out of the car for fresh air. As I slammed the door behind me I saw Det. Miller coming out of the station with the blonde channel four reporter coming up to her. What was her name again? I couldn't remember, at least not then; my feelings were making it hard to think.

I was just close enough to hear their conversation from where I was. Jared stepped out of the car, starting to say something when I held up a hand to stop him. His eyes followed mine to the two women. Something wasn't right.

"So what did you want to tell me?" the reporter asked, a pen and notepad in hand.

"Lucan Harroway," Det. Miller said.

"Pardon?"

"Lucan Harroway," the detective said again, "he's the suspect that was in jail before, and he's just been arrested again. He's an Eidolon and he's committed the murders."

"Oh, no," Jared said quietly.

"What evidence do you have?" the reporter asked, a little surprised at the detectives words. The mention of evidence stalled Det. Miller, she knew she didn't have anything real but it wasn't about to stop her.

"We have enough," was all she said. The journalist wrote down what she said, probably word for word. I took a small step forward, wanting to intervene but Jared grabbed me again.

"Hold it honey," he said pulling me back to whisper in my ear, "you'll just make it worse."

"Or I'll expose that witch for the Etheric hating racist she is," I said but he yanked on my arm once more, dragging me to the passenger side door of his car, shoving me inside. After he shut it and moved I tried to open it but it was already locked, every time I unlocked it he would press a button and I was trapped again. He sat down next to me and drove away from the station.

Maybe it was better that way, it's not like the reporter would believe anything I said, especially with a cop standing right there saying something else. Begrudgingly, I put my seat belt on and crossed my arms. I knew what was coming. And no matter how hard I tried to convince myself that it wouldn't happen, I knew I was wrong.

Jared drove around the block a few times before the

two women went their separate ways. He then led me to my car and made sure I drove straight home by following me there, not letting me talk to anyone inside the station. I forced him to promise to contact me the next day after he said he had plans to find the real killer. I was going to make him know that I was going to be with him every step of the way whether he liked it or not. He just agreed and walked me into my apartment, all the way to the front door. I had considered going back home, to see my family for comfort…but it was useless and I would only feel worse by answering their questions. So I stayed in Luke's apartment, wondering if I would ever get to sit with him again.

The next morning I turned on the news to find Luke's face on every channel. He was declared the major suspect in the investigation; all that meant was the world would see him as the criminal. Even after he was proven innocent, nobody would look at him the same; he was a killer, whether that was the truth or not.

Chapter 11

I had to give myself a little credit for being able to stay so calm, considering the situation. I mean, my best friend, whom I considered family, had just been arrested a second time for murder and now it was public. Everyone knew his name, his face. Everyone was talking about him; friends, coworkers. He was now known as a killer for something he didn't do. It didn't help that he was an Eidolon too. Soon enough everyone was calling *him* the killer The Ellengale Nightstalker.

I gripped the steering wheel in my car, trying to ignore the thoughts that Luke may never be freed. My phone began to ring on the passenger seat but I ignored it, knowing it was my family. My brothers and my father had been leaving endless messages ever since the first news report; I never called them back. I would fix this, I would make Jared find the real killer and fix everything. First I just had to find Jared.

Last night I had gone into a zombie-like state. After listening to Det. Miller tell the reporter all about Luke and "his" victims my hands were shaking, I couldn't even see straight. I had wanted to rush over to her and just push her to the ground. But Jared stopped me, which was a good thing…I guessed. It was oddly out of character for him to help me the way he did; he escorted me back home, made sure I got into my apartment. He wanted to check that I didn't do anything crazy, say like break into a crime scene. I didn't even say "thank you"; in fact, I didn't say a single word to him. I should probably do that when I saw him next.

I checked the time. I had to leave, but I stalled in the parking lot. Luke may have not been with me, but I was still going to go to the third class with Dr. Wineman. I needed to talk to him, ask him why he tried to help Luke and maybe ask for help finding the real killer. He knew something; the only question was how I could get it out of him. I thought Jared's gun would have been quite handy about then.

The drive to the college seemed excruciatingly long without Luke to keep me company. I was so used to him changing stations on the radio like he did on the television, used to him talking about how excited he was for the class or for something else. I glanced at the empty seat next to me; Luke had only been gone a short time but I really missed him.

As I drove down the dimming streets my mind wandered to Cindy, the blonde, bright-eyed reporter that had released Luke's photo. Not very responsible reporting on her part, but then again she was fed misinformation by a cop with a grudge against Eidolon's. My grip on the wheel tightened again, my knuckles beginning to change colour just slightly. Everything was just getting out of hand with the Eidolon's. Honestly, who cared if you weren't human? We had managed to live together this long, what difference did it make if someone had a tail or could fly? It didn't bother me, so why did it bother everyone else so much?

I finally made it to the college and by the time I had

gotten there most of the parking lot was full. I pulled in where I had the past two visits and made my way through the maze of cars till I reached the B Hall entrance. A part of me was really hoping to see Jared's car sitting there, with him awaiting my arrival. No such luck.

Walking through the doors I saw two new women working the desk. It only occurred to me then that they may not let me in, seeing as I was only a "plus one". I strolled over to the wooden doors, hoping I looked like I belonged; neither of them even glanced my way. Breathing a sigh of relief I opened the doors to find almost every seat already filled.

Sitting where I usually did, I ignored the whispers and frightened glances. I was there to talk to the doctor, help Luke and nothing else. Yet, it finally occurred to me that I could have waited until class was over...

Moments after I sat down Dr. Wineman came in, appearing to be a happy medium between his two previous moods. He was neither bouncy nor tired, he just seemed...average.

"Hello class," he said, setting his briefcase on the table. "I'm glad you could all make it to our third official class. Today's lesson will be—"

"What about the killer?" a girl interrupted from the front row, raising her hand in the air.

"I beg your pardon?" Dr. Wineman asked. He must have what she meant, but just wanted her to clarify. She was about to ask what was on everyone's mind.

"The man that killed those women," she said, her head beginning to turn towards me but suddenly stopped, "he was in this class..." A few people around me risked a glance, but I tried not to give them any notice. I wasn't completely sure they were looking at me and not the empty seat beside me. Dr. Wineman looked uncomfortable.

"I'm sorry, but we aren't here to discuss that," he said, his eyes didn't even flick towards me. "Now, today's class will be a little shorter than our others as I have to leave early." He shuffled through his bag and pulled out a laptop. I tried to stay focused on him while he plugged it into the projector; I tried not to focus on the classroom and their accusations about Luke. I did wonder though, what the woman wanted to know about it. Why would she ask the professor? It's not like he would really know anything. I knew he knew something, but the rest of the world shouldn't know that.

"In this world there are humans that are truly evil," the doctor said, bringing my attention back to him from the woman in the front, "and there are humans that are good. It is the same for Etheric's; some are just born…bad." He kept his eyes on his computer, searching for a file. I had a hunch that he just didn't want to look up at the class, or me, because of Luke. How wonderful, Luke was arrested for murder, twice, and now we were in a class talking about evil. Somebody up there had a twisted sense of humour.

"Etheric's are a little different though," the doctor continued, "when they're evil it isn't because they were raised in a violent household, or because they need to be medicated, it's because it's in their nature. It's simply in their nature." The doctor clicked a button and an image popped up on the screen behind him.

Three women sat atop a pile of bones and jewels, every one of them naked. Cloth covered their lower halves as the one on the right held open arms to a boat out at sea. The middle woman played on a flute while the other dipped her hand in the nearby water, her mouth open as if singing. It wasn't a very detailed drawing, but it could still be considered good; I knew I couldn't draw anything like that.

"Can anyone tell me what this is?" Dr. Wineman asked, looking around the classroom. Nobody answered, not even daring to guess.

"I can tell you," someone said by the door. All eyes

turned, including mine, to find Jared standing there, hands in his pockets. "They're sirens. The sketch is a little inaccurate though." His hands came out of his pockets as he walked up the stairs, directly towards me. Taking two steps at a time, the room watched him; they must have seen him as some mysterious, attractive man with all the answers. Nobody seemed surprised when he sat down next to me in what had once been Luke's seat.

"That's correct," Dr. Wineman said, not asking who Jared was once he sat down. "Why do you say it's inaccurate?"

"Well, Greek mythology had a couple of different stories for sirens; one was that they were servants to Persephone but when she was kidnapped by Hades and brought to the underworld her mother Demeter cursed them, making them half bird." Jared leaned back in his seat and all I could do was stare at him in disbelief. "Another story was that Demeter gave them to bodies of birds to search for Persephone but eventually gave up and made a home in Southern Italy. But none of that is true."

I was at a loss for words. Jared was...Jared was actually kind of smart. He sat there, looking smug, most likely because he knew exactly what I was thinking. I had known he was a bounty hunter, but I had never expected him to actually...know things.

"That's right," the doctor said slowly, walking around the projector, "there are many different tales of how the sirens came about. They had the bodies of birds, but the heads of women and the truth is that there were only three sirens, daughters to the Greek river god Achelous. Eventually they all left the riverbank where they decided to remain on an island in Southern Italy."

"But why did they leave?" a student asked.

"All children have to leave home some time," Dr. Wineman said, opening his arms out wide. "The sirens were not always evil either. They challenged the Muses to a musical contest but were defeated. As punishment the

Muses plucked their feathers and kept them as a trophy, turning the sirens into creatures that had a woman's torso, but legs of a bird. It was then that they started to lure sailors to their death on the rocky shore."

"Are they still around?" someone else asked. Jared let out a quick and quiet laugh, obviously knowing the answer. The doctor caught it and gave him a stern look, warning him not to insult the students.

"There are two types of sirens still alive today," he explained, "there are the ones with birds legs, kept hidden from the world with magic amulets. They are the most dangerous ones of all as they could be anyone around you and you would never know until they strike." The man that asked the question paled a little.

"And the other one?" he asked, swallowing loudly, his mouth most likely drying from fear.

"They are what you know as mermaids," the doctor clicked a button on his computer and the image behind him flashed to a woman with a fish tail, combing her hair in a mirror on a single rock. "Mermaids can only live in the sea, in rivers and streams or in waterfalls, so they cannot attack as easily as their bird-like sisters. In many cultures they are mistaken for an undine, or water-spirit, but are almost always seen as a symbol of coming doom.

"They came about over many years as some of the sirens changed their image to continue luring men to their death, especially after they were defeated in the Odyssey. The mermaids are much more powerful than their avian counterparts, and their scales are highly regarded for their magic. A mermaid's scale can actually sell for thousands on the black market."

"Are they really that powerful professor?" the same man from before asked. Dr. Wineman thought for a moment.

"Though they are incredibly strong, they are sold for such a high price because it is almost impossible to get one."

"Is it possible to get one right from a mermaid?"

The doctor thought for another moment and considered the question. "Maybe," he finally said, "though there has never been a documented case. I suggest if you ever come across a siren that you get away as quickly as possible. They're extremely dangerous, to both men and women."

"Got that right," Jared mumbled harshly, his hand covering his mouth so I barely made out the words. I was about to ask him what he was doing here when he turned to me and whispered, "We need to talk."

"Not now," I said, trying to ignore not only his remarks but his very presence in general.

"It's important," he prodded, watching the doctor speak about the sirens. I guessed he was cataloguing which facts were right and which were wrong. He was no longer scoffing at the material so most must've been correct, at least in his mind. Just how many sirens had he come across in his travels?

"I need to talk to Dr. Wineman after the class," I said, crossing my legs away from him, "that's more important." Jared sighed and sat back in the chair. Obviously he wasn't going to go away; instead he was going to wait out the class with me. That seemed rather out of character for a bounty hunter; shouldn't he have just dragged me away in front of everyone?

"Next on the list of dangerous Etheric's," the doctor said, clicking to another picture, "are Ghouls." The photo behind him was...repulsive. It was a black and white sketch of a large hairy creature with fangs protruding from its mouth. It almost looked like a twisted version of Big Foot or even a werewolf.

"I hate Ghouls," Jared mumbled to himself. Apparently I was going to get commentary through the rest of the class. Splendid.

"Ghouls are not exactly...evil," Dr. Wineman continued, ignoring Jared's comments. "They feed off of freshly buried cadavers in graveyards so you can most often find them in abandoned mausoleums.

"Most of their history comes from the East, where they were known as an inferior form of Djinn. But Western stories tell them to be a sort of… vampire elemental, preying on the energies of humans, haunting places where tragedy occurred."

Dr. Wineman took a few questions from the class, but I was having trouble concentrating with Jared sitting next to me. He had moved as close as he could to me, trying to make me uncomfortable enough to leave. I could smell the leather of his jacket and the dirt-caked steel scent of his skin and underneath that some kind of cologne. It wasn't going to work though, his tactics that is. I needed to find out why the doctor lied for Luke and what he was hiding. Nothing could stand between me and those answers, not even a bounty hunter.

The doctor moved on, clicking his button to switch photos. An hour and a half later the doctor finally dismissed the class. Honestly I hadn't expected it to end so soon, the class was extremely interested in the topic, most likely because of the recent killings though. A few people stood and left, leaving the doors open on their way out.

"Doctor," said a girl, the same one that was so interested in Luke, "what about that man? Is he something that can't help but be evil?" Dr. Wineman flinched and a few of the people that were so ready to leave froze in place, waiting for an answer.

"No," the doctor said, carefully choosing his words, "he is not."

"So he's just…evil by choice then?" the girl asked. I clenched a fist over my phone in my pocket. I would not say anything. I would not say *anything*.

"I'm sorry, but if you wish to know something please consult a newspaper." The doctor turned and began to pack his bag. The girl seemed surprised by his response but quickly left once realizing she had upset him. When the room was empty I climbed down the stairs and approached the doctor; it was clear he was expecting me to talk to him. The only thing that caught him off guard was Jared, who was on my heels the entire way down.

"What can I do for you?" Dr. Wineman asked, desperately trying to stay casual.

"I just wanted to ask you a couple questions," I said, also trying to stay casual, "why did you help Luke?" The doctor glanced at Jared over my shoulder then back to me. Was he trying to tell if Jared was trustworthy? Good luck with that, I still wasn't sure myself.

"I'm aware that he is innocent," the doctor said, folding his arms behind his back, "I didn't want him to seem more suspect than he already had." His eyes darkened, thinking about how that didn't matter anymore; Luke had been thrown into jail once again thanks to the person directly behind me.

"But how do you know he's innocent?" everything the police had said was pointing to him being guilty. Everything that was reported said he was guilty. Dr. Wineman sighed and gave me a sympathetic look.

"Because of the smoke," he said, attracting Jared's interest.

"You know what that is?" Jared asked, pulling on my shoulder to get closer to the doctor who merely nodded. "What is it? How do I kill it?"

"I can't tell you," the doctor said, not budging when Jared stepped forward. I had to give him credit for that, at least. Jared reached forward to hold Dr. Wineman by the collar but I grabbed his hands before he could.

"Why the hell not?" he shouted. "This thing is killing people and you're not gonna do a damn thing about it?" Jared ripped his hands from mine, grabbing the doctor's collar and shoving him against the wall.

"Stop it!" I said, trying to pull Jared off the doctor. I was angry too, but this wasn't going to solve anything.

"It's not doing the killings," the doctor panicked, "Shadeland doesn't kill humans like this." Oh, but they *do* kill humans? Dr. Wineman froze, realizing he told us what he never intended to.

"Shadeland?" Jared said as if realizing something I wasn't. Suddenly he smiled and released the doctor. "Fine, I've got enough information from you to do this on my own."

"No!" the doctor yelled to him as he stormed away. "You're wrong!" He looked at me, then back at the door, not knowing what to do. I debated staying with him, asking him more questions but I couldn't afford to lose Jared now. I chased after him, hearing the doctor dialling a phone as I ran out the doors.

By the time I caught up with Jared he was already at the front doors. I almost risked yanking on his arm to make him stop but decided against it again.

"What are you going to do?" I asked, pacing his long strides.

"I'm gonna kill this thing," he said, "I just need a little help."

"From who?"

"That doesn't matter to you," he said, pulling out a set of keys from his jacket.

"Yes it does!" I yelled back. Suddenly he stopped in his tracks and turned to me.

"All right," he said and suddenly he grabbed my arm, dragging me across the lot, "if you aren't going to leave me alone, I'll make you leave me alone."

"What?" I shouted. Jared brought me to my car and threw me into the driver's seat, slamming the door shut. I was so flustered, I didn't even question as to why my car was left unlocked. My arm hurt where he had grabbed it but I was too focused on him to really notice.

"I'm going to do what I do best," he said through the window, his breath creating a slight fog over the glass. I tried to open the door, it opened an inch before he slammed it shut again; the difference in our strength gave me a severe disadvantage. Jared's voice was harsh, "And to make sure you don't follow me, I'll tell you what I was going to tell you sooner; Luke got released again. He's waiting for you to get home. You're welcome." He banged on the window and walked away. Jared came all the way to see me...to make sure I knew about Luke?

I stared out the window, his words registering in my head; Luke was released from jail and waiting for me at home.

I broke every speed limit driving back to the apartment and back to Luke.

Chapter 12

The door slammed against the wall as I burst through it, not even glancing at the yellow tape across Charlie's doorway as I moved.

"Luke?" I called into the apartment to find him sitting on the couch, watching the news. I left the door hanging open as I jumped over to him. "Are you okay?"

"Hi Liv," he said, a fatigued smile on his lips, "I...I've been better."

"Why did they release you?" I sat down next to him and touched his arm. It was so good to see him again, even though it hadn't actually been that long. It had felt like a lifetime to me, I didn't even want to ask how long it had been for him.

"Watch," he said and pointed at the television, "they've been playing this on repeat since I got out." I looked at the television to find Cindy there, a concerned expression painted across her face.

"Just two hours ago," she started, "Lucan Harroway was released from police custody after being arrested under false pretences." An image of Luke flashed on the corner of the screen. "The Detective that called for the arrest was suspended as well, here's what her partner has to say about it."

"I would like to apologize for the trouble caused to Mr. Harroway," Det. Young said, standing in front of the police station, "Det. Miller arrested him on the sole evidence that he is Eidolon and she has been suspended until further notice. Mr. Harroway is no longer a suspect in the case and has been cleared of all charges. If you have any further questions please direct them to—" Luke shut off the television, deciding I'd heard enough. Or maybe he just couldn't watch it again; knowing that they only reason he was a suspect was because of his birth family's history. I couldn't understand why they would out him as an Eidolon, since most people were still having trouble telling the world what they were. It was just cruel but it wasn't like they would care or even realize what they had done.

Luke sat on the couch, slumped over, defeated. I wasn't really sure what to do; I had never known anyone that had been arrested, humiliated on a national scale and then released. Instead, I just asked what I really wanted to know.

"Why was it Jared that arrested you?" Jared had told me one thing, but it didn't really add up in my mind. I highly doubted he had brought Luke in just because he thought it was the right thing to do.

"Hm?" Luke looked at me with dim eyes. "Oh, after the Detective decided I was guilty he brought me in so nobody else did. I think he just wanted the reward money though." Of course he did.

"Reward?" I remembered the paper he had stuffed in his pocket; a cheque?

"Yeah," Luke covered his face. "There was some reward to whoever brought me in or told the police where I was or something. How am I going to go into work now?" He fell over on the couch, his head hitting the cushion and groaned.

"It's okay," I told him. "It won't be long before they forget all about it. Especially after the killer is caught."

"The cops have nothing," he said, "so what if the killer is never caught?" He leaned up again, looking at me. "If the real murderer is never caught, they'll all think it's me! I'll lose my job, my friends, my whole life will be in ruins!" That stung, just a bit but he never caught on to how he had insulted me. It didn't seem to matter to him that I thought...no, I *knew* he was innocent.

"Jared's working on it," I said, hoping that would make it better, "I'm sure he'll find out what's going on." Luke just rolled his eyes.

"Great, the guy that arrested me is on the job," he stood, "I just...I need to be alone for a bit. Sorry." He waved his hand at me and walked towards his room. I only sighed when I heard the door gently click shut. I wished there was something I could do or say that would make him feel better, apparently.

What now? I was so happy Luke was out but he seemed less than impressed by it. It could've been worse; they could've left him in there and let everyone think he was a murderer. Although, the more I thought about it the more I realised that everyone at work would think he was a murderer anyway, until they were convinced someone else had done it. Which means...

"We need to find the killer," I whispered to the darkness. I wanted to rush out the door to find Jared, to tell him I was going to help him. But honestly, what could I do? There was a knock at the door, causing my rather depressing train of thought to come to a halt. When I didn't answer, whoever was on the other side knocked again, louder this time.

I stood and walked over to the door, taking a brief moment to glance down the hall towards Luke's room. There was no movement inside, so he was either asleep already, or ignoring the world. He rarely did that, but then again, he rarely got this depressed.

When I opened my front door I came face to face with a desperate doctor.

"You can't do the summoning spell," he said, grabbing my shoulders and pushing me inside to the kitchen. "It's not what you think!"

"What?" I said, confused and taken aback by his very presence. How did he know where I was? "Summoning spell?"

"Please," he said, "don't do it! You could get hurt, both of you. Where's Jared?" The door hung open behind him, allowing an eerie yellow glow into the room, his face shadowed.

"What are you talking about?" I asked again. Dr. Wineman's grip on my shoulders was tight, and I was too surprised to try and push him off. At least he didn't seem to want to hurt me.

"You cannot summon a creature from Shadeland," he told me, "it's not only very difficult, you need an experienced witch to do it. If you or the bounty hunter tries it yourselves you will most likely get hurt." So the killer really was from Shadeland? That was why Jared had run off so quickly?

"A witch?" I said, Jared's actions from the previous hour suddenly made sense. He was going to get Yamuna to summon the thing that killed the women. She was the one he was going to for help. As if the sound of my thoughts slowly clicking together could be heard, Jared appeared in my doorway, gun drawn. Dr. Wineman turned to face him after hearing the gun cock.

"Come on," Jared said, waving his gun towards himself, "time to go." The doctor didn't seem intimidated by the gun, so much as Jared himself. He took a step towards the bounty hunter. "Not you, moron. Her." His weapon pointed at me for a split second before returning to the doctor.

"What?" I said again, feeling repetitive.

"I need you to give me a hand with something," he said, "let's go." I didn't question why he was suddenly so willing to let me help, instead I listened and embraced the opportunity.

"Stay," Jared said to the doctor and pulled me out the door.

Chapter 13

Yamuna's house seemed even more dilapidated than I remembered, now that I was seeing it at night. Looking at it from Jared's car made my stomach turn just a little bit and his lecture on the ride over didn't help any. Wasn't the dark supposed to make things look better or at least skew the perspective a little? Today it didn't seem to be doing its job.

"Do you remember what I said?" he asked, turning to me from the driver's seat. I thought back to how he took me from my apartment and shoved me into his car, explaining how he didn't need my "help". He really just needed my help though.

Yamuna wouldn't help him unless I was there, apparently. I could understand her logic. She hated Jared, Jared disliked having me around, and therefore, to annoy him, she demanded I be present. I was thankful for that though, her distaste for Jared was allowing me to help out in what little ways I could and I didn't think I could handle Luke at the moment; he was sleeping anyway, I hoped, trying to hide from the world.

"I remember," I said, wondering if he was always going to be this...aggressive when asking for help. I imagined he would be, though he never admitted to needing my help; he strongly avoided the word in fact. We climbed out of the Charger and walked towards the gate. Just as the gateway creaked open I saw Yamuna opening the front door but quickly closing it again. We weren't going to have to force our way in again, were we? Although that might give me the opportunity to see what Jared had shown her on his ankle...

"Open up," Jared called as we came head on with the door. On the other side I heard a bolt click shut, ensuring us no entry. "Come on! You wanted her here, now she is."

"You weren't supposed to bring her," Yamuna said from inside, "you never bring anyone..." I wasn't sure I was supposed to hear the last part and I peeked at Jared; he didn't react to it. Despite the commotion around me I noticed the scent of lilacs filling the air. I glanced around but couldn't find the source; where could it be coming from?

"Well I did," Jared said back, "so open up before I kick the door down!"

The lock clicked again and slowly creaked open. Yamuna looked through the tiny crack, blue hair hanging loosely over her grey eyes as a sliver of light hit them. Suddenly her hand shot out, grabbing me and dragging me inside, neither I nor Jared fast enough to stop her. It probably didn't help that I was looking around the area, not paying attention to either of them. As I stumbled backwards into her hallway she locked the door again, leaving Jared to bang on it with a lot of force. He shouted, "What the hell are you doing?"

"Don't like you," she said to him, as if he was right beside her and not behind a heavy door, "I'll talk to her...not you." Yamuna's eyes darted back and forth between the walls before they finally settled on me.

"Tea?"

"Sure," I said, not entirely certain why I was there. At least she let me into the house. Yamuna walked into the kitchen and set a kettle on the stove. I glanced at the door for a moment, listening to Jared's curses and kicking, before finally going into the kitchen. It was still strange to see what the inside of her home, or prison as she called it, looked like; so new when the exterior was so…broken. I wondered why the porch was so torn apart when she was able to walk on it, maybe she just didn't care enough to bother.

"Sit," Yamuna said, gesturing to the same chair I had taken before. "I need you to get some things before we can do the spell."

"Spell?" I questioned, looking up at her from the table.

"The summoning spell," she said, turning to face me. She must have guessed by my expression that I was completely clueless. She watched me, thoughtful.

"What spell?" I asked. I already knew what she meant, to a certain degree, from what I had learned from Dr. Wineman. He told me that it was too dangerous to do the spell as well, so why was Yamuna willing to help us?

"If the thing that's killing women is an ancient creature from Shadeland," she explained, sitting down while the kettle boiled, she was careful not to look at me, "we need certain…ingredients to summon it into our realm." It bothered me a little, how sure everyone was that this creature was committing the murders. Where was their proof?

"It isn't…already in our realm?" I pondered. "How is it killing if it isn't…here?"

"Shadeland is as old as the world itself," she brushed her hair behind her ears and gazed out the black kitchen window, "it's not just in the triangle like they tell the humans, it's everywhere. It exists all around us; it's just not visible to us."

"So if something is in Shadeland," I started, "and we

can't see it, can it see us?"

"Only if the thing in Shadeland is powerful enough," she tapped her fingers on the sleek furniture, "which most of them are since they only allow purebloods in now." We sat in silence for a while as I thought everything over.

"That doesn't explain how it kills when it isn't in our realm." Yamuna twitched, annoyed by how little I understood from her explanation. I only knew what most humans knew, since I had never actually met another Eidolon besides Luke. It was unfair of her to hold that against me.

"It moves around in Shadeland," she said, trying to stay calm but clearly losing the battle, "but when it kills it comes into this realm. It can only be killed when it is fully formed on this plane of existence."

"So the smoke…" I said, allowing my thought to trail off.

"Yes," Yamuna agreed with a nod, "the smoke that Jared mentioned is a partly formed Shadeland ancient." The kettle began to whistle with a trace of steam coming from its mouth, its shape reminiscent of what I had seen recently hanging over dead bodies. She got up from her chair and poured the hot water into a teapot.

"How can it be killed?" I asked. She froze, her back to me.

"Sound like the hunter," she mumbled to herself but the room was quiet enough for me to hear her. She prepared the tea in small white cups and brought them to the table, handing me one. "Don't worry about killing it."

"What should I worry about then?" I ignored her comment, partly because I knew how true it was. When this was over I would be sure to never ask how to kill something again. I didn't like how it sounded coming from my lips; like a murderer.

"The spell," she said, taking a sip. I jumped when Jared banged on the front door again but Yamuna didn't seem bothered. "I need certain ingredients to make it work."

"So what do you need?" it was my turn to take a drink. I hoped Jared wouldn't bang again and make me spill it; I had been dangerously close only seconds earlier.

"A mermaid's scale," Yamuna said, making me almost spit out the tea. She handed me a napkin and I dabbed my mouth with it, setting down the cup. It would be safer if I didn't hold onto it, it seemed.

"A what?" I asked, remembering Dr. Wineman's previous lecture. "A mermaid's scale? Aren't those impossible to find?" Yamuna shook her head.

"They're quite simple to find," she said with another sip, "they're just hard to hold in your hands." A small smile curled her lips but I didn't understand why.

"Where can we get one then?" Yamuna shook her head again, blue hair shivering on her shoulders. It looked spectacular against her dark skin tone.

"That's for you and the bounty hunter to find out," she said. I didn't try to fight her, not wanting to risk changing her mind. "I also need the venom of a dragon, the dust of a pixie and the blood of the latest victim. I would suggest getting that one last, it will take time to get the other supplies."

"Why get that last?" I watched her, curious.

"Because there will be more victims before you can get everything ready." Her grey eyes were an unsettling calm. We sat in silence once more and I found I couldn't look away from my teacup. Eventually the quiet began to bear down on me, twisting the atmosphere into something uncomfortable.

"Why do you need these ingredients?" I questioned, wondering as to how they mattered. I could understand the mermaid's scale, since it was so powerful, but everything else? I didn't have a clue.

"Why does a spell need anything at all?" Yamuna questioned back taking a small tea spoon between her fingers and stirring her drink. She didn't answer my enquiry or perhaps avoided it altogether. The scale, venom and dust were all magical properties...but why the blood? I asked her and she replied, "Connection."

"Connection?" I repeated to her and she made a small disapproving noise under her breath. I had a feeling I was going to get this a lot, from just about everyone.

"Need a connection to it," she explained, carefully controlling her tone and keeping her eyes down, "otherwise the spell would just summon the closest one. Blood will give us the connection to the creature." I was about to ask why it had to be the latest victim and not just any of them when I came to my own conclusion; the latest victim would have the strongest connection. They would be the...freshest so to speak. I pursed my lips, thoughtful.

"Why do you think it's doing it?" I asked towards my teacup as the witch picked up her own. "What does it want?" Yamuna set the cup down and continued to stare out the window. Her hand touched her face gently.

"To kill, I imagine," she said plainly. There was a hint of boredom in her voice, as if I should already know the answer. Because killing something for no reason was just so common? This must've seemed so uninteresting to her, as I tried to figure out the why.

"But...why?" I couldn't understand why it wanted to kill. I needed a reason, like most of the world, I needed to know why it chose these people, why it chose now to start killing. Another question occurred to me, and it seemed to stand out from the others. Has this happened before? Were Charlie and Rosa and the others not the only ones killed?

"Some things don't need a reason." She looked down at her cup and turned it back and forth on the table. She whispered, desire clear in her words, "Some things just like the *power*." The tea began to bubble and swirl around. As I watched her I saw her eyes change; her pupils contracted to mere dots before exploding to erase her irises. It was only a second before they returned to normal along with the tea. I knew I was staring at her, but she didn't seem to notice. Something about the way she whispered her words sent a shiver through my body.

"Is that all you need?" I asked, ready to leave and possibly find my own answers.

"Hmm?" Yamuna looked up at me, oblivious to what she had just done.

"A mermaid's scale, the venom of a dragon, pixie's dust and... blood of the latest victim," I repeated, "that's it?"

"That's all I need you to get," she said with a sigh. I typed the ingredients into my phone. It wasn't that I thought I may forget them, I just wanted to play it safe; I doubted Jared would be very forgiving should something go wrong. And I would never be able to forgive myself if something went wrong because of me and we never caught Charlie's killer. I doubted Luke would be able to forgive me too, despite his high threshold for mistakes.

"One more thing," she said just as I was about to stand. "I won't be doing the spell."

"Then who will?" I asked, confused.

"I'll show you how to do it," she took a sip, an attempt to hide her devilish smile "but that's where I draw the line." Was this the catch? If we needed such a powerful witch to do the spell, why would she let me do it? Or maybe she meant Jared should do it? I was about to ask her another question when she waved her hand at me, telling me to leave. What was she thinking? What was she *planning?*

I stood up and made it to the kitchen doorway before thinking how strange it was that Yamuna was suddenly helpful. I didn't know her that well, but she hated Jared, so why help him? Was it just to catch a murderer? Somehow, I doubted that. There was something else she wanted, something that might have to do with me helping Jared.

"Why are you helping?" I asked her, trying not to sound too insulting. Yamuna gave a low, almost menacing chuckle.

"Does that really matter so much?" She looked up at me, causing another shudder to run through my entire body. It was the same feeling I got when Luke used his abilities on me but her stare felt...dark.

"Sometimes," I said, suddenly feeling the urge to flee. I walked out the door, my pace giving away my true feelings.

When I got outside I took a deep breath and found Jared pacing back and forth on Yamuna's small walkway. He jumped on me the second our eyes met.

"What the hell was that?" he shouted, pointing at the door behind me. I made sure to shut it quickly, in case he wanted to go inside and give Yamuna a piece of his mind...or possibly a bullet.

"She didn't want you around," I stated, knowing it was the truth and ignoring my instinct to tell him everything. It was probably best he didn't know *everything*.

"Don't do that again," he growled and stomped off towards the Charger.

"Like it was my fault? Yamuna just grabbed me and pulled me inside; I didn't exactly have a choice." Jared slammed his car door shut, making me a little surprised. His car seemed to be a large part of his life; I doubted he slammed the door very often.

I followed him into the car, leaving the crisp night air for the smell of leather. I made sure to be gentle with the passenger door. Jared sat gripping the steering wheel.

"So what do I need to get to summon this thing?" he questioned, not looking at me. I told him the ingredients and with each one his knuckles got a little whiter on the wheel. "Perfect."

"I want to help," I said fast, already knowing his reply.

"Not happening," Jared laughed, starting the car. "You'll get in the way." I wasn't about to win this argument so I went with what humans did best in this situation; I lied.

"Yamuna said I have to go," I said, "otherwise she

won't do it." Okay, it was a lie, but it was necessary lie.

"Oh, come on," he groaned. Jared wasn't about to talk to Yamuna and by the time he found out I lied, if he ever did, it would be too late. He was stuck with me, whether he liked it or not. Besides, Yamuna technically wanted us to do the spell. I mentioned that part to Jared and he took a deep breath in through his nose before pulling away from the broken house.

Chapter 14

The next day Jared didn't have to say a word to let me know I wasn't welcome. It was obvious in the way he glanced at me without moving his head, and in the way he held the steering wheel with both hands, as opposed to his usual one. I knew that what we were doing was dangerous, but that didn't matter to me; some part of me wanted to catch the killer that had caused Luke so much trouble and another part wanted to do it just because it was...interesting. That sounded wrong, even as I thought it.

We had gotten lucky that Luke was released again, but that didn't stop people from still believing he was the killer. It didn't stop any of the humans, at least. Most of the Eidolon's seemed to know that he didn't do it, yet none of them wanted to say anything, making sure to keep it a secret. It made me wonder if they knew who was really behind the killings. Dr. Wineman knew something that he wasn't telling anyone and if he wasn't going to help us then maybe Yamuna could.

Though she had probably needed some convincing, she

agreed to help us in the end. What I didn't understand was why she didn't want to do the spell herself. Was it really so dangerous to summon this thing? And how did she expect us to do it?

"Do you know how to kill it?" I questioned Jared, the tension in his arms not getting any worse. He was stiff, and after driving for nearly an hour I imagined it would get sore or at the very least tiring. Still, he kept his position.

"Kill what?" he asked back. What else would I be talking about? Was there something else out there that needed to be killed? I hoped not...that thought led me astray, into a direction I didn't want to go.

"Whatever's killing these women," I said, resting an arm on the door of his car. "When we summon it, do you know how to kill it?"

"First off, there is no 'we'," he waved his hand in front of himself, finally losing a bit of control, "you refused to get out of my car, so I'm stuck taking you with me to get the stuff Yamuna wants. When *I* summon this thing, you won't be there. I will be alone, and I will kill it *alone*."

"So you do know what it is," I said, ignoring the tone of his voice and how he was going to make sure I wasn't around. "You know how to kill it?" He placed his hand back on the wheel and kept his eyes forward.

"Can't be that hard," Jared said, "everything can die."

I found his choice of words interesting. As a bounty hunter I would have thought he would say that everything "can be killed", but instead he said everything "can die". So who did he lose that he thought would never die? I considered asking him, but he probably would have stopped the car and left me in the middle of the forest. My mind began to mull it over, trying to figure him out without being given any clues.

I said nothing and stared out the window watching tree after tree after tree pass by. It was a bright day out, despite the fact that later today we may be killing a creature as old as the world itself; somehow whenever I imagined the future it was dark and usually black and white. I began to think about what it must have seen in its lifetime, the wars, the revolutions and the changes, until soon enough the paved road turned into dirt and the car began to bump along with its curves. Jared had refused to tell me where we were going, as if I would go there alone at some point. Of all the ingredients on Yamuna's list, all of them were nearly impossible to get; a mermaid's scale being at the height of impossibilities.

I eyed Jared, he didn't look like he had thousands to spare; he wore the same outfit almost every day, or every time I saw him, anyway. So where did he plan on getting the scale? His answer to almost every question I had asked was "I know someone" or "I know a place" or sometimes just "shut up already". Not the most informative or nicest person around.

The Charger came to a stop on the dirt lane, the fender just inches away from the knee-high grass ahead of us. I grimaced, glancing down at my moccasins, they weren't exactly hiking shoes.

"I suppose if I told you to wait here you wouldn't," Jared said, putting the car in park. He stepped out without waiting for a reply. I opened the door and quickly shut it, just in time to hear him say, "That's what I thought." He was wearing his sunglasses now and as I looked around I regretted not having mine with me.

"What are we looking for here?" I asked, tailing him through the trees as he tromped down the grass. He stepped down hard on the blades, making sure they stayed down for a while after he moved on. I followed in his footsteps, wondering if he did it to help me walk through.

"The first item on the list," he said, holding up the piece of paper, "the mermaid scale." I stopped and looked up at him, knowing that if I tried to walk it would end in disaster.

"But the doctor said those were almost impossible to get," I continued forward, since Jared didn't stop to chat.

"They are for normal people," Jared laughed. If I were him I would probably laugh too, knowing how not normal I was. Maybe his laugh wasn't at how others couldn't do what he could, but at himself, for how not normal his life was. The puzzle that was Jared seemed to be falling together, piece by misshapen piece.

"So where are we going to find a mermaid's scale in the woods?" I asked, catching up with him easily as he forced the grass down to the earth. I hoped saying "we" enough would get into his head; make him start saying it so I was included. It was bad enough Luke was stuck in a depression at home; I didn't need to join him there. Being productive would be the only way I could stay sane, or so I hoped.

"Like the good doctor said," Jared pulled a compass out of his pocket and suddenly turned right, "mermaids are always mistaken for undines. They can be found pretty much wherever water is." I paused and listened to the stillness in the air.

"I don't see any water," and I couldn't hear any. We pushed our way through the grass; it almost seemed to be getting thicker, stronger. As a child I had walked through many woods surrounding Ellengale, but this area was unknown to me, with no designated pathway.

"Just hurry up," he ordered, still stomping down the grass to make my journey easier. At least, I hoped that's why he was doing it; I couldn't think of any other reason. It was only about two minutes later that the silence between us started to really bother me.

"So do you know a lot about the Eidolon's?" I asked, and it almost sounded like I was making polite conversation. This was new to me, I never really bothered talking to people but for some reason I really wanted to talk to Jared then. He was...scary but still interesting. I had never met anyone like him.

"I hunt them daily," he told me, "of course I know a lot about them. Watch your step." He hopped over a fallen tree branch and paused to look back at me from the corner of his eye. I did the same and we kept moving.

"You said you've only been hunting Eidolon's for about a year, since they came out," I wanted to call them Etheric's, to be politically correct, but I didn't think Jared would care what I called them. "How much can you learn about them in a year?"

That made him stop; I counted to three before he started walking again and I decided it would be best to keep my mouth shut. After a few more minutes I could hear water falling over rocks but still no animals. The hushed woods were unnerving and the sunbeams streaming between the leaves only made me feel a little safer.

We stepped into a small clearing in the sunlight. A few feet away was a river and at its head a small waterfall, probably only fifteen feet high. The water was clear, allowing me to see the smooth pebbles on the bottom; I had never seen a river so clean. It almost appeared to glisten as we walked over to it. Jared moved away from me and surveyed the area looking, I assumed, for the siren but I couldn't take my eyes off of the water; it was just so beautiful.

I moved a few inches closer to it, not having a single thought in my head. Kneeling down I reached my hand out to the water, almost able to touch it when a small yellow butterfly landed on my fingers, wrenching me out of my trance with a cool puff of air.

I felt its legs tap along my knuckles as it founds its balance, its wings fluttering to create another oddly cool breeze on my hand.

"What are you doing?" Jared asked, grabbing my shoulders and wrenching me back up. The butterfly glided off on the air and I looked up at Jared, confused.

"Huh?" I said, wondering why he would sound so mad. Well, then again, he always seemed upset over something.

"You wanna die?" It didn't sound like a threat so I

asked him what he meant. He sighed and pulled me away from the water before explaining. "Mermaids are pure magic, that's why their scales are so rare. When they're in the water, they give off this…pheromone,"—he waved his hands around slightly—"it makes the water like a trap." He set his aviators on his head to show how serious he was. That explained the stories of sailors diving into the water near a mermaid.

"That's why it glows?" I looked towards the water for a second before Jared pulled my face back to see his.

"Yes," he stressed, "so don't look at it for longer than a few seconds otherwise you'll get trapped." He grabbed the sunglasses off his head and put them over my eyes. "Here, these'll help."

"What about you?" I asked, touching the sides of the glasses. They were a little large for me so they slid down my nose just enough to be irritating.

"Can't you just say 'thanks'?" He sighed and walked away, towards the waterfall. I stood there and watched him, holding my left arm for comfort.

"Thanks," I mumbled under my breath and followed after him. I tried not to look at the water again, but it was hard since we were looking for a mermaid. At least we knew she would be there, since the water was glistening. I didn't say anything to Jared, but at some points I actually thought I could hear the water almost calling to me; it sounded like a ringing chime in the air that I couldn't ignore. It was a song sung just for me.

Jared stood at the edge of the waterfall, staring into it. I almost thought he was in a trance like I had been minutes earlier but he would look away every few seconds, ensuring he wouldn't be ensnared in the mermaid's trap.

"How did you know there would be a mermaid here?" I asked, still trying to fill the quiet, and drown out the chime. Jared brushed his hair back.

"I did a little research," he told me, "and ten years ago a woman killed herself here." I gave him a blank expression through his sunglasses, hoping he would elaborate. I expected him to roll his eyes or sigh like Yamuna so often did with me, but he did neither. "She jumped off the cliff after finding out her husband cheated on her. There's a legend that above the River Rhine in Germany that a woman did the same thing over a faithless lover and she became a siren. There are a few different versions to that though."

"I've only heard of two cases when the woman actually becomes a siren, or more specifically a Lorelei." He began walking down the river but I stayed by the waterfall; it was… quieter there.

"So if you only know of two other times a woman has become a Lorelei, how did you know this one would?" It was one hell of a lucky guess. Jared crouched down by the water and touched his mouth in thought.

"Over the past decade there have been a few mysterious drowning's and disappearances, all of them started after the woman killed herself."

"That's really…professional of you," I said. I really hadn't expected him to do research on the subject, or to even think about looking into the history. Jared was just full of surprises and apparently deserved more credit than I gave him…for now at least.

"Well that and there were reports of seeing a mermaid here over the years," -and it was ruined. He straightened himself and shot me a toothy grin. "It's about time you showed up."

"What?" I asked, confused.

"Well neither of you were going to go into the water willingly," came a voice that felt like silk across my skin. I twitched, resisting the instinct to jump away as I turned around to face the caressing voice; in front of me stood a woman with chestnut dark hair and deep, empty blue eyes. Taking a careful step back I watched her, unable to look away as I had the water; this time because of fear though, not magic.

129

"What can I say? I'm not that easy," Jared was beside me, pulling my arm to keep me back. He stepped between us, just enough to emphasize that I wouldn't be another one of her victims. It was exactly what Luke did in elementary school when someone would try and pick on me; they were both protecting me.

A soft breeze came from my left and lifted the sirens hair with it. I noticed that her hair was dry, not wet as I had imagined it would be. Her red and white flowered sundress moved with the wind while her toes played with the grass below. She was absolutely gorgeous, if you ignored the hollow abyss in her eyes.

"We want a scale," Jared said, almost as if she would just hand one over. Her laugh came out like a bark, mocking us both.

"As if I would give one of my scales to anyone," she said, covering her mouth while she laughed, "besides, you have something much more powerful on your side." Her eyes fell on me, sending a shiver through my body. She continued, "But I'll die before you get one of my scales."

"Well, if that's what you want," Jared's arm shot from his side and swung at her, hitting her across the face. I jumped back at that point.

"What are you doing?" I yelled at him with a jump backwards. Somehow I didn't think she would hand over a scale if we beat her. Jared turned to me for only a second.

"We need her to show her true form," he yelled back, "we need to get her mad!" The siren straightened herself and laughed again, the punch barely fazed her.

"Hitting me won't work human," she scoffed, "you'll never get my scale, you'll be dead soon enough." Jared punched her again, this time I could see more power in it. I stayed still, not knowing what to do but knowing I couldn't just punch a mermaid. The only person I had ever considered hitting was...well, Jared.

The siren moved in to attack Jared and my heart began

to race even more. I started feeling the same as when I had found Charlie; totally useless. She hissed at him as he prepared to swing again, holding up her hand in defense. I had thought she simply would have blocked his attack, but instead she countered it.

A large stream of water poured from the center of her palm, moving like a serpent and hammering Jared in the chest. I stumbled aside just in time to avoid him crashing into me. He flew back a few feet past me before landing on the grass. Jared stood, soaked.

"Okay," he said, removing his jacket, "happy birthday to me." He tossed his jacket at me and I caught it, trying not to get wet. Jared's white shirt was almost completely clear now, showing multiple scars that he must have gotten during his years as a bounty hunter. His gun was holstered by his side but that quickly changed when he ripped it out of its holster to point it at the siren.

Jared's hair was matted down from the water, almost covering his eyes. I wondered if he could see very well like that, if he would be able to aim the gun. He pulled the trigger, the sound echoing through the woods. Hopefully nobody was close, or they would have easily heard the shot.

The siren burst into a million strands of water, disappearing into the ground. I looked around the area but couldn't find her anywhere, she was gone.

"Bullets," said the siren, reappearing behind Jared in seconds, "how...simple."

Jared spun on his heels but it was too late, the mermaid stuck her hand in the air and blasted him with another torrent of water. He was coming right at me again, and I ducked as I heard him sail over me, feeling the air whip my hair back. I was gripping his jacket as though my life depended on it, not caring that the water was soaking into my clothes.

I turned around, still on my knees to see Jared rolling over on the ground. I imagined he was seeing stars as he

131

climbed to his hands and knees. How did he still manage to get up? Looking back, the siren had disappeared again. This wasn't going as well as I had hoped it would.

With shaky knees I stood and backed up towards Jared. I almost shrieked when I bumped into his chest and he touched my arm.

"Watch yourself," he warned, eyeing the trees around us, "she could be anywhere." He stepped in front of me, holding his gun low in front of him with both hands.

"What should I do?" I asked in a whisper, clutching his jacket in my hands.

"Just stay out of the way," he said, his voice as loud as it usually was, "I need to make her show her true form and the only way to do that is to make her lose the glamour."

"Glamour?" I whispered back to him.

"Yeah," he said, glancing at me, "it's like camouflage; makes her look human. Almost all the things use it to blend in."

"And how do we make her lose it exactly?" I was still whispering, feeling as if that would ensure she couldn't hear us. He had said something about making her mad but that seemed too easy.

"You can't," said the siren from behind me. I turned to see her empty eyes staring back at me as she lifted her hand for the attack.

"Down!" Jared shouted and I dove to the ground, covering my head by instinct. He fired the gun and I heard the siren screech. I had to hold my hands over my ears; the sound could shatter glass and the river next to us rippled from the exuding power, an echo resonating around us. The leaves rustled and in the distant birds took off, screeching. When the scream died down I opened my eyes and peered upwards, where the siren was standing.

"How is this possible," she questioned, her voice hoarse. "They're just bullets." Her eyes were wide as she stared down at her bleeding hand. Jared had managed to shoot directly through her palm, leaving a bloody hole in the center. Her left hand clasped at her wrist, unsure of what to do with the wound.

"Hurts, huh?" Jared said with a wicked smile, a deadly smile. I was glad I wasn't on the receiving end of that look; that look that said he knew something that you didn't. That look that said he was about to kill you. For a brief second I wondered if he had ever looked at a human with that smile.

"It isn't healing," the siren said, finally ripping her eyes to look at me, "why isn't it healing?" She fell to her knees, her dress soaking up the water as it touched the ground.

"Liv. Here. Now." Jared pointed to the spot next to him and I obeyed. I didn't care that he was treating me like a dog in that moment; I was too focused on the woman in front of me. Though she was evil, she looked very human, appearing as a woman in pain and scared.

"It won't work," the siren laughed, hysterical, "I won't change, not completely. You will never get my scale." She held onto her wrist, blood trickling down her arm before dripping onto her dress. Jared lifted his gun again at her.

"Guess I'll have to shoot you again," he said, "kinda sucks when you're shot with a cursed bullet. Believe me, I know." His smile was gone, replaced with a stern and thoughtful look. He rotated his left shoulder, remembering something from the past. As he prepared to shoot I stopped him, touching his forearm. He looked down at me. "What?"

"You said the first Lorelei had killed herself because of a cheating husband, right?" I asked and he nodded. I turned to the siren, still crumpled on the ground. "Is that why you did it?"

"What does that have to do with anything?" she asked, looking at me with her bottomless eyes. This time they weren't empty though, they have a flicker of something in them…despair. She had jumped down onto the sharp rocks below to kill herself because her husband cheated on her. I felt a twinge of guilt over what I thought I was about to do. Telling myself it was necessary didn't make me feel any better.

"You probably deserved it," I told her, trying to act as if I didn't care about what was happening. "Clearly you weren't enough for him."

"What?" She said, anger taking over her beautiful features.

"What are you doing?" Jared whispered to me, never taking his gun off the siren. I ignored him and gently swatted his shoulder.

"I mean, come on," I said with a hint of a laugh, "you're pretty and all, but I'm guessing the woman he slept with was way better than you. Blonde maybe?" The siren flinched. "Yeah, guys always have a thing for blondes."

"Shut up, child," she warned, "you don't know anything." Water began to drip down the strands of her hair until it was plastered to her head. She watched me through her bangs, ire rising in the deep blue irises as they began to swirl with power.

"I know that you loved your husband, but know what?" My hands fell to my sides, Jared's jacket hanging loose in my fingers. "You didn't *satisfy* him. *He didn't love you.*" That was enough to set her off. That was enough to make her lose her glamour.

"No!" she shrieked and leapt at me. A cyclone of water circled her as she showed us her true form while still in the air before us. Her dress was gone, revealing a smooth grey torso leading to a classic mermaid's tail, long and shining in various blues, violets and greens. The blue that had once been so gorgeous in her eyes took over the whites and the pupils. As she screamed she bore fangs and her arms reached for me, her nails two inches too long, fingers rigid.

I could hear the chimes in the water and covered my ears instead of ducking. It was too loud, I couldn't hear anything else; I was paralyzed. Jared grabbed me and threw me to the ground, shielding me from the water. He didn't waste any time jumping from me and aiming his gun but the siren was gone again, already hiding in the river she deemed hers. As I hit the ground his sunglasses flew from my face.

"Mind telling me what that was?" Jared said, on high alert scanning the river and waterfall. I sat up and rubbed my head, thinking about how close I had just come to death…again. I picked up the sunglasses and placed them back on, careful not to look at the water without them.

"I figured if she killed herself over her husband then it would upset her enough to make her change," I was yelling, trying to drown out the chimes of the water. I adjusted Jared's sunglasses on my face and got to my feet, cautious of another attack.

"Well, warn me next time, 'kay?" I was about to say something back to him when the river began to bubble and flow backwards. A whirlpool began to form in front of where Jared and I stood, sucking water from the waterfall and further down the river. We stood watching it, water dripping from our bodies and flowing towards the pool. He stared down and said, "That's not good."

I took a step back and Jared raised his gun just as another cyclone shot out of the river. I could see the form of the siren inside it and had to cover my ears again because of the song. I counted off two bullets Jared shot into the cyclone by watching his trigger pulls. He jumped out of the way, leaving the siren to fall to the grass below, dead and in her true form as the water fell around her.

"Stay back," Jared said and he walked over to the lifeless Etheric. She was lying on her stomach so I couldn't tell where she had been shot. Her face was elegant, as if she was sleeping; no fangs. Jared tapped at her torso with one foot and her eyes jumped open.

She screamed and reached for me again with one free arm. I fumbled backwards and fell to the earth, frightened. Jared swore and shot two more bullets into her back, both hitting her heart. She slumped over on the earth again, her eyes slowly closing as she died. I was still shaken from the sudden outburst, my ears ringing.

"What was that?" I shouted at him. I had thought she was dead the first time.

"Guess I missed," he shrugged and reloaded his gun before putting it back in its holster. I stayed where I was, still holding onto Jared's jacket too tightly again as he knelt down next to the siren.

He reached into his back pocket and pulled out a switch knife, flicking it so the blade came out. Slowly he lifted off one of the colour scales from the tail, pulling it upwards with sickening "*shtick*" noise.

"C'mere," he said and again I obeyed on wobbly legs. He held out a hand when I reached him and I gave him his jacket back. "Hold this."

Jared placed the scale into my hand possession, careful not to break it. As it sat in my hand I could feel it buzzing with energy, so much so that the center of my palm grew hot. I was just glad it wasn't singing to me like the water had. With that in mind I glanced over at the river; it was flowing as it should be. It no longer had that same alluring glow to it, its bottom obscured by the rustled mud; it was just regular water now that the mermaid was dead.

Jared threw his leather coat on and pulled a plastic container out of it. If I hadn't known any better I would have said it was a petrie dish. He stuck the scale inside and tucked it safely back in his pocket. I bent over and picked up Jared's sunglasses off the ground.

"Let's go," he ordered, taking his sunglasses off of me before leading the way back to the car.

"What about the body?" I asked, holding onto my phone in my pocket. I was a little surprised it hadn't fallen out when Jared tackled me. He turned to face me and smiled, setting up his aviators on top of his head to get a clearer look at me. Jared asked the question back to me, still smiling. His question confused my already scattered mind so I looked down at the body of the siren.

Just three feet away from the body began to evaporate and melt at the same time. Like she had done before, parts of the siren started to turn into water and soak into the ground, but a thin mist also floated up and away from her into the air. It was only a matter of seconds until she was completely gone, leaving nothing behind besides the greenest grass I had ever seen in the shape of a what had once been a lonely, heartbroken woman.

Chapter 15

"Are all the ingredients going to be as hard to find as the mermaid's scale?" I questioned from the passenger seat. Jared tapped his fingers on the steering wheel, staring out the front window with an upsetting amount of intensity.

We sat parked in front of the diner he had once taken me to. Jared remained silent most of the ride here, the mermaid's scale safely in his pocket. For some reason I imagined something on his mind, but it's not like he would ever tell me should I ask. When he had decided to speak to me, he just said that "this" was the reason he never worked with others. I had gotten in the way, but then again, I *had* gotten the mermaid to reveal her true form. It's not like I was completely useless, not this time.

"Yes, now c'mon," Jared said as he got out of the Charger. I followed suit and walked behind him into the diner. He seemed to be ignoring answering my question in detail and I couldn't tell if it was because he was mad I was there or mad that I had actually managed to help him. We sat down at the same booth and asked for two coffees, Jared adding the daily special to his order.

"You're eating?"" I asked a little surprised. I felt as if I hadn't eaten in days, ever since Charlie had died. It had only gotten worse after Luke had been arrested for the second time, and I knew it wasn't going to get better once we returned to work.

"Yeah, so?" Jared said, grabbing a knife and fork from the end of the table and placing them beside him. I shrugged, wanting to get back to finding the ingredients for Yamuna. I didn't like taking this break, even after getting the mermaid scale. If all the other supplies would be hard to find, didn't that mean we should pick up the pace? I poured some cream and sugar into my coffee and took a sip.

"What did you mean back there?" I asked him, peeking up at him.

"What?"

"When the mermaid hit you...is it really your birthday?" I had almost missed what he said. But it was an odd, and kind of sad, thing I thought if today really was his birthday.

Jared stayed silent for a moment before answering. He sighed and said, "Yes, technically."

"How old are you then?"

He leaned onto the table, shifting his entire body towards me. Under the table one of his boots hit my foot and I resisted the instinct to turn away. A piece of hair flipped into his eyes but he didn't brush it away. For a moment my heart rate sped up, wondering what he was going to say and as I thought of reaching over to brush that piece of hair out of his eyes.

"Twenty-four," he finally admitted, a hint of a smile on his lips.

"Happy birthday," I said. For some reason my mind calculated automatically that that made him only seven years older than me, technically six since my birthday was so late in the year. I had never calculated a man's age before.

"I guess," he shrugged. I didn't say anything after that, since his response was a little strange even by my standards. Instead I started to look around the room, my face felt too warm.

The diner was busy but that only made sense considering it was almost lunch time. As I peered around the area the normal hustle and bustle began to bother me until a woman caught my eye. She was staring at me from another booth, just behind Jared. We made eye contact and I realised who she was; Cindy the reporter. The same reporter that had first put Luke's picture out to the world but she was also the first reporter to apologize for it. I wondered if it was because she was actually sorry or if it was because her boss told her to say it.

Cindy was sitting with a small, dark skinned man with black hair from what I could tell by the back of his head. His shoulders slumped over the table towards her, either showing interest in her or he was exhausted, I couldn't tell. The reporter suddenly stood, paying no attention to her friend and approached me.

"You're his girlfriend, right?" she said to me, making an alarming amount of eye contact. I wanted to look away but I found I couldn't, her eyes hypnotising me as the mermaid's water had. At least this time it wasn't because of magic. "I'm so sorry for what happened."

Finally, I tore my eyes away from her to look at Jared. He was watching her, leaning back in the booth, completely at ease. It made me uncomfortable, the way he looked her up and down, as if sizing her up. I guessed what I said was true; men really do prefer blondes. I played with my still-growing-out brown bangs and pouted a little.

"I'm not the one you should apologize to," I said and shifted my body away from her. She took the hint and slunk out the glass doors, leaving the man she was with to pay the bill. I saw him take the piece of paper and stuff it into his pocket as he stood. I risked looking at his face, just for a moment, to see that he had large bags under his eyes. He blinked at me and continued forward, not even realizing who I was connected to. Or maybe he just didn't care; he looked rather distraught.

"That was harsh," Jared said, eyeing Cindy as she quickly walked past the window by us. I couldn't believe he was saying that, after what had happened to Luke. "She seemed honest." I shrugged my shoulders again and took another drink, tucking my hair behind my ears.

"What are we getting here?" I questioned as Jared stopped in front of a pet shop downtown. I looked into the windows at the kittens playing and tapped on it gently with my knuckle. One grey tabby fumbled his way to me and put his paws where my hand had been, pressing his nose against the glass.

We were only two shops down from the diner and Jared looked back at it, thoughtful. In one smooth motion he grabbed my arm and pulled me back to the car, sitting me onto the passenger seat. Jared was ignoring my questions again.

"You're staying here," he said as he opened the glove compartment, pulling out an extra clip and leaving the other gun already there inside. He tossed the mermaid's scale inside next to it, not even trying to be careful. What would he do if a cop searched his car? Seriously? "This is too dangerous for some novice who wants to play hero."

"But--!" The door slammed shut, cutting me off. When I went to open the door it suddenly locked, the small silver tab hiding inside of the frame. I was trapped, or so I wanted him to think.

Jared never looked back at me; he didn't even glance through the windows of *Pete's Pets & More* before walking inside. My heart was beginning to clench a little, just imagining what might be happening. What could be more dangerous than a mermaid determined to kill everyone that crossed her path?

I looked around the car, Jared never really thought his

141

plans through it seemed. At least he never thought his plans through when they involved locking me inside something, or *to* something. How he survived as a bounty hunter was beyond me. I chalked it up to having more than one gun.

I rolled down the window of the passenger seat, since the car was so old, it didn't have power windows. After some simple manoeuvring I managed to crawl out the open window and land unsteadily on the sidewalk. Glancing around I only received a few strange stares but nobody said a word to me. Acting as if nothing had happened I straightened my sweater and marched towards the pet store. I resisted tapping the window with the kittens again and found it a little difficult as the small grey tabby that had looked at me with such hope was still there, watching.

As I opened the door a bell rang to announce my presence. There goes any possibility of Jared not noticing my entrance immediately. He stood at the counter talking to a man but when the bell rang he turned to me with a scowl. The older gentleman behind the counter seized the opportunity and struck Jared in the cheek before running towards a back door behind him.

"Son of a—" Jared called out and leapt over the counter and dashed after the man. I stood at the doorway, unsure of what to do. The animals surrounding me seemed to know something was wrong and began to make noise. The birds tried to fly from their cages but found they were trapped, settling to just shake their cages loose and fall to the ground. I rushed after Jared and the man when something crashing in the back room jolted me to attention.

I turned the corner of the counter when my foot caught on a heavy box. Tumbling forward I caught myself on the doorway just as a bullet whizzed past my head. If I hadn't tripped, I would probably be dead.

"Get down, moron!" Jared shouted at me from

behind some shelves. The backroom to the pet store was filled with various foods and unlabelled boxes. Jared crouched to my right, just out of sight behind a large box with holes in it. Two more shots rang through the air but not towards me. I ducked down, realizing that there was now more than one shooter facing Jared and myself. "Over here, now!" Hastily, I crawled to Jared.

"What's going on?" I asked, understanding why Jared didn't want me involved.

"How the hell did you get out of the car?" he took the time to bare his eyes into me, thinking exactly what I thought he was.

"The windows can roll down you know," I said, trying not to lean against the box with holes in it. Over the gunfire I could hear something shifting inside. Jared didn't seem to have a problem using it for leverage though as he stuck his gun out and fired. I covered my ears; his weapon was just too loud, even for a gun. More shots came back at us but none even came near.

"What?" Jared asked, looking at me. "Son of a—" A bullet clipping the corner of the wooden box cut off his realization. He fired back and I heard a man cry out in pain, hit. "Ha!"

More bullets came at us when suddenly Jared let out a shout. He thrust his chest forward and tried to hold onto his back.

"What is it?" I asked, afraid he had somehow been shot through the box.

"Something bit me!" he went to look in the box but whatever was inside retreated to the far side. When he turned to fire another shot at the men I could see a small amount of blood dripping through his leather jacket. It wasn't gushing out, so I considered that a good thing. If his jacket hadn't been there it probably would've been a lot worse.

"Listen up, honey," Jared said while reloading his gun, "I'll deal with these three, you find the dragon's venom. It should be somewhere in here." I looked around.

"What does it look like?" I asked, I doubted it would be in a bottle labelled "Dragon's Venom". Or would it...?

"It should be purple." That was all he told me as he leapt out from behind the box and dove behind another, bullets narrowly missing him as he rolled to safety.

I began reading the labels on the boxes, careful not to get too close to the one next to me. Jared was occupied and not going to be much help. So what did "Purple" mean exactly? Would it be a purple liquid or in a purple container? This was frustrating and the gunfire wasn't helping me think any clearer.

"Good to see you so lively, Jared," said one of the men on the other side. Great, they knew each other. "Last I saw you were about to get eaten alive by a werewolf." Jared laughed.

"What can I say?" he said back. "I have a knack for surviving." I glanced over at him, crouched down and saw he was smiling. Was he enjoying the gunfight or the conversation? Either way it wasn't good. When he saw me watching him he yelled, "Find it already!"

Looking back at the shelves I didn't see anything that appeared to be dragon's venom. When the gunfire came to a sudden halt I crawled around the shelves to see the other side, another bullet narrowly missing me.

"So to what do I owe the pleasure of seeing you again?" said the same man as before.

"Just thought I'd drop by," Jared called, "say hello, that sort of thing. I can see you're doing well. I'm in the wrong business, shoulda gone into exotic creatures." So *Pete's Pets & More* really did mean *"& More"*. It had been downtown ever since I could remember, so had it always been like this? I remembered coming here for my first pet with my mother; had it always been run by gangsters? I hoped not, not wanting to lose such a cherished memory.

Staying low to the ground I searched the bottom

shelves. Some of it was regular pet store supplies; dog food, cat toys but as I looked I began to find stranger things. I cringed wondering why people would ever want some of these things as pets until I remembered they probably weren't all pets. A shot flew over my head and I heard glass break. A purple liquid began to drip down the shelves and onto my hand, it almost felt like it was being absorbed into my skin. I quickly wiped it away on my pants when a thought occurred; purple liquid!

"Business is wonderful," the man said and the gunfire ceased. "But I am curious, who's your friend? She's cute, a little plain, but cute. Kind of young for you though, if you don't mind my saying."

Looking up I could see some small vials, filled with a glowing purple liquid. There were only four there so I grabbed two, they were small enough to each fit into the palm of my hand.

"How many do we need?" I asked Jared, hoping he would hear me. My ears were starting to ring louder with all the explosions.

"She's nobody," Jared said to the man and turned to me as I peeked behind the containers. I held up the vials for him to see and he nodded. "That's it?"

"Yeah...I think," I said, since I wasn't completely sure it was the venom.

"You think?" Jared ducked lower as the top of the box behind him blew up into tiny pieces. I stuffed the vials into my pocket, hoping they wouldn't break. "Good enough!"

He dove towards me, no gunfire following him.

"What now?" I questioned.

"Well," he said, trying to rub where he had been bitten, "we need to get out the back door."

"Why not the front?"

"There's two of them there."

"There is?" I leaned to take a look but Jared grabbed the back of my hoodie, holding me back. "Where's the back door?"

"Behind Violet," he said. He nodded in the direction of where some of the bullets came from. It wasn't too far from us and we could actually be seen rather easily from where the girl crouched. I could just make out the top of her head, streaked with a dark blue. How she hadn't shot us yet was a mystery.

Near the girl was the back door, to get to it, we needed to get rid of her.

"How do we get there?"

"Like this." Jared grabbed my hand and ran for the door, bullets trailing behind us with every step. The adrenaline coursing through my system made it hard to see or to even feel my legs. He shoved me to the ground when we made it to Violet and she gave us a hardened look. Was she not expecting us to run towards the enemy? I guessed I wouldn't have, if I were her. Jared mumbled, "Sorry Vi."

Violets narrow eyes became very wide then as she tried to back away. Jared hit her with the butt of his gun, knocking her out. I was a little surprised he would hit her so easily, but I was more surprised that he apologized first. He must have known her, what else could it be? He had called her "Vi" after all…

"C'mon," Jared said, holding my hand again and pulling me out the door. We fell out into an alleyway, covered with old boxes that had been used to store "exotic" animals. Jared began pulling me to the mouth of the alleyway and into the light.

"Gun," I managed to say before we hit the sidewalk. He shoved his gun into its holster, finally releasing my hand. He had such a tight grip on me I thought I was being crushed. Shaking my hand out of his titans grip we walked around the block towards the car.

"What part of 'stay in the car' did you not get?" Jared said, his voice filled with anger. I was hoping it was just left over adrenaline from the fight, but somehow doubted it. When we passed the front window I couldn't see anyone inside and took one last look at the small grey tabby. He and the other kittens didn't seem frightened by the gunfire.

"I just...I just wanted to help," I said, my body beginning to calm down now that we were safe. Jared opened the passenger side door and ordered me in. When he climbed into the driver's seat he sighed. "I helped, didn't I?"

"This time you did," he said, "next time you could die. You could've died this time!" He groaned and struggled out of this jacket, tossing it into the backseat. His white shirt was stained with blood on the back but didn't seem to be bleeding anymore. "Damn it."

"Did you know her?" I suddenly blurted out and immediately regretted it.

"Yeah," he said, "why?" Jared reached into the glove compartment in front of me and pulled out a white bandage and some tape. It must have been his idea of a first aid kit. "Stick this on for me." He lifted his shirt and handed me the supplies.

"You said sorry before you hit her," I told him, almost sounding jealous. Not that he hit her, but that he seemed to know her well enough to actually apologize to her. Some silly part of me wanted him to apologize for how he had treated me, for giving me so many sleepless nights. But I knew that would never happen, he didn't even know how much grief he had given me. Plus his apologies looked rather....painful.

"'Cause we used to...know what? It's none of your business." I stuck the bandage over the wound, not paying any attention to the various scars he had. I tried to see what might have bit him but there was too much blood, all I could make out was what looked like a snake bite. I patted on the white cloth, making him wince, but it was only to make sure it would stay. Really.

"What now?" I asked, not bothering to pry into

147

Jared's history with Violet.

"Let's see the venom," he said rubbing his forehead, one hand held out to me. I handed him the glowing vials and he inspected them. "We'll give these to Yamuna, that way they can't get lost while we get the pixie's dust."

"How would we lose them while getting the pixie's dust?"

"Clearly you've never met a pixie." He started the car and drove off, not even checking if we were being followed. I tried to make sure of that though; I didn't want to be in another gunfight today.

Engine purring, Jared stopped the car in the same spot in front of Yamuna's house. Our car ride back had been silent and for some reason I couldn't keep my mind off of Violet. She was small for an illegal animal's dealer, or even a henchman, but Jared knew her. He even said sorry before hitting her, and she seemed surprised that he would do such a thing. Whatever their relationship, Jared didn't want to talk about it. Jared didn't want to talk about a lot of things with me.

My thoughts were consumed with questions again, always about the bounty hunter I was working with. His very existence invaded my mind but maybe that was because he was always saving my life? I had lost count as to how many bullets he had helped me dodge, and how many ancient monsters. That was all it was though; fear, adrenaline and unfortunate situations that made me think about him.

Yamuna opened the front door as we stepped onto her decayed porch.

"Do you have it already?" she asked, peeking through the crack.

"Almost," Jared said and handed her the container holding the mermaid scale and the vials with dragon's venom. She held the scale in the air and watched it glitter with a smile. Jared finished, "We should have everything by tomorrow morning."

"Better hurry," Yamuna said, still holding her smile. She blinked at me and then waved her hand at us, telling us to leave. Jared turned and walked down the steps, with me just a foot behind him. "Wait."

I stopped on the last step, hearing Yamuna walk out the door. Jared stood in front of me on the concrete path, and faced the witch, a sour expression on his face. It didn't seem to be from his hatred of her though; it seemed more like...pain.

"What?" he rubbed his forehead again, like he had been through most of the car ride.

"What happened to your back? Get shot?" she laughed, mocking him. Would she really enjoy him getting shot that much? Probably. He grimaced and began to walk away, ignoring her.

"He was bitten at the pet store," I told her, if she really wanted to know. Her pasty complexion paled even more as her eyes flashed black.

"Stop!" she shouted and took another step forward, stopping just before the stairs. I stumbled backwards in surprise, my feet just catching their balance on the pathway. Looking to Jared I saw him fall to the ground, unconscious.

"Jared!" I called, trying to rush to his side. Yamuna grabbed me though, reaching too far out of her confinement, causing an electric current to run through her body. She screamed in pain as she threw me backwards onto the wood. Falling to her knees she gasped for air.

"Don't touch him," she managed, "not yet."

"What are you talking about?" I asked, tugging on her to get free. All she did was point at him, and together we stared.

Slowly, starting from his wound, he began to change colour. Jared's skin and clothes hardened, changing to a deep grey as he turned to stone. The line separating him from human to rock engulfed his body and he lay there,

149

frozen in place; a statue.

"He was bitten," Yamuna gasped, "by a Child of Medusa."

"Will he be okay?" I asked, knowing it was a stupid question. I didn't like Yamuna's face then because it answered me more than her words did.

"What do you think?"

Chapter 16

I stood in Yamuna's kitchen with her, as she calmly sipped at her tea and nibbled on a cookie. She didn't care for Jared, so obviously she didn't care that he was...well...made of stone. But she had stopped me from getting near him and that had to count for something, didn't it?

"What was that?" I asked, pointing in the direction where Jared had fallen and was now staying. "He just...he just..." I trailed off, unable to actually say what I was thinking. Despite what I knew about this world I found it hard to comprehend.

"He was bitten it seems," she said, offering me a chair but I refused, "a shame too. We need to know exactly what bit him in order to cure it."

"But you said that it was a child of Medusa right? So it's easy to find the cure."

Yamuna rolled her eyes lazily at me. I had no idea what a child of Medusa was, but I was hopeful she knew how to cure it. She said, "There are many children of Medusa, we need to know which one bit him. They all have very different cures." The teacup rose to her lips, an attempt to hide her smile?

"So if we figure out which one it was, we can cure him?" I sounded horrifyingly hopeful.

"I suppose," Yamuna shrugged. She didn't seem interested in helping Jared. Part of me thought she really just wanted to keep him there, a token of her enemy's defeat. "This isn't really my area of expertise, now if you don't mind, maybe you should finish finding the ingredients?"

"But what about Jared?" I held my arms, knowing I could never get the final ingredients without his help. But finding them wasn't my first priority now either.

"I'll look after him," she said, without the evil smile I had anticipated.

"Shouldn't we cure him first, and then finish with the ingredients?" Yamuna sighed.

"Jared isn't going anywhere," she told me, "but don't you want to stop the killings? We don't even know what bit him; it could take weeks to find a cure. Go get the dust and the other blood, and then worry about the bounty hunter." Her tone was so harsh. Yamuna crossed her legs and waved me to the door, showing me that I didn't have a choice.

I walked out the door, knowing it was pointless to argue. I could understand why she and Jared didn't get along; they both needed things to be their way. Stepping outside I took a deep breath before I could look at Jared, lying frozen on the ground.

Carefully making my way down the steps, I kept my eyes on the Charger telling myself I would not even glance in his direction. But curiosity got the better of me, and I looked down at him as I brushed by.

Jared only looked like he was sleeping, taking a nap on the concrete path. Pushing my thoughts of him aside, I had to focus on the other current situation; finding out how to catch an inter-dimensional killer, not curing Jared.

Both seemed impossible though.

To top it all off, I had no way of getting anywhere. When I made it to the car, I realized that Jared still held the keys in his hand, which were also made of rock now. The walk back to my apartment was too far, so I reached into my pocket and pulled out my phone.

Scrolling through my contacts I considered who I should call. My first thought was Luke, but he was probably still sulking in his room; I doubted he would even answer the phone. My next thought was my father, but he would only ask questions, and try to stop me from doing anything involving the Eidolon's. It wasn't that he didn't like them, he was one of the few that accepted them, but he still thought they were far too dangerous for humans to deal with. After him came my brothers; all of which were busy with their own lives.

That left nobody else in my phone to call, my only other contact being...deceased. As I set my phone back into my pocket I felt a small piece of paper. Forgetting what it was, I pulled it out of my pocket to read; it was Dr. Wineman's phone number, written in Luke's elegant cursive.

I remembered he had given it to me during out first lesson, when he thought I should have it. I hadn't thought the doctor's number would be important enough to write down, so Luke insisted on doing it for me. I hadn't even remembered it was there, with everything that had happened.

Weighing my options, I decided that I had to call him for help. I didn't want to do it, because there was a very slim chance that he would help me, but he was the only option I had. My keys clicked as I dialled his number, hoping he wouldn't just leave me here to figure out a different solution.

"Liv!" Dr. Wineman answered after two rings. "Are you all right? Are you hurt?"

"Uh...no?" I said, surprised that he knew who was

calling, and that he wanted to know if I was hurt. I heard him breathe a sigh of relief.

"Thank goodness," he said, "so you decided not to summon the Shadeland ancient?" He was so full of hope; it made me feel a little guilty to answer.

"Not...quite," I told him, "I need your...help." I looked up and down Yamuna's street, a car nowhere to be seen besides Jared's

"Of course," Dr. Wineman said and I could picture him waving his hands, "what do you need?"

"A ride," I said, "and maybe an escort?"

Twenty minutes later Dr. Wineman pulled up behind Jared's Charger in a small, red, four door convertible. The top was down, letting in the warming spring air. He smiled at me, still thinking I had changed my mind of the subject of summoning the Shadeland creature, but he was wrong. Very wrong.

Dr. Wineman stepped out of his vehicle and walked around to see me.

"I'm very glad you have changed your mind," he said, grabbing me into a hug. I didn't wrap my arms back around him, instead I stood there again, feeling awkward. Again. Why did he insist on hugging me? I barely hugged my own family. When I didn't say anything he let me go and looked at me, the expression on his face telling me he understood. "You haven't changed your mind, have you?"

Taking one last glance at Jared I said, "Not exactly." Dr. Wineman looked behind me, his eyes staying on the house, rather than Jared, where I thought they should be.

"Let's get you home," he said, hurrying me into the car. As he shut the door and walked around to the other side I looked back at Yamuna's house, just in time to see the front door shutting. Dr. Wineman quickly started the car and drove away, leaving Jared and Yamuna behind.

We sat in his convertible in silence, neither of us saying what we were thinking as he drove down the street. I guessed he was trying to think of a way to convince me not to do the spell while I had to figure out a way to make him help me actually do the spell. Somehow I thought both of our goals were rather improbable.

In the past, whenever I had to say something I didn't want to say to Luke, I just asked him to read my mind…it was so much easier then. Maybe the best thing to do right now would be to convince him to help?

"I need your help," I said, finally breaking down and speaking.

"I cannot help you summon the Shadeland creature, Liv," he told me, "it's far too dangerous."

"I'm going to do it with or without you," I said, frustrated, "and with Jared out of the picture I'm on my own so it would just be—"

"Jared?" he asked, "why is he no longer with you?" I stared at him from the passenger seat. Had he actually not seen the stone version of what was once Jared back in the garden?

"He was…bitten by something and…turned to stone," I said, not really sure how to explain it. It seemed to make sense to him though, as his eyes widened and he screeched the car to a halt, pulling to the side of the road with a jolt.

"He was… he turned… what bit him?" Dr. Wineman waved his hand in the air towards me, flustered.

"I don't know!" I said, beginning to panic. "I never saw it, it was in a box at the pet store!"

"*Pete's Pets & More?*" I nodded and he sighed. "Anything that could turn him to stone like that means there is a limit on the cure."

"What do you mean?" I could feel my stomach drop inside of me.

"I mean, if he doesn't get the antidote soon," Dr. Wineman gave me a cold look, "he could very well stay like that forever." He put the car into drive and began back down the road, no explanation, just the horrifying truth hanging between us.

"Where are we going?" I said, hoping he wouldn't say he was taking me back to Luke.

"To find out what bit Jared," he said, "so then we can figure out if we can save him." *If?* I thought.

Dr. Wineman pulled up in front of the café Jared and I had been to earlier, only two spots down from the pet store. I felt like there should be a broken window, cops surrounding the store but everything was normal; people were walking past it and looking at the animals inside, nothing out of place. That bothered me, knowing what was really hidden inside the backroom.

Dr. Wineman rested his arms on the steering wheel, watching the store.

"How many are in there?" he asked, as if readying himself for an attack. For some reason, I couldn't quite remember the number of people that were there. It was all blurred together.

"Um...about three or four?" I guessed, trying to focus but finding it difficult. There was a nagging feeling in the back of my head, as if we were being watched. As I tried to look around the area the doctor was already out of the car and heading for the shop. What was he planning?

He barged into the pet store just as I walked past the kittens in the front window. Waving at the small grey one that seemed to recognize me and hop over to the edge of the glass to see me. I smiled at him, and walked into the store.

"You there!" Dr. Wineman said to the man behind the counter. I didn't think he was one of the men that had shot at me, but then again, I didn't get a very good look at any of them.

"What are you doing?" I whispered to him as we approached the counter.

"Follow my lead," he said, sounding as if he was making this up as he went along. He suddenly banged his fist on the counter, surprising both me and the man behind it. "I want answers."

This attitude was strange on the doctor. He had seemed so…mild-mannered, and even as he was being forceful, it was awkward. It was like trying to watch a child act like an adult. I was embarrassed for both him and myself.

"Answers?" the man questioned. His nametag was written on a dog bone, reading Steven. His tan polo shirt and matching khaki's seemed oddly disarming and I didn't recognize him as one of the shooters. What if he didn't know anything about what was in the back?

"You know what I'm talking about," Dr. Wineman continued, banging his fist again, "tell us what we want to know!"

"Maybe we should tell him what we want to know," I whispered closely to him. The doctor went still, thinking.

"Right," he said, "tell us about what's in the back." Steven's eyes widened further, so he did know about the secret operations. His eyes narrowed at us, testing our knowledge.

"What do you want to know about what's in the back?"

"What bit the bounty hunter?" Dr. Wineman loomed over the counter, trying to appear imposing but missing the mark completely; he merely looked like he was leaning casually. Steven reached under the counter, his muscles tensing as he gripped something.

"That's enough Steven," came a voice from the door, the bell chiming as the person stepped in. Steven set both his hands back on the counter innocently. Dr. Wineman and I turned to find a girl with a dark blue streak in her hair; Violet. "I'll take care of these two."

Her expression didn't give away what she was thinking. I knew she had history with Jared, so maybe that meant she would be willing to help us. Unless her history was similar to Yamuna's…

"You sure?" Steven asked.

"Yeah," she said back, "c'mon." She nodded her

157

head towards the door and walked out. Dr. Wineman looked to me and I shrugged at him before we followed her out. We tracked her all the way back to the doctor's car as she leaned on the passenger door. Before the doctor could open his mouth I cut him off.

"Do you know what bit Jared?" I asked, hopeful. She looked up at me, her thin eyes boring into mine. I couldn't tell what she was thinking at all.

"Yeah," Violet said, "what are you gonna do if I tell you?" She crossed her arms.

"We want to help him," Dr. Wineman said, reverting to his usual self. He must have felt comfortable enough to not threaten Violet. She snorted at his comment.

"Good luck with that," she said, "he was bitten by a Cockatrice." She got off the car and put one hand on her hip, challenging those around her. If she and Jared had a history, it was clearly a negative one; he seemed to have that effect on a lot of people.

"Are you sure?" the doctor asked, troubled by her words. She nodded with a hint of guilt in her eyes. She turned to me then, her face changing with determination.

"What were you two doing there, anyway?" she questioned me. I didn't answer and instead looked to the doctor. His features didn't give me much hope that we would be able to help Jared.

"What's a Cockatrice?" I asked. Dr. Wineman touched his hand to his lip in thought and I didn't think he had heard me.

"Hmm?" he said, coming out of his daze. "Oh, it's a creature from around the twelfth century; it has the ability to turn one to stone with simply a look, or a touch."

That must have been why Yamuna called it a "Child of Medusa", I thought, remembering the story of Medusa turning people to stone with just a glance.

"Or a bite," Violet chimed in, unimpressed.

"Ah, yes," the doctor agreed, still touching his face. Violet didn't ask me again what Jared and I were doing there earlier; she just walked back towards the pet store, mumbling something under her breath. The way she walked in her black jacket reminded me of Jared; there was something very similar in the way they both held themselves. Or maybe it was just their overpowering arrogance that bothered me so much.

"So is there a cure?" I asked meekly, feeling as if there was no hope. Jared was turned to stone, and Luke would forever be labelled as a killer. There was no way I would be able to collect the final ingredients on my own, let alone summon and kill the Shadeland being.

"Yes," the doctor sighed and pulled his car keys from his pocket, "but it will take some time to acquire." We climbed into his car and drove off, towards an unknown destination.

"So what is it?"

"It is something that a human should not concern herself with," he scolded, "I will help Jared, but you must stay home." He turned down all the streets that told me I was going home. That wasn't all he made me realize though, he just proved that he was in fact, an Eidolon. As he pulled up in front of my apartment building I touched the door-handle.

"What are you going to do?" I couldn't help but ask. He let the car idle as he watched me, weighing his options as I had when deciding whether or not to tell the cops about Luke. Dr. Wineman was deciding if he should tell me the truth, because it was the right thing to do, or if he should lie to me, for my own good. When he finally came to a decision it was written clearly on his face.

"I'll tell you everything you want to know," he said, "when I get back with the cure." Not another word passed between us as I got out of the vehicle. He drove away, and there was nothing I could do to help anyone now.

Chapter 17

"So what you're saying is that while I've been in jail, you've been going around with some bounty hunter, collecting ingredients for a spell to summon an ancient demon so you can kill it and prove my innocence?" Luke stared at me from across the couch, eyes filled with disbelief. When he put it like that, even I found it a little hard to believe. I also found my reasoning a little confusing and yet there I was…

Right now though, it was easier to tell him the truth rather than lie to him. He had finally come out of his room and talked to me, I thought it was best to update him on the situation, especially with Jared and Dr. Wineman out of the picture.

"Yes," I said, reassuring him with a nod, "but now that Jared is… a statue and Dr. Wineman is doing something else, it all came to a standstill." I looked away from him, not wanting to see his reaction. There was a dark feeling inside my chest that told me everything was hopeless; I didn't need to see Luke's expression to know he would be disappointed.

"Have you lost your mind?" he shouted, jumping to his feet. "Do you have any idea how dangerous that is? What would your brothers think? What would your *father* think? I…I can't even…you could have been killed!" He threw his hands in the air and stalked to the couch.

"I just wanted to help," I said, caught off guard. His face was red, his eyes just a little too narrow. The way his shoulders didn't do their usual slope downwards worried me; I had expected him to be upset, but not this mad. I had never seen him this mad before.

"Of course you haven't seen me this mad before," he stood in front of me, "you've never done something like this before! Though I should have seen it coming, after you broke into—" he began to pace around the coffee table when I cut him off.

"What?" I asked. "What did you just say?" I stood, watching him as he realized what he had done.

"Sorry," he said, "I didn't…mean it…I just…it just happened." His voice was quiet.

"You promised," I whispered, feeling a lump in my throat, "you promised."

"I'm sorry, it was an accident." I could see the pain in his eyes over his mistake. When we were kids, he had promised to never use his psychic powers on me, unless I let him or a situation arose that he could use them without penalty. He'd never accidentally done it before, not like this, and there had never been a time when he used them and I hadn't felt it. This time, I never would have noticed unless he had said something. It made me wonder if it was really an accident. It made me wonder how many times he had done it and I hadn't felt a thing. It made me wonder if he was still listening in on my thoughts.

I pushed those ideas away quickly, not wanting to persecute him, after everything we had been through and everything he was *still* going through. Sitting down I took a deep breath. It was an accident, and that's where I was going to leave it.

161

"Have there been any more killings?" I asked, wanting to change the subject quickly. I didn't have the time or the energy to feel angry as we sat back down on the couch.

"No," Luke said, sitting down next to me, for the first time there was a space between us. "What are you thinking?"

"That I hope the doctor gets back soon to cure Jared so we can continue collecting the ingredients for Yamuna."

"We don't need him," Luke said, almost sounding angry again. "Why can't we just do it ourselves?"

"Do you know how we can get some pixie's dust and the blood of the last victim?" I questioned, as if he would really know. He's either been locked in his room, or locked in a cell for the past week. There was no way he was getting anywhere near the victim's blood, wherever that was. "Or have you developed a new ability you haven't told me about?" He went rigid in his seat. So much for not having the energy to be angry…

"Well, about that," he started playing with his hands, "I've been meaning to tell you something." He crossed his legs away from me as I turned to face him head on. He had never hidden anything from me before; this Luke was very different than the Luke I had grown up with. I didn't like it.

"What is it?"

"I'm…well you know I was adopted, right?" I nodded my head, growing more anxious with each passing second. "And my parents had always just sort of said I was psychic so that's what we always said, because I could get glimpses of the future and get into people's minds and…some other things."

"Does this have to do with why Dr. Wineman wanted to talk to you?" I touched his shoulder, hoping to comfort him, at least a little. Suddenly my anger was gone, replaced with concern. Luke was rarely this serious. He looked down at me and I knew I was right. This was also probably why the doctor had taken such an interest in him, in both of us.

"I'm not really psychic, like we thought," he admitted, "Dr. Wineman told me what I am; I'm a Fae." He gave a meek smile and shrug. I had no idea what I was supposed to say. For years I had thought, I had *known*, that Luke was a psychic, but now he was telling me that wasn't true. I could see in his eyes that he was happy with what he was, or maybe he was just happy that he *knew* for sure what he was. Or maybe he was happy because he had finally found someone he could truly confide in about himself...

"A Fae?" I asked, not recognizing the term and trying to not think the way I was. Later I would have to search the library to see what came up. "What's that?"

"Well, remember in class how I asked about purebloods?" I nodded again. How could I forget the doctor's reaction? He had looked completely confused as to why Luke would ask such a thing. "Well," Luke smiled knowingly, "I am one; at least according to Dr. Wineman."

"You're a pureblood Fae?" I leaned back on the couch, still trying to organize my thoughts. So that was why the doctor had pulled him aside after class, that was why he vouched for him to the detectives. Jared did say something about them protecting each other.

"Yeah," he leaned back with me, "I've been doing a little research on them...me...and I haven't really learned too much. I think I really need to talk with Dr. Wineman to find out more."

I wondered if the doctor would still want to talk to him after Jared and I summoned the creature. Or *if* we summoned it that is.

"So what have you learned so far?" I asked, hoping to keep my mind off of Jared.

"I'm going to live for a long time," he said, sounding a little sad, "but I can still die from wounds and stuff. Apparently I can die from a broken heart as far as the myths go." Luke looked down into his hands, despair written all over him. I could understand that, if he had ever been willing to date someone and they happened to break up with him, he could be dead.

"Can't everyone?" I asked, wanting to make the situation sound better. The mermaid had died from a broken heart after all so what I said wasn't completely untrue. Luke glanced up at me, surprised at my answer before realizing that it wasn't technically a lie. Everyone can die from heartbreak, one way or another. "Anything else?"

"Just that there are different classifications of Fae, like Light and Dark," he scratched the back of his head. "I can't find anything else that sounds real; a lot of the information contradicts itself in other areas."

We sat in silence for a moment, becoming aware of how real everything was. It was one thing to see murders reported on television, to see how the world was changing but it still never felt...real. I grew up knowing that the things that hid in the dark existed, but now...it was just hitting me now how dangerous everything was. Before now Luke was really the only Eidolon I had come in contact with. I was almost killed by a mermaid earlier, then I was almost shot, more than once and I could have been turned to stone by a Cockatrice.

To top it all off, I was trying to kill an ancient creature from what sounded like an alternate dimension. I rested my head back and closed my eyes; this was insane. But if I didn't try and do this, then who would? My eyes opened, staring at the ceiling but not really seeing it.

Now that Jared was out of the picture, I was the only one left. Yamuna wasn't going to go and get the ingredients; she couldn't even if she wanted to. The doctor wasn't about to do it either and the police seemed to have less than nothing on the case, at least in terms of suspects other than Luke. I was the only other person that was willing to do it.

"We need to get that dust," I said aloud, "we need to

stop these murders." I looked to Luke to see that he had turned the television on, leaving the sound off. Cindy sat on the screen again, reporting the news that Luke was in fact innocent. Luke didn't seem to hear me as he watched the screen, a hardened expression on his gentle face.

"I kind of like her now," he said, "this Cindy woman. I know that's stupid, but she's the only reporter that actually seems sorry for accusing me."

"She apologized to me," I said, "the other day in the diner. She was there with a guy and she said sorry." Luke's lips hinted at a smile but he kept his eyes on the television.

"She said it to me too," he told me, "she came by the apartment earlier with the weather girl and they both apologized. I had no idea what to say especially since the weather girl wasn't really involved in it."

"What did you say?"

"That I forgave her," he turned the television off, "that she was given misinformation by the detective and that she was just doing her job." Luke shrugged the topic away, wanting to leave it at that. He was always taking the high road and I let it go, following his lead. It was a better way to go anyhow.

"I think we need to get to work," I said, determined to find the killer, "nobody else is going to try and stop it."

"Where do you want to start?" he leaned his elbows onto his knees and looked to me.

"The pixie's dust should be easiest for now," I said, praying that while we got the dust, the doctor would have a cure for Jared and he would know how to get the blood. "I just don't know where to find that." We sat and thought about it, I came up with nothing though.

"There is a place downtown," Luke said slowly, "they sell witches supplies and stuff. Maybe they have some dust?"

Well, it was worth a shot.

Chapter 18

Luke and I parked on the bustling downtown street. We were only a few blocks away from the pet shop that I had nearly died in and I wanted to stay far away from it. Despite the fact that Violet had told us what had bitten Jared, I doubted she would be so nice next time we met. I doubted any of them would let me live if I ever walked in there again. I couldn't understand how such violent and deadly people could sell kittens and puppies; it just didn't make sense.

Luke wore his black sweater, being sure to keep the hood up as we went out into the public eye. This was the first time he had left the house and he didn't want anyone to notice him.

He led me two stores down from where my car was to a dark yet oddly inviting shop. It was one of the many stores downtown that I had never noticed; its windows had large red letters reading "50% off" while purple curtains hung on the edges. The display was filled with candles, crystals and stones; I recognized one of them as the stones I found in both Charlie's and Alice's homes. I made a mental note to ask about them.

"This is the place," Luke said, peering into the windows, "I've never actually been in but I hear they sell a lot of weird stuff."

There was no name on the shop, no sign telling me what to call it. I guessed most people just called it the magic shop; that's what I would call it from now on anyway.

Luke and I walked through the glass door, another bell alerting the shopkeeper of our presence. For some reason the chime put me on edge; maybe it was because it reminded me of the shooting. Or maybe because it sounded like the mermaid's song, the very same song that almost led me to drown myself in a glowing river.

Forcing my mind to focus I observed the shop. The lights were dim, just barely illuminating the shelves around us. Large, old books sat at the back of the room while newer ones were at the front. Candles and vials of unknown liquids lined the walls only to be complemented by incense and charms sitting beneath glass counters. It gave off a nice atmosphere, a strangely safe and homey feeling rose in me. That was something I hadn't felt in a while.

I tried to find something that may look like pixie's dust but there was nothing. I wasn't even sure what I was looking for. It probably didn't look like the dust that came from Tinkerbell.

"Hey," said a man behind a glass counter, "anything I can help you with?"

He certainly didn't fit in with his surroundings. I had expected a slender woman to be there, dressed in all black and adorned with silver pentagrams or crosses, but he wasn't that at all. This man stood around at least 6'4" with enough muscle to make sure nobody was going to try and corner him in a dark alley. His brown hair was kept short and his brow was furrowed naturally, just barely hiding his green eyes. He reminded me a lot of my older brother, imposing but not quite threatening because of his baby face.

The man set aside a book face down on the glass.

"Uh, yes," Luke said from beneath his hood, also taking note of the man's resemblance to my family with a simple raise of his eyebrows at me, "we're looking for pixie's dust, do you have any?" The man thought to himself before holding up a finger.

"Give me a second and I'll check the back," he said, "we might be sold out."

He walked around the counter and through the back door, past all the ancient texts. I began to wander around the store, reading book titles and admiring the charms. When I finally came across the stones I got a flash of Charlie's body in my mind, and another image of the blood coating Alex's living room. I hurried back to the counter, hoping Luke didn't notice my mood change.

"Somehow I doubt they'll have it," Luke said, putting his hands in his pocket.

"Why's that?"

"Because it would be too easy." The man came out of the back room, nothing in hand. Luke's doubts seemed to be accurate. That's my psychic...err...Fae for you.

"I'm sorry," the man said, "but we've sold out of it. We should be getting more in by next week." He walked back behind the counter. "Is there anything else you need?" Luke and I both grimaced.

"Do you know where we could get some then?" Luke asked.

"Well you could always just catch a pixie and shake it out of him," the man didn't smile as he spoke showing that he was actually serious about his answer. "There's tons of 'em up in the northern woods; they usually come out after sunset and fly around."

"Really?" Luke said, surprised. "Aren't they hard to catch?"

The man swayed his head, thinking.

"Yes and no," he told us, "I can sell you some stuff to help get them if you like, but they are fast little buggers." The man turned and walked to the end of the counter, reaching underneath it and pulling out a jar. He then grabbed two butterfly nets from behind him and brought them to us. "These are enchanted, so once you get a pixie in the net it'll transfer right into the jar where you can collect the dust. Just be sure keep the lid on, 'kay?"

"Sounds easy enough," Luke said to me with a shrug, I caught a glimmer of a smile on the man's face as he punched some numbers into the register. "How much?"

"Comes to $56.38," he said and Luke pulled out his wallet to pay. Once the transaction was done he said, "You guys look new at this, so I'll give ya a tip; put anything you don't wanna lose somewhere safe. Pixie's love to take stuff."

"Thanks," Luke said, "what's your name?"

"Carson," he replied, "I own the store." Luke introduced us to be polite, though I honestly don't know why he would ask for the man's name. Just as we were about to leave I asked what I needed to know.

"Do you sell a lot of agate?" I looked up at Carson who seemed a little surprised that I said anything at all. Unfortunately I got that a lot.

"Sometimes, why?"

"Have you sold two or more stones to one person lately?" I wondered if there were more stones elsewhere. Charlie and Alice had them, but did anyone else? Did Rosa and Heather have one too?

"Actually I did," Carson said, rubbing his mouth, "a couple weeks ago a guy came in and bought a few."

"What did he look like?" I asked, feeling as if this man was involved. He had to be, right? I put my hands on the counter with anticipation and Carson leaned on with his arms crossed, coming to my eye level.

"Why do you want to know?" he smirked, amused by

169

something.

"Because I think this man may be involved in the series of murders across town that are being blamed on Luke," I said and he lost his smirk, "I know you recognize him from the news."

"Yeah," Carson said, quickly straightening his back, "but I know your boy didn't do it." Luke resisted a smile hearing someone other than myself saying he was innocent. If so many people felt Luke was innocent, why didn't they say so? Why let the rest of the world accuse him?

"So what did this man look like?" I was determined to find out. There was nothing that would stop me from finding this man.

"He was pretty small, not much taller than you really," Carson leaned on the counter again, "dark skin, black hair. Had a bit of an accent, when he asked for the agate he seemed to be in a hurry too. He looked exhausted, like he hadn't slept in days."

"What kind of accent?" I asked, trying to narrow it down.

"Sorry, don't know that," Carson said, "but he was with some skinny blonde chick, she never said a word though. Her hair was weird, all different colours."

"Thanks," I said, starting to think about who it could be. This could be the mysterious B that had taken the photograph I found in Charlie's apartment and the woman could be the fourth victim; Heather.

I walked towards the door, leaving Luke to grab the nets and jar. I heard him thank Carson, who called to us as we left with a resonating ring.

"Happy hunting!"

"What was that about?" Luke said as he caught up to me. I opened the trunk of the car for him to drop our supplies into and shut it hard.

"I don't' know," I said, still trying to think, "something about that description just set off a flag in my head." I pushed my hair behind my ears. "I just don't know, I need to think about it."

"Well, let me know," he said rubbing my shoulder, "are we going out tonight?" There was probably only a couple hours till the sun set, leaving us time to prepare before we went out to find a pixie.

"Yes," I said, "the sooner we get the dust the better." Then all we had to worry about was getting the blood, saving Jared and killing a powerful creature as old as time. See? There wasn't *that* much left to do.

I sat in the car next to Luke, staring out into the dark woods ahead. The sun was almost down, creating a light orange and blue glow across the trees. Beneath them was black, no sunlight getting through the thick fresh leaves.

"Here," Luke said handing me a flashlight. We got out of the car and collected our nets. Luke put the mystical jar inside his satchel, making sure to secure the zipper in case the pixie's wanted in. I had done a little research before we came out, making sure to know roughly what to expect. Pixie's liked to take things, and they also liked to lead people astray.

"Let's make sure to stick together," I said to reassure myself I would not get lost, "remember what we found online." Luke nodded and we turned on our flashlights, the sun running away beyond the horizon.

We were lucky to have grown up here and to be so familiar with the northern woods. It was a well-known hiking path, but people could get lost at night, the trails suddenly becoming strange and twisted. I had never been there at night before though, so I wanted to stay with Luke as best I could. One pixie was all we needed, that should be enough dust for Yamuna.

Stepping into the woods everything was quiet. The world had gone to bed already, leaving only the crickets and owls to fill the air with noise. Staying on the path our flashlights gave us what we needed to keep walking, the moon only peeking out from behind the clouds and barely penetrating the treetops.

"How do you think we'll find them?" Luke asked. All the information I found didn't say how to find them, and we were currently just going on what Carson told us.

"I guess I don't really—ow!" Something hard smashed into the back of my head causing me to drop my flashlight. I held my new wound, making sure to not to let go of the net.

"What is it?" Luke flashed his light onto me, blinding me.

"Ow, Luke!" He shone the light lower.

"Sorry, what happened?"

"I don't know, something hit me!" I bent over to pick up my flashlight when it suddenly flew to the side. It floated through the trees and without thinking I chased after it, my instinct kicking in.

"Liv!" Luke called, chasing after me. "Wait!"

As I dashed through the woods I could hear laughter, it surrounded me until I tripped and tumbled into a small patch of moonlight. The flashlight dropped in front of me when I stood and whatever had grabbed it flew off. Behind me Luke stumbled into the light.

"Sorry," I said, realizing what I did. After reminding him we needed to stick together I decided to stupidly run off. Good idea. I picked up the flashlight and shone it around the area while Luke gave me a dirty look, thinking exactly the same thing I was.

"I think we've found the pixies," he said looking around. In the moonlight around us tiny creatures came out from behind the trees and flowers. They looked just like people, covered in tiny bits of cloth and giving off a soft yellow glow. None of them had wings, as I had expected they would.

"Let's get one then," I handed my flashlight to Luke, opting to use both hands on the net.

"Wait," Luke said, "maybe we can just reason with them?" He took a step forward, lightly holding the net in

172

one a hand.

"I don't think—"

"We don't want to hurt you," he called into the night air, "we just need your dust! Please, it's to save lives." Some of the pixies giggled.

"If you didn't want to hurt us," one on a flower said, "you wouldn't have enchanted nets!" Three flew at Luke, knocking him off balance to the ground as he tried to avoid their aerial attack. His net was grabbed by two pixies and he quickly chased after them as I had earlier.

Multiple sets of eyes watched me, daring me to try and catch them. With Luke gone I wasn't feeling as confident. I heard a giggle come from my pocket and when I looked down I saw a small female pixie there, hanging out of the cloth. When I tried to pull her out she had my phone in her small hands, and flew off before I could stop her.

I reached out for her but missed. She passed by another pixie and threw my phone to him, allowing him to fly off in the opposite direction of Luke. I chased after them, and every few feet they would pass my phone between then, laughing. It was like I was in second grade all over again, having my favourite doll thrown between my brothers. Unfortunately my mother and father weren't about to show up to save the day this time.

The moon was hidden again behind the clouds, leaving me in the dark and without a flashlight to help. I could barely make out the glow of the pixies as they disappeared behind the trees. The only way I knew they were there was from their constant giggling.

The girl flew out towards me and I swung my net at her, missing.

"Nyah, nyah!" she taunted, making a face and wiggling her fingers at me. While I watched her flit about my phone dropped in front of me. I lunged for it when two more flying creatures rushed for my ankles, the branch between them tripping me up. My face planted into the ground and they laughed harder.

I jumped to my feet and chased after them after grabbing my phone. If I was going to fall this much, I may as well fall and catch one of them. Running through the woods I swung at the pixies when they came into sight, but never got one. When I stopped to catch my breath I leaned against the net for support. Then I saw a familiar yellow butterfly land on the top of it, resting. Did butterflies come out at night? And when had it gotten so cold? I could just make out my breath in front of me, coming out in wisps. When the creature flew away I finally I stopped to clearly think about how to catch one of the pixies since flinging the net wildly wasn't working.

Listening to the sounds around me I tried to map where the pixies were.

"One," I whispered, "two...three!" The female pixie came at me again and this time when I swung at her I got her trapped inside the net against a tree.

"Hey!" she yelled and beat against the net. In an explosion of yellow and green sparks the pixie disappeared. Her comrades weren't too happy about that. The other three that had been tormenting me came out of hiding, angry expressions set. Guess they didn't like that I had caught their friend.

They seemed to glow brighter as they glared at me, slowly floating closer. A clicking resonated through the air and the pixies scattered, hushed screams coming from them. Other pixies came out of the trees and whisked past me, not caring that I had a net with me. One flew into the enchanted weapon and burst into sparks as the other one had.

In a matter of seconds the world was silent. Not a single cricket chirped and the pixies were no longer laughing; when they passed by they all looked scared, terrified even. That was making me nervous. I held the net closer to me and took a wary step back.

I heard the clicking again, this time it was further

away, at least I thought it was. I knew I wasn't alone but I didn't know who or what else was out there. With the sound of beating wings a dark figure shot out of the shade and into the sky. I could only make out the shape of bats wings as it passed in front of the moon; they must have been at least four feet long and as it flew I could still hear clicking.

Not bothering to stand there any longer I ran back the way I had come. I could no longer see whatever had flown into the air; I couldn't even see the ground beneath my feet. After a while I managed to find my way back to the clear patch of moonlight.

"Liv!" I heard Luke call and he burst out of the trees.

"Luke!" I said. "Did you see that?"

He held up a jar filled with three pixies, banging on the sides.

"We got them!" He said triumphantly. "Are you okay?" He took in my appearance.

"Uh...yeah," I said, taking a wary glance behind me. Maybe it was better to just not tell him. After all, I wasn't even sure of what I saw and I did take a blow to the head minutes earlier. "Let's get back to the car."

Somehow, we got back to the car and it was only then that I noticed Luke didn't have his net with him, or his bag for that matter. I asked him what happened.

"The other pixies got them," he told me, his cheeks turning red in embarrassment, "it's okay though, I got the jar back and we have the dust now, right?" I set my net into the backseat and Luke and I closed the car doors. We peered inside the jar at the three Eidolon's, which seemed to have given up on getting out. They sat cross-legged in the jar, surrounded by a golden haze of dust. It coated the base of the jar and when the pixies saw us watching them they stood.

"Let us out," one demanded, "you have your dust, now let us out!" He pouted and crossed his arms, not enjoying that he had lost the game they had played on us.

Luke looked to me, as if I would know what to do. I shrugged at him and cracked his window down, low enough for the pixies to get out. Carefully he opened the lid of the jar and they were gone, leaving nothing but a trail of dust behind them. Luke sneezed from the essence left behind and quickly rolled the window back up.

"We got it," I said with a smile. "We actually got it." Now all that was left was the blood of the latest victim.

Chapter 19

The roads weren't very busy for nine o'clock at night and I chalked it up to an Eidolon killer being on the loose. Nothing like that had ever happened in Ellengale before; we were just a quiet suburban town filled with quiet people wanting a quiet life. At least we used to be, these killings seemed to have put us on the map and made the humans fear Eidolon's even more.

That was something that I found frustrating. People were afraid of the Eidolon's because of their abilities, because humans didn't understand them. Why couldn't the humans just give them a chance? Somewhere inside of myself I knew that was never going to happen, since humans didn't even give their own kind a chance. I was beginning to understand why Dr. Wineman had been so elated to see me in his class.

I pulled the car to a stop with a sigh, behind an unfamiliar red mini cooper in front of Yamuna's house. I was so tired of this and it wasn't going to get any better. I looked past Luke into Yamuna's yard. Jared's body was blocked by the dead plant life but I knew he was there; I was going to have to walk past him to get to the door after all.

"Just wait here," I told Luke, "I'll only be a minute."

"All right," he said with a concerned expression. Taking a deep breath I stepped out of my vehicle. Strong yet wary steps took me to the gate and I moved onto the dead grass beside the pathway. I closed my eyes and before I knew it I was at Yamuna's steps, clutching the jar of pixie's dust to my chest.

"You know nothing will happen if you look at him, right?" Yamuna said as I peeked at her with one eye. She stood at the top of the broken stairs, watching me. What she said was completely untrue. If I looked at Jared in his current state, something would definitely happen; and it would happen inside me.

"We got the dust," I told her, passing her the jar. She observed it for a moment before finding it was acceptable.

"So how do you plan on getting the blood?" she asked, walking back into her house. After glancing back at Luke I followed her inside; somehow I knew she was going to tell me something useful.

"I'm not really sure," I said, "I thought Jared would know…" my sentence trailed off as I turned the corner to her kitchen to come face to face with Violet. Arms crossed tight across her chest she raised one eyebrow at me, telling me to move.

"What are you doing here?" she asked me, as if I wasn't allowed to be in Yamuna's house.

"Calm down," Yamuna said, taking her usual seat at the round table. "She's helping *Jared*." The sly grin on her face as she said those words disturbed me. Violet flicked her eyes towards the witch then quickly turned them on me, looking me up and down.

"Huh." I wanted desperately to ask why Violet was there, but I knew I wouldn't get an answer from either of them. They all had such a mysterious history, them and Jared, and I wasn't sure if I would ever find out. Jared seemed to be connected to everyone, somehow, like he was the center of a sinister spider web. I tried to leave it alone, telling myself that it was none of my business and would be over soon, but my brain wouldn't let it go and I found I was jumping eagerly onto that web. I swallowed my questions and focused on getting the final ingredient. Stepping around Violet to show her that she didn't scare me I faced Yamuna.

"How should I get the blood?" I asked. Yamuna's eyelids lowered at me, bored; it seemed Violet hadn't reacted to my presence as the witch wanted.

"You won't be able to do it on your own," she told me. Her smile grew again as she gently touched her finger to her cheek and there was something rather sinister behind it. "Violet can help you."

"Like hell that's—" Violet argued when Yamuna interrupted her. She rushed to her feet and clenched a fist at Violet, her eyes turning black. The chair she was sitting on screeched backwards, almost falling over from the force.

"You'll do as I say!" I stepped backwards just as Violet fell to her knees with a groan. She held her stomach, crying out in pain.

"Fine!" she coughed back and Yamuna released her fist. Violet put her hands on the ground for support and looked up at the witch through streaked hair to growl, "Fine."

"Are you okay?" I asked, going to hold her arm to help her up. She swatted me away and I guessed she would have done that to anyone, not just me.

"Don't touch me," she warned. Pushing off the ground she straightened her clothes, careful not to look at Yamuna. I couldn't tell if it was fear, but it didn't seem so; if I didn't know any better I would say it was from shame. "We need to go then."

"Take care," Yamuna said, as if she had done nothing. I made a mental note not to get on her bad side.

It was only then that I realized she wasn't a victim, she was a villain. I had felt sorry for her before, but maybe it was a good thing she was locked out of the world.

"Let's go," Violet said, grabbing my elbow and dragging me outside. She and Jared seemed to have a lot in common, so much so that their facial expressions seemed to be the same. As we stepped out onto the porch I gasped when I saw Jared was not where I had left him. The pathway was clear, no evidence of him at all. Violet hauled me along until we got to the fence. Reaching into her jacket pocket she pulled out a set of keys. She didn't look at me as she said, "Get in."

I heard a car beep, the Mini Cooper that I had parked behind. She released my arm and walked to the driver's side, opening the door. Luke sat in the passenger seat of my car, patiently awaiting my return. When he saw me he immediately got out.

"What's going on?" he asked, clearly wondering who Violet was as she sat down and slammed her door shut.

"I just—"

Violet honked the horn, telling me she wasn't going to wait. I tossed Luke the car keys and said, "Tell you later."

Dashing away before he could protest, I jumped into the Cooper. Hopefully he wouldn't follow us, wherever we were going. The second my door was shut Violet sped off, leaving Luke in the rear-view mirror. I sent him a quick text, telling him to go home for now, that I would contact him later. He only sent back two words, "Be careful."

The first thing I noticed while driving with Violet was the way she held the wheel. She kept her hands high, gripping it tight. It was rather aggressive but matched her speed and the way she swerved around other vehicles. Exactly like Jared.

"What are we doing?" I asked with as little hesitation as I could muster. I still didn't have any idea as to how we were going to get the blood. My hand kept on the arm rests by my sides, posture growing more tense with each sharp turn, checking my seatbelt.

"We're getting the blood of the latest victim," she said. So she knew about the spell then. What else did she know?

"How exactly?" I flinched as she turned again, causing her to smirk. Was she doing this on purpose?

"By finding the latest victim's body and sticking a needle in it," she gave me tight smile that didn't reach her eyes. I faced the windshield, picturing how we would get the blood.

The sky grew darker as we drove until finally lightning streaked across it. The booming thunder made me feel at ease, just slightly; I had always found storms comforting. Violet turned down a suburban street lit by flashing red and blue lights, her speed finally reducing. Slowly, she rolled the car past an ambulance and multiple police cars. Drops of water hit the window while I stared out of it. I could see Det. Young standing at the doorway of a pretty white house speaking with a middle-aged man. A small crowd had gathered on the outskirts of the property, just like at Alice's house. As we rolled past, I saw a large black bag being lifted into an ambulance.

"Someone else has been killed," I said, not asking a question.

"Then we have to go to the hospital," Violet said, stopping on the side of the street to let the ambulance pass. Once it was around the corner she began driving again; taking the same path to the hospital.

"Why?"

"Because that's where the morgue is." I looked back out the window, a heavy feeling in my stomach.

Violet's driving was slower now, calmer. Her hands rested at the proper positions and she no longer dodged around the few cars that were on the road. My fingers finally loosened on the rests and I began to relax my legs.

I didn't understand what had changed her mood so drastically.

My mind began to wander around, but never straying too far from Jared or Luke. Had Violet been at Yamuna's house because of what had happened to Jared? And what had Yamuna done to her?

"How are they connected?" I mumbled to myself without realizing it. I gave Violet a glance, wondering if she had heard me; her grip on the steering wheel told me she had.

"Shouldn't I be asking you that?" she said.

"What?"

"I think I'm the one who should be asking how you're connected with Jared. Not the other way around." She glared at me from the corner of her eye. She thought I had meant Jared, not Yamuna. Though I was wondering about that connection as well.

"He's helping me catch the one responsible for the recent killings," I explained carefully, "so that my friend can be proven innocent." She laughed, quick and bitter.

"Jared doesn't help people," she said, "if he's trying to catch this thing, then he's in it for the money. You and your friend don't mean a thing to him."

It was true, Jared had told me he was looking for the killer just because he was paid for it; Rosa's mother was the one willing to pay him even. But I felt like that wasn't all it was. A part of me felt like he was doing it because it was right, because he didn't want to see anyone else die. A part of me hoped he was doing it to help Luke and me as well.

"How do you know that?" I asked, beginning to feel a little upset. He was a good person, despite certain behaviours.

"Because I know Jared, and he doesn't just help people without him gaining something," she thrust her hand at me, end of discussion.

"How do you know Jared so well?" I questioned. I

wasn't going to convince her otherwise, but I would at least try and get something from this conversation.

"I think I know my own cousin bett— damn it." She banged a fist on the wheel, realizing what I had made her tell me. Resisting a smirk I kept my view forward. "That's dirty." I shrugged her off, not apologizing.

So they were cousins then. That explained a lot. But they had so many similarities it must go past simple genetics.

"I'm guessing you were raised together, then?" I said, more telling then asking.

"Did he tell you that?" she asked, frustrated.

"No," I said, not choosing to explain myself. I could tell it bothered her. This made me feel better, being the one who was able to read between the lines rather than the one who couldn't. I might have been the one asking questions, but I could read her better than I could Jared. "Then are you a bounty hunter too?"

"Not exactly," she said. Her knuckles began to turn white on the wheel.

"So you just work selling exotic animals then." Violet was easy to manipulate. Say the right things when she's mad and she'll tell you anything you need to know. I made a mental note to try it on Jared, when he was better. Who knows? It might work…

"Like I would work for scum like that!" she shouted at me, making me jump in my seat. "For your information I'm only working there undercover to save all those animals! What he's doing is wrong and I will not let him continue doing it!" She pointed her finger at me for a split second.

"So you're a…" I said thoughtfully, "animal activist then?" It was a reach, but lately my life had been full of reaches.

"Not exactly," she huffed, placing both hands high on the steering wheel. Violet was speeding again, but thankfully not as much as before. I stared her down, hoping she would just tell me. After a moment she finally sighed and confessed. "I used to be a bounty hunter with Jared. But once all the…supernatural things came out of the proverbial closet I saw that the creatures weren't being taken care of so I started hunting …poachers, so to speak."

"So you're an Eidolon animal activist."

"That's one way to put it," Violet said.

I was content knowing her connection with Jared, oddly enough. I actually felt relieved to hear that they were family. Why did I feel so much better about that?

"What about Yamuna?" I said.

"What about her?"

"What has she done to get her locked inside of her house?" I asked, wanting to really just ask how she knew Jared. I didn't think it was as simple as he was paid to catch her; it couldn't be that simple.

"Leave it alone," Violet told me. "It's between her and Jared."

"But-"

"Alone."

"Why—"

"Leave. It. Alone." Her tone told me that I wasn't going to get anywhere. Not tonight anyway, and not with her.

Turning my attention to the street, I saw that we were only two blocks away from the hospital. The ambulance that had taken away the latest victims body was nowhere in sight, even though Violet had driven like a madman behind it.

This was it; the final ingredient was so close that it made me start to think about what would happen after we got it. I didn't like where my mind took me.

Chapter 20

The bright fluorescent halls of the hospital basement said the same thing as the college. They tried to appear non-threatening and positive but I knew what was at the end of the hallway; the morgue. Those bright green and yellow lights made me feel as if I was walking into a zombie horror movie and I knew how those ended.

A few silver carts used to move bodies sat down the hallway, always opposite an open door. The walls were freshly painted and a thick, bitter chemical smell hung in the air, reminding me of the time I had to dissect animals in high school. I held my arms to my stomach, trying not to breathe through my nose.

Violet certainly had a different way of dealing with things compared to Jared. When we had walked into the hospital she didn't ask where to go, or who to talk to, she just went straight for the elevator and nobody stopped us. We rode it all the way down to the morgue, clearly the hospital didn't want people accidentally getting off on the wrong floor; the dead were stored just above the parking garage.

There was nobody in the hallway, the only sounds coming from our footsteps. It reminded me of being in the forest not two hours earlier when that thing had flown overhead. Nothing had made a noise then, too scared to even take a breath. The only difference now was that anyone nearby wasn't capable of breathing.

As we passed the second to last door, Violet came to a stop. The wooden door was open to an empty office, appearing just as positive and "safe" as the hallway. She stepped inside.

"What are you doing?" I whispered, feeling as if I wasn't supposed to make any sound. Poking my head in, I saw her grab two white lab coats off of a hanger in a change room, tossing one to me.

"Put this on," she ordered, "we need to look the part." I threw the jacket on over my sweater and followed her down the rest of the hall. Checking if I had a nametag, I didn't; at least that would make lying easier, if it came to that. Violet put the identical jacket on and slammed open the doors to the morgue.

The large silver room only had one living occupant, a young intern asleep at his desk. At least, he *was* asleep, before Violet woke him. He jumped to attention in his seat, frantically looking around for the cause just as Violet stuck a wedge under the door to keep it open. When he saw our lab coats he quickly pushed up his glasses and straightened his clothes, attempting to save himself. If we were actually doctors he might be in trouble... I remembered Violet carried a gun and decided that he was still in trouble, just a different kind.

"C-can I help you?" he asked, keeping his eyes on Violet.

"Yes," she said, "I'm Dr. Ryder and this is my intern, we're here to take over your shift." She flipped out a white ID badge and flashed it to him, not long enough to see anything clearly but the picture. When she put it away he looked to me for one. "She doesn't have one yet, so don't bother asking. She doesn't even speak any English; fresh off the plane from Germany! Now get out." She thrust her thumb at the door, almost nailing me in the eye. I leaned back fast, narrowly dodging her most likely intentional attack.

"But I was never told—"

"That isn't my problem," Violet said, "this girl needs to learn how to…uh…" she looked around the room, "handle being around the bodies, so leave us to our teachings."

"I think I should call the night manager…" he said as he stood. Picking up the phone he punched in four numbers and I heard it begin to ring.

"Well I tried to be nice," Violet grumbled, reaching into the back of her pants to reveal a black gun, similar to Jared's. It only took one hit from the butt to knock out the intern, leaving the person on the other end of the phone confused. He fell onto his chair and Violet hung up the phone before the person could ask anymore "hellos".

"Why did you hit him?" I asked, watching her walk around the desk. She shoved the intern underneath as I heard the elevator ding down the hallway. Sitting in the chair she looked up at me.

"Can you see him on that side?" Not thinking I looked down.

"No," I said, leaning backwards to check down the hallway to see a woman dressed in a paramedics outfit wheeling a black bag towards us. "What are you doing?"

"You should hide," she said, folding her hands in front of her on the desk. "It'll look suspicious for two of us to be here."

"What?"

"Hide. *Before* they get here." She rolled her eyes at me, like this should make any sense? I wasn't really sure where she expected me to go. The morgue walls were lined with boxes, labelled with names and there were no carts around to dash behind. That only left the doors.

I took one last look down the hallway at the paramedic wheeling towards me. Her attention was on the large body bag in front of her so I took the chance to rush behind the open door. Leaning back as much as I could against the wall, I heard the wheels squeak to a halt when she got into the morgue.

"Johnny not here tonight?" she asked Violet. I wondered how often she came here, if she knew who should be working when. Did that many people die in Ellengale? Lately, they did. Well, maybe they were just good friends...

"Nope," Violet said with what I assumed was a fake smile, "he's taking a personal day. What have ya got for me?"

"Another murder," she said, "from that Nighstalker bastard!" I clenched my fist, feeling as if she was talking about Luke. But I was just being overly defensive; he had been cleared of all charges.

"Well put her over there," Violet said, very nonchalantly. I heard the wheels roll further into the room and then footsteps coming back towards me. Peeking through the window I saw the paramedic facing Violet at her desk when suddenly a moan emerged from beneath it.

"What was that?" the woman asked, staring down at the floor, trying to look for the source of the noise. She couldn't see anything, that much I was glad for.

"That was nothing," Violet said with a jolt, kicking the poor intern under the desk. She stood and walked around, putting a hand on the woman's shoulder. "It was really nothing. Are you doing something after this?"

"No," the paramedic said slowly, "I'm done my shift but—"

"Good," Violet said. With one swift movement she clocked the paramedic over her head as she had to the man moments earlier. The woman went down easily, landing on the tiled floor with a thud. I stepped out from behind the door.

"Stop hitting people!" I tried to order her. Violet stuck her gun into the back of her pants and shrugged.

"They asked too many questions."

"They were just doing their jobs!" I huffed away my frustration, knowing she was just like Jared; the little people didn't matter too much, especially if they got in the way. Violet dragged the paramedic behind the desk and left her with the intern.

"Let's just get this over with," she said coming back towards me, opening her palms.

"Agreed," I said. We both turned to face the body bag then. It sat only a few feet away, beside an empty silver set of tools. As we walked over I tried not to breathe too deeply, the smell beginning to make me feel woozy.

"Wait here," Violet said, "I need to get a needle." She walked away from me but I kept my eyes on the black bag. Was this what they took Charlie away in? Was this where Charlie was right now?

I looked at the rows of storage containers on the wall and at the metal trays around the room. Is this where they did her autopsy? Suddenly I could see her smiling face in my mind and unexpectedly I remembered the time she had taken me to get her hair cut before a date.

"What do you think?" she had asked me, holding up a magazine to her head. The photo had a woman's hair up in a ponytail, with just simple bangs falling to the side. "These?"

We had been sitting in the hair salon, the smell of chemicals had made me feel dizzy there too. Her hair was long and straight, without a fringe. Quite different from the curls she sported the day she died. For some reason she had decided she needed a change for her date at the time.

"I don't think I'm the person you should ask," I told her, still uncomfortable around such an exuberant person. We had only recently met, then, and she was determined to be my friend.

"Well I want to look good tonight!" she threw the magazine into her lap. "You never know, this guy could be The One!"

"Really?" she sounded so positive I couldn't believe it.

"Haven't you ever met someone you've just had an instant connection with, Liv?" she laughed at me, as if love was the most common emotion to feel about a person. My name echoed in my head with her laugh.

"Liv? Liv!" Violet elbowed me in the ribs, bringing me back to my current and morbid reality. She moved me down to the head of the body, syringe in hand and asked, "Where the hell did you just go?"

"A memory," I said under my breath, "nowhere but a memory. How do you know my name?" I had never introduced myself and it had just occurred to me.

"Yamuna told me about you," Violet said as she unzipped the body bag, "she finds you disturbingly interesting."

The victim's body was exposed to us to the hips. She had a clean, white peasant top on, flowing over her stomach. I hadn't realized it at first, but she was pregnant. She had just the slightest baby bump showing underneath her shirt and just like all the other victims, there was no blood; no evidence of any kind.

I could say the same about how interesting Yamuna was, I thought with a tilt of my head. Actually, I could say the same about all of them. Damn them all for being so mysteriously intertwined.

This woman wasn't quite like the other victims; she was middle aged, she looked like a common housewife. She didn't fit the image of some young party girl. This woman probably had a husband, maybe a child, and she was expecting another, just like Heather... Something in my mind clicked.

Violet stuck the needle in the woman's arm and

withdrew blood. It was thick and dark, like the blood at Alice's crime scene. I began to purse my lips as I stared down at the woman's stomach. Something about the fact that they were both pregnant bothered me, a lot. Could it simply be a coincidence? Nothing so far seemed like a coincidence though.

"Let's go," Violet ordered, "before anyone else comes here." She zipped the bag back up, covering the woman's face with the black plastic.

"Wait," I said, grabbing her forearm before she could leave. "Where would they keep the coroner's reports?"

"They would go to the forensic lab," she told me, "and a copy would go to the coroner, which he would file away somewhere."

"Would they be in one of the offices down here?"

"No, none of these offices are occupied," Violet said, wrenching her arm from me. She pulled a vial out of her pocket and injected the blood into it. "They're going to be doing construction down here to make the morgue bigger."

"Why?"

"Because nobody wants their office next to the morgue." I tilted my head again, imagining that to be true.

"So where would they be then?" I asked, following her down the hallway.

"Who cares?" she shrugged out of the white jacket and tossed it into an open office. I stopped and twirled in a circle as I took mine off to do the same, jogging to catch up with her. She pressed the elevator button and watched the numbers above the doors change.

"Because I need to see something that might help us," I said, pleading. It was a slight lie, I mostly wanted to indulge in my own curiosity but there was something just...off about this.

"Hmm, fine," she said, deciding not to bother arguing with me. "You have five minutes when we get there. That's it."

"Okay," I smiled slightly as the doors dinged open and we stepped inside. She pressed for the second floor and the elevator shuddered as it raised us up.

She never asked me what I wanted to know and it bugged me a little. Wasn't she at all wondering why I wanted to view the coroner's report? If I was her I would want to know what I was doing.

The doors opened to another fluorescent hallway. There were only a few nurses, walking in and out of rooms to behind the oval desk between them all.

"This way," Violet tapped my arm and took a sharp left down the empty hall, which had nobody there. "These are the offices for the coroners." She stopped at the door labelled 205 and pulled a key from her pocket; where had she gotten that? I wondered. Checking over her shoulder, she unlocked and opened the door. I glanced behind myself, to see if anyone was looking but the coast was clear when Violet yanked me inside with a whisper, "Hurry it up."

She shut the door behind me as quietly as possible and I looked around the room. The only light that I had to see by was from the hallway and the moon outside, neither of which gave much. Violet never turned the light on so I assumed that meant we couldn't.

"Here," she said as I stumbled through the darkness. She passed me a mini flashlight that hung off of her keys. "Try the cabinet."

"Thanks," I said taking it from her. The grey filing cabinets sat just behind the door and opened with ease. "Shouldn't these be locked?" I rifled through the file names, trying to find the victims.

"This is Ellengale, honey," she said, sounding exactly like Jared, "they don't lock up much here. Trust me, I know." She shot me a tight lipped smile. I didn't ask what she meant.

Continuing through the files I noted they weren't in chronological order as I had anticipated. Once I reached the end of them all I saw they were actually simply alphabetical, the first recognizable name I went for being Rosa's. Pulling out the last four files took longer than I had hoped, but I managed to find them all and carefully opened Heather's first. I knew what Rosa's would say; it was the rest I wanted to check out.

It contained a lot of jargon that I wasn't familiar with so I skimmed it quickly, looking for certain words. Once I found what I wanted I checked Alice's, and found the same. That only left Charlie's file. Going over her name with the light I began to reminisce again, my mind wandering back to the salon.

"Whadyathink?" Charlie had asked me as she spun in the chair, hair bouncing through the air.

"It looks nice," I told her, not sure of what I was supposed to say. After she had paid and we started walking back to the apartment building to pick out her outfit for the night. "Why did you bring...*me*?" Charlie was popular, she had plenty of other friends that would actually enjoy this, so why me?

"Because we're friends silly!" She playfully pushed me on the arm and quickened her pace, making me stop in my place.

She had really impacted me at that moment; I had never made a friend so easily.

"Hey, hurry up!" Violet jostled me back to the present. "We need to get going."

"Uh...oh, yeah," I said, reading the cause of death. Each victim had died from blood loss, but the coroner couldn't figure out how; there were no cuts, no marks, nothing. It was as if most of their blood just...disappeared. As I continued to look over the files I came across something shocking. I think my mouth must have been hanging open, it was the only explanation for Violet's next sentence.

"What is it?" I looked up at her, the hallway lights reflecting onto her face.

"She was pregnant," I said, "they were all pregnant." I thought my words would impact Violet more.

"So?" she asked, grabbing the files from me and shoving them inside the cabinet. Once they were inside she slammed the drawer shut.

"Don't you think that's a little strange?" I followed her out the door and back to the elevators. "Five victims, four of them knew each other and all of them were pregnant."

"Coincidence," Violet shrugged as she hit the elevator button. The doors opened instantly and we got in, heading back to the first floor.

"How often are things like this a coincidence?" I questioned. It couldn't just be that simple.

"Lots of times," she said, "look, you got the blood, Yamuna'll summon it, the thing'll die and it'll be done."

We got out of the elevator and headed for the front doors. Nobody looked at us as we walked outside, our pace fast. The rain had calmed down a bit, but was still coming down. She made it to the car before me and opened her door.

"Would Jared think it was just a coincidence?" I called to her, a few feet away from the car. I opened my arms under the crashing sky, awaiting her reply. She stopped and faced me. I moved the few steps to the door, lessening the distance between us

"Yeah, he would," was all she said before slamming her door shut and coming around to my side. She grabbed my collar and shoved me against the Cooper. She was close enough for me to see the water running down the strands of her hair, to see the tears welling in her eyes. "And don't you think for a moment that you know what he'd think."

"I—"

"No!" she pushed me harder against the car, her voice cracking. "He is *my* family, not yours. *I* grew up with him, *not* you. So don't you think for one second that

194

you know him better than me."

I didn't see it before, how much it hurt her that Jared was turned to stone. She had seemed so indifferent, she never gave off any indication of caring. But now that she was inches away from my face I could see it quite clearly. Her brown eyes were red, her breathing shallow, trying to hold back the tears.

"I'm sorry," I said. I had never actually tried to say I knew Jared better than her, but...I didn't think he would consider it a coincidence. Violet released me from her grip, walking back around the car and carefully facing away from me. I saw one hand reach to her face, wiping away a tear that I wasn't supposed to see.

"Just because he lets you go around with him doesn't mean that you matter," she said, wrenching on her door handle, "you're just another girl in another town that he is going to forget." She slammed the door again and started the car. I stood for a second next to the Cooper, thinking about what she had said. That kind of hurt, just a little bit.

Chapter 21

I stood, yet again, on Yamuna's front steps. I felt like I was always there, and being there gave me such a dark feeling. The guilt I felt over hurting Violet's feelings wasn't helping me either. I was a little glad she had left, though she didn't take the uncomfortable tension with her. At first I had thought she was leaving because she couldn't stand the sight of me, but she had received a phone call prior to arriving at Yamuna's; it was clear that whatever the person wanted, it was more important than finding the killer.

She had given me the blood, barely saying two words to me and sped off down the street to an unknown destination. The blood was in my hand now and all I had to do was knock on her door and she would show me how to do the spell. Simple, oh so…simple. I sighed and lifted my hand to knock.

"Wait!" called a voice from behind me. I turned to see Dr. Wineman rushing in my direction, with Luke just behind him. He pulled me down the stairs by the wrist. "You can't have her do the spell!"

Luke stood behind the doctor, his eyes serious but not exactly agreeable.

"She wasn't going to do the spell," I said, pulling out of his grip gently. "I was." He didn't seem to like that.

"But you're not a witch," he said, as if that would matter, "you're not even Eidolon; you can't do magic."

Oh. I didn't say anything, understanding what he meant.

Only Eidolon's could do magic then? So why did Yamuna say I would have to do the spell? Old questions that I had long forgotten bubbled to the surface of my mind when the door behind me creaked open and we all faced the witch in her home.

"Did you get the blood?" she asked, not caring about Dr. Wineman or Luke. The doctor pulled me further away and spoke to me in a whisper.

"You don't want to have her do this," he told me, "she has a…history of betrayals."

"Liv," Luke came into the conversation, replacing the doctors hand with his own, "I know you don't like leaving things alone, and I know you're just trying to help in your own way…but if he says it's too dangerous for you to do it, then don't." His eyes pleaded to me.

"If I can't do it alone, then why don't you help me," I said to him, holding back my tone, "and how do you know that this thing is so innocent? How do you *know* we're wrong about it?" I turned to the doctor and waited for a response. He seemed to be at a loss for words.

"You have to trust me," he said, "you just have to trust me." I shook my head, resisting a bitter laugh.

"No," I said and tore my arm from Luke's grip, something I had never done before with such seriousness, "I won't let any more women die like Charlie did. I won't let there be any more victims even if I have to kill this thing myself."

"Tick tock," Yamuna chimed from her porch, waving her fingers to the beat in her head. I turned and walked up the steps to the witch, showing the blood to her with an open palm. "You know I could do the spell for you."

"I thought you didn't want to," I asked, confused. "You said it was too dangerous."

A smile spread across the witches face, her white teeth showing through; with an expression so sinister I felt she needed fangs. She had wanted me to ask her to do the spell. She had planned all of this to happen.

"It comes at a price," she said, plucking the vial from my hand. "But you can afford it."

"Do not make a deal with her, Liv," Dr. Wineman stepped forward, to the edge of the steps. He tried to move closer but couldn't, an invisible barrier keeping him out. "Whatever you do, do not make a deal."

Yamuna laughed. "I've learned a few things about fences, *Dick,*" the witch said, "and I might not be able to get out, but I certainly can control who comes in." She touched the vial of blood to her cheek, pride flowing off of her for being able to keep him out.

"Except for Jared," the doctor said, and Yamuna grimaced.

"Well," she began, "exception that proves the rule, I suppose. Come inside, we'll talk."

She glided into her prison, and I stopped myself from looking back at Luke clenching at my sweaters sleeves. This wasn't just about him anymore; it wasn't *just* about proving his innocence. With a deep breath I stepped across the threshold, making my decision in that very moment about making a deal with a witch.

Yamuna was in her kitchen, lining up all the ingredients on the round table; the mermaid's scale, the pixie's dust, dragon's venom and finally, the blood of the most recent victim. All of our hard work was set out for me to see and could fit into the palm of my hand.

"Where's Jared?" I asked, my mouth feeling dry. I knew I was avoiding the topic at hand, and that I didn't have any time to waste, but I still wanted to know. I still wanted to stall.

"Oh, Violet took him away," Yamuna said waving her hand at me, "as lovely a lawn ornament he made, he was an eyesore to the neighbours."

I imagined the entire house was an eyesore to the neighbours, but it was rather isolated for anyone to care. The nearest houses looked exactly the same as hers.

Yamuna continued, "You can ask your little friend out there, I believe he sent my girl on a mission to get the cure."

"Your girl?"

"Violet and I made a deal," Yamuna said, sitting down, "like the one we're about to make."

"What kind of deal?" I asked, not even sure which one I was talking about; mine, or Violet's.

"I do the spell, summon the creature from the Shade," she waved her hand in a circle, "and you give me eternal servitude." Oh, was that all?

"Eternal? As in forever?" I stayed at a safe distance a few feet away, though I knew it wasn't going to help much. She was probably capable of killing me with just a look.

"Just until you die," Yamuna giggled. "It's not so bad, Violet made the same deal after all." She leaned towards me in her seat when I began to hear Dr. Wineman speaking to Luke through the open door.

"What are you talking about?" Luke asked the doctor.

"You have to go inside," he told Luke, "she can't make the deal. I'll do the spell; just get her out of there! I can't go in, but you can." Yamuna flicked her wrist towards me and the front door slammed shut.

"Pay no attention to the purebloods," she smiled, "just say yes, and it's done."

"If I refuse?" I gripped my phone in my pocket, as if it would actually help me.

"If you refuse then that's your choice," she rested against the back of the chair, attempting to mask her eagerness. "But you'll have to figure things out on your own. So just say 'yes'."

"You said you would show me," I pointed a finger at her, taking note of the difference while I could hear Luke trying to open the door. Yamuna leaned on the table, eyeing me.

"Liv come outside! Richard will do the spell!" he called and banged on the door. I had never heard the doctor's first name before, but I knew that must be it. They had gotten close while I was away...

"Things change," Yamuna shrugged and crossed her legs, triumphant. I could see now this was her idea ever since she told Jared I needed to be around; this was why she never gave him a choice. What I couldn't understand was why me. Why would my specific "eternal servitude" benefit her?

Getting someone like Violet to make a deal made sense to me, Violet had skills. What did I have? I couldn't think of a single thing and that made me feel a little worse than I already did.

"If I refuse, do I get to keep the ingredients?" I pointed at the table. The witch rolled her eyes and walked over to the stove in a fluid motion. She poured steaming water into a cup and stirred it as she turned to me.

"You collected them, do what you want with them." Not asking anymore questions I scooped up the magical supplies and hurried to the door while Luke continued to call my name. Yamuna stopped me at the doorway to the hall, appearing next to me in an instant and lifted my hands into hers. "Interesting..."

"W-What?" I asked, watching her eyes turn black as she stared upwards. Yamuna smiled again, just like before.

"You may want to hurry," she warned, "your time is running out." She didn't need to say anything else to quicken my pace out of the house.

I tried best I could to not drop anything when I reached for the door handle. When I opened it Luke came running at me, prepared to smash the door down. He scraped his feet on the wooden floor before he slammed into a barrier in the threshold. Luke fell backwards and Yamuna chuckled as she stepped around the corner with a cup of tea.

"Luke…" I said, helping him to his feet.

"I lowered the fence for a moment, just for that moment," she looked down into her tea thoughtfully and laughed. For a witch, she was fast.

"Splendid," I handed Luke the pixie's dust and blood, keeping the venom and scale to hold myself. Pulling him to his feet we walked down the steps to Dr. Wineman, who held his hands out to both of us. Once we reached him he breathed a sigh of relief, for reasons I was only beginning to understand.

"Good, good," he said, "come on, I'll take you home." The crickets chirped around us, something I hadn't heard in what felt like a lifetime. We walked the pathway back to his car and once we were safely inside I risked a glimpse backwards.

Yamuna wiggled her fingers at us, or more at me, to say goodbye. I had a feeling that her invitation to make a deal was always on the table, should the need arise. I hoped that need would never come up as it had for Violet. What did Violet want so badly from Yamuna, that she would offer eternal servitude to the witch?

"Jared," I mumbled. He was the only thing I could think of that would make someone as headstrong as Violet sell her freedom for.

"Don't worry about him," Dr. Wineman said starting his car, "I called Violet earlier and she's getting the cure for him." He pulled away quickly and Violet's haste made a lot more sense, and it was appropriate. I almost wanted to join her in her search for the cure.

"You'll do the spell?" I asked from the passenger seat. Luke remained silent in the back and the doctor continued to drive. "You said you would."

"I will," he said, "but we do things my way." He

wagged a finger at me, something that seemed to be happening a lot. "You *will* do what I say." I nodded, knowing it was either that or serve a witch for the rest of my life.

It was two in the morning and we still hadn't performed the spell. I sat on my living room couch with Luke and... Richard with no action. Doing nothing was starting to take its toll on my body; I was finally beginning to realize how truly tired I was.

"Why aren't we doing anything?" I said, standing in frustration and hoping to rid myself of my fatigue. "There could be more deaths while we just sit here waiting on...on what?" I brushed my hair backwards and then looked at my hand. It really was no wonder Jared did that so often.

"Well I'm waiting for the sleeping pill to take effect," Richard said, crossing his legs. "Then we can talk in the morning, when you've actually had a full night's sleep." He took a sip of the tea he had made and I stared at my own cup.

After we had gotten home he had kindly offered to make us some tea and I didn't think anything of it. As if knowing what he had done triggered effect of the drug I felt even wearier than I had before.

"Why..." I groaned and Luke seated me down onto our chair.

"You'll feel better," he told me, "you haven't slept since this started."

"But if we don't hurry...someone might die," I pleaded to Luke, hoping to get the message across. He sat down next to me in the chair, lifting me slightly into his lap like my father used to do when I was a child. As comforting as it was, I didn't like it; it felt wrong for some reason. Luke didn't feel like himself to me anymore.

Luke said something to me, but I couldn't quite hear him. My eyes were closed and I was falling asleep. My dreams that night were filled with running through a forest, running from a clicking noise behind me but whenever I looked back all I could see was black.

Chapter 22

I woke up feeling groggy, my mouth was dry and the room was kind of moving on its own. It took me a few moments to remember what had happened; Luke and Dr. Wineman had given me some sleeping pills, how many, I didn't know. I looked around and found I was in my room, only a light blanket covering me.

Groaning, I sat up on my bed, swinging my legs over the side and rubbing my eyes. What time was it? I checked the clock and saw that it was already a little past ten. Being drugged by my closest friend was not something I saw coming, but then again Luke was just full of surprises lately. Quickly, I changed into fresh clothes and stepped out the door, the apartment quiet.

When I reached the living room there was nobody there; where did they go? I checked the refrigerator for a note but there was nothing there either. Leaning my head against the fridge in defeat I noticed the metal felt oddly cooler than normal against my skin. My eyes opened and I saw that the spell's ingredients were sitting out on the counter. So they weren't doing the spell without me then.

Maybe it wasn't so bad that Luke had made me sleep; I was ready to do the spell alone after all. I was even prepared to sell my freedom to Yamuna to have her do the spell. What had I been thinking? For some reason I had temporarily lost my mind and I wanted to blame it on my lack of sleep. At first it was just because of Jared that I couldn't sleep, but then it was stress from Luke being in jail and then…well, then everyone around me started to disappear.

Charlie was dead, Jared was stone, Luke was keeping secrets and to top it all off I had opened some kind of wound in Violet. The past two weeks had been completely insane and it wasn't getting any better.

While I stood in the kitchen, thinking about everything, a noise from the apartment next door drew my attention. Feet shuffled around and at first I thought it would be the police, but they had no reason for being in Charlie's place anymore. I opened my front door, hearing Charlie's door shut first.

In front of me stood a small, dark-skinned man with large, sunken in eyes. Her stared at me, wide-eyed with panic. Immediately he dropped the book he was holding and ran down the hall, not a single word to explain what he was doing. He wasn't a cop, that much I knew and he looked strangely familiar. I had seen him before, but where? It was right there, his on the brink of my mind but I just couldn't focus on it.

"Hey!" I called after him but he was already at the stairs. I didn't chase after him and instead looked at what he had dropped. I picked up a thin, bright yellow notebook that read "Journal" across the cover. It didn't look like something a man like him would carry and when I flipped open the cover I saw Charlie's name, written in her bubbly handwriting.

I walked into Charlie's apartment, the police tape that once covered her door gone. Flicking on a light I made my way into her room to put the journal back but I found it beckoned to me. I could feel its weight in my hand, just begging me to read it, to find out if she had known she was pregnant. The coroner's report said she was eight weeks pregnant when she died, so she must have known by then?

Standing in her room I tried not to look at all the pictures of her with friends and family. I sat down on her bed, staring down at the cover of the journal. This wasn't right. I shouldn't be reading a girl's diary; reading all of her deepest thoughts and emotions. But my hands and eyes wouldn't listen to my brain and suddenly I was flipping through the pages of the yellow journal, finding her most recent entries.

Most of them were just about her day, people she didn't like and people she really liked. Her large, loopy writing made me smile and the way she dotted every "i" with a large circle was just very...Charlie. There was nothing incriminating, nothing to say she was in danger. When I found the last entries I read them, word for word to ensure I didn't miss anything.

Dear Diary,

Rosa was killed today. I don't even know what to think about that! I didn't know her very well, she was just the bartender we hung out with sometimes, but still...she's gone. She was murdered too, by someone, right after she finished working. That could have been any of us! We were all at The Corner; any one of us could have been attacked.

Also, I've been feeling sick lately in the morning too...plus I'm late. I've never been late before...what if I'm pregnant? What will my parents think?

So she did know she was pregnant? Or she at least had an inkling to it. I read down to her final entry, written the day she died. *The* day she died, though it was hours before she did; it was written after she had gotten home from The Corner. I didn't understand why she kept going there, if she was so concerned with Rosa's murder. The party stopped for no murder it seemed.

Dear Diary,

You will never guess who I met today! I met the weather girl from channel five and the blonde anchor host...what was her name? Oh well, I couldn't believe it! They were at The Corner today and I got some great advice from them, on how to get into the industry but school is such a big part of that; do I really want to go back?

And, I found out that Alice and Heather are pregnant! It's not just me! Although, they at least got pregnant with their boyfriends...I got pregnant with a guy that isn't even in town anymore. I don't even know how to contact him...I wish he didn't leave in the morning, I really liked him. I thought we had something...

I could see small, round stains on the paper; Charlie had been crying when she wrote this entry. I traced my fingers over the tear marks, feeling her pain for being left.

"Liv?" Luke said behind me. I turned around to see him standing in the doorway to Charlie's room. "What are you doing?" I snapped the journal shut, caught in the act. It was a strange reaction though, since it wasn't like it was Charlie that was catching me.

"Oh, uh..." I started, not sure if I should tell him the truth, "I was just...looking for clues in Charlie's diary." He was going to find out anyway.

"Clues to what?" he asked, stepping in and sitting next to me on the bed. "We already know what killed her, and we're going to stop it today."

"I know...I just feel like something's off," I said, "I just feel like...I mean, it feels right, that the ancient is the one doing the killings but it feels wrong. Especially after that guy tried to take this and..." I trailed my sentence off, thinking that maybe it was better if Luke didn't know she was pregnant.

"Someone tried to steal Charlie's diary?" Luke asked, putting an arm around me. I bit my lip and decided that I would just tell him everything; I didn't want to keep any secrets from him though he didn't seem to have a problem keeping them from me.

"Yeah," I said, beginning to play with the edges of the journal, "and…"

"And what?" Luke gave my shoulder a squeeze, an attempt to comfort me.

"And she was pregnant," I said, feeling him flinch, "they were all pregnant."

"All of them?" He brushed past the flinch and no longer concerned with the mystery thief. I knew he had had a crush on Charlie, hearing she was pregnant must have bothered him.

"Yeah," I said, "that's why something just feels…different now. And with this guy trying to steal her diary…I don't know what to think anymore." I looked up at Luke, feeling a lump in my throat, my words coming out as a whisper. He hugged me tighter to his chest and I took a deep breath.

"Why is this so important to you," he asked, "what happened to my utterly indifferent best friend who stays out of everyone's business but our own?" He laughed and I actually did too, for a quick second. It wasn't like me to get so involved in something and no matter how many times I told myself it was for him, I knew that wasn't true. I was never doing this for Luke, was I?

"I don't know," I said, "I just don't want anyone else to die." Luke rubbed my shoulder and sighed.

"She's not your mother," he said, "finding Charlie's killer won't solve your mother's death." I hadn't thought of that, not really. Charlie was a lot like my mother was when she was alive; outgoing, positive, nothing holding either of them down for very long, if at all. Until she was killed, that is.

"I know," I said, "but it'll make me feel better. When mom died and it was declared an accident I didn't know what to do. I know that's not true; something happened to her. There was something else in the car, I *saw* an Eidolon in the fire then. You know—"

"I know," he cooed, "I know." Luke moved away

from me to look me in the eyes. "Let's go back to the apartment."

"I can't have another unsolved death on my mind, Luke. I-I just can't."

"We'll figure it out."

This was why Luke was my best friend; because he never told me I was crazy. While other's told me I had been traumatized by my mother's death, that I was seeing things in the fire she died in, he believed me. I had shown him what I had seen and he believed it too.

"Luke, Liv!" Dr. Wineman rounded the corner into Charlie's room, a sympathetic look on his face. Had he heard us? I hoped not. "What are you two doing in here?" He glanced around the room, curious. A little too curious, I thought.

"We were just going back," Luke said standing. The doctor nodded and left us alone, knowing that he had just walked in on something he shouldn't have. I set Charlie's diary on the bed, the yellow leather contrasting with the blue comforter. I smiled at the bears across her pillows and sheets; Charlie was gone, but I certainly wasn't going to forget her. Luke reached his hand to me and I took it, leaving the room and feeling just a little bit better. I couldn't tell if the doctor had heard what we said, but I was going to choose to believe he didn't.

When we got back to our apartment I found Violet sitting on our couch. Legs and arms crossed she glared at the television news, reporting about a break in at the hospital morgue. It claimed there were no suspects so we were safe, but I had a feeling Violet didn't like that fact that we were almost caught.

"That was your fault," she said to me, pointing at the television. "If I'm caught for your crap, I'm not going down alone. Now can we do this already, doc?"

"Yes, yes," Dr. Wineman said, "please call me Richard. But I thought Liv might want to be there for it."

"For what?" I asked, a little too eager. "The spell?"

209

So we were finally going to do it then? The doctor's eyes told me I was wrong. It was clear to me that he didn't want to do it, that he was determined to prove to me that the Shadeland ancient was innocent. I was even beginning to believe him, after everything that had happened.

"No," Richard said, "to cure Jared." My eyebrows raised and he smiled, knowing I was trying not to do the same.

"You have the cure?" I asked, excited.

"I do not have it," he said and gestured to Violet, "but I sent our dear Violet to go get it...I admit I could not have gotten it myself."

"Damn right you couldn't have," Violet came in, "so if you don't mind, I'd like to get this done so my cousin can turn back into a real boy." She shot daggers at me with more than just her eyes; her very stance was telling me what she was thinking.

"Yes, yes," the doctor said, trying to keep her at bay, "I just need to examine the piece before using it; make sure it is authentic." Violet snorted and rolled her eyes.

"Fine," she said. She yanked a bag from the couch and reached in to pull out a long black box. Handing it to Richard he pulled the lid off, thanking Violet as he did. "How are you going to check if it's real?"

"Just a touch," he said, pulling his eyes away from the item in the box. Luke and I peered into it, leaning closely in as the doctor's hand hovered over top.

Sitting on a red velvet piece of cloth was...something. It looked familiar but I still didn't know what to call it. It appeared to be a foot long piece of twisted ivory, gleaming in what little light came to its surface.

"What is it?" Luke whispered. I smiled, feeling like he was his usual, socially awkward self as he whispered for no reason. The doctor touched it for a brief moment and replaced the lid.

"It is an Alicorn," Richard told us, "it is what's going to cure Jared. Did you bring him then?"

"Yeah," Violet said, throwing her side-bag over her shoulder, "he's downstairs."

Standing in the parking lot behind a van made me feel a little shady. Violet had brought Jared in a windowless, white van, since he wouldn't just fit inside of her Mini Cooper. She threw open the back doors of the van and displayed Jared for all of us to see. How she had gotten him into the van was a mystery to me and I wasn't about to question her methods now.

He was in the same position, made of rock. I was thankful Violet had parked with the back against the trees, ensuring none of the other tenants would see him by chance. That was something I wouldn't have an explanation for.

"So how will that cure him?" I asked, breaking down and voicing what most of us were thinking.

"This is an Alicorn," the doctor explained, displaying the object in his hand, "it is believed to neutralize any kind of poison. Back in the day people who feared being poisoned would drink from cups made of Alicorn to protect themselves." Ever the history teacher, he was and I wondered what he had considered "the day".

"But what is an Alicorn?" Luke wondered aloud. I caught Violet rolling her eyes again.

"It's the horn of a Unicorn," she said. She kept her arms crossed tight and her attitude made a little more sense to me. The Etheric Shade animal activist had to get a Unicorn horn; it must have actually hurt her, depending on how she got it. She grumbled, "Just do it already."

"All right then," Richard agreed, "now Liv, where was he bitten by the beast?" I pointed to Jared's left shoulder, cautious not to touch him. "Thank you." Violet and I almost screamed when the doctor raised the Alicorn and thrust it into Jared. Bright orange and red sparks flew from Jared's stone form, lighting up the doctor's greying hair. Luke and I shielded our faces but Violet just stepped back, watching with amazement.

211

When the fireworks died down, the doctor pulled the Unicorn horn from Jared. I had expected a hole to be in Jared's shoulder, but there was nothing there. The same thing seemed to happen as when he turned to stone; slowly, his jacket turned back into leather, his skin turned from solid rock into the same soft texture. When his eyes fluttered open I smiled to see the blue of his eyes. Jared groaned as he leaned up onto his forearms.

"Oh God," he moaned, "this is the worst hangover ever." He held his head and Violet rushed to help him up. She pushed him back, holding him as he sat upwards.

"Are you all right?" she asked him. He nodded his head until he finally remembered what had happened. He looked up into Violet's eyes and finally past her, at me.

"Are you all right?" he asked back. The last thing he remembered was being at Yamuna's, so I understood his concern.

"Yeah I'm—" Violet started but he held up his free hand to stop her.

"Not you," Jared said, "you can take care of yourself. She can't." He pointed at me and Violet turned around, fire burning behind her irises. I was a little insulted by his statement despite the fact that it was partially true.

"I'm fine," I said, trying not to antagonize the situation but noticing I wavered on my feet. Why was that? And why did Jared have to notice? I tried to get his focus off of me. "Uh, how do you feel?"

"Like I just went five rounds with a vampire," he inched forward till his feet could touch the ground, "and lost. What happened?"

"You were bitten by a Cockatrice," Richard said after clearing his throat. "But Violet was able to find the cure at her...ah, job and give it to you. And here we are." The doctor opened his arms, displaying everyone around him. He seemed uncomfortable but I didn't know why; he had no reason to feel that way. No obvious *reason*, anyway.

"Great, thanks," Jared stood up, leaning one hand on

Violet's shoulder for support. "Why are you here?" He was talking to the doctor.

"I have...reluctantly agreed to do the spell," he said, "I had no other choice." He gave me a sideways glance.

"Why?" Violet asked, looking at both of us. "You told me you didn't want to do it."

"It was either I do the spell, or Liv make a deal with Yamuna, among other things." Richard gestured to me, his eyes careful to avoid anyone else's. This was his way of ratting me out and I found it rather underhanded.

"You what?" Violet was the one that was furious, something I was not expecting. "Do you have any idea what that means?" She tossed Jared aside and came towards me.

"But you...you did the same thing," I said, panicking. Her eyes widened, as did everyone else's.

"Vi," Jared said in a low tone, "you made a deal...with that witch?" His words were soaked with anger, disgust and...concern. The sound of a broken heart, I thought, but Jared would never admit to caring so much. Violet turned on her heels, face drained of all blood, her pupils contracted.

"I had to..." was all she managed to say without releasing her tears.

"You *had* to? You know better than to make a deal with her!" He banged his fist on the inside of the van and gasped, anger taking over his other emotions now. Jared bent over, holding his legs for support, his breathing becoming weathered. He straightened his back as the doctor touched Violet's arm.

"I didn't... I didn't know," she whispered, her eyes beginning to fill with tears again.

"Luke, please take her inside," Richard said and he pushed them both away. I stood with Jared as he tried to control his breathing. The doctor told us both to sit down in the back of the van once Luke and Violet were out of sight. "Understand, at the time she didn't believe she had

213

a choice."

"What in hell does that mean?" he questioned, holding his chest as his breathing returned to normal. "There is always a choice."

"She made the deal with Yamuna to try and save you," Richard explained, "but we both know how that witch is. She tricks people," he looked to me, "*betrays* them." He was trying to drive the point home in me, but I still couldn't quite comprehend the situation. If I asked what evidence they had I doubted I would learn anything. But how could I just leave it to trusting them when they didn't even seem to trust me in return?

"What, you were ready to sell your soul to save me?" he asked, flashing me a tired grin.

"No, I was going to have her do the spell..." I said, feeling a little bad that I had never considered him. He looked away from me and patted my leg. In my defence I didn't *know* about Yamuna's deals or that she had planned on making one with me. It made me wonder why she had never offered me the same contract as she did Violet.

"Oh, well, good...that's...a good choice," he said and left his hand on my leg, not thinking. I could feel my face heating up as it stayed there. When he noticed both the doctor and me staring at it he took it away and rubbed at his old wound. "Anyway, what ingredients are left?"

"None," Richard informed him, "Liv has collected everything we need." Jared laughed but it was cut short when he realized the doctor wasn't actually joking.

"You?" he pointed at me. "You got everything else?"

"Well she wasn't alone," Richard said, "Luke and Violet helped as well."

"Then what are we waiting for?" Jared got out of the van. "Let's do the spell." He stumbled back with a grunt, holding his side. I reached my hand out to touch him, help him but quickly withdrew. There wasn't anything I could do for him, not really.

"I think we should wait a bit, maybe just a couple of

hours till you're feeling…better." The doctor patted him on the shoulder and walked away, I assumed to check on Violet. They had a strange familiarity between them, but it seemed everyone I met recently did. I stood up and observed Jared's condition.

"Do you…need help?" I asked, moving my eyes around the area.

"I need my car," he said, "where is it?" I thought back, remembering that his car was still parked in front of Yamuna's. I stared down at his baby blue's, anticipating how badly this next conversation would go.

Chapter 23

Jared kept his head rested on the passenger side window as I drove, the air between us uncomfortable only in my mind. Why did I always have to feel uncomfortable around him? He looked tired and I told him he should rest, but he insisted on getting his car first. I wasn't looking forward to what he might do when we arrived at Yamuna's. She had just made a deal with his cousin and tried to make one with me; Jared was furious, though I thought it was more because of Violet.

Wanting to talk with him, I found the only common thread we had; the creature.

"Do you really think the creature from Shadeland is committing the murders?" I asked, shifting my hands on the wheel. I felt like I was the only one having doubts, besides Dr. Wineman that was. Luke seemed sure, so did Jared and Violet…was I the only one feeling this way?

"What else would it be?" Jared said, rolling down his window. The fresh breeze blew his hair back and he closed his eyes, enjoying it. "The doc said it wasn't it, so it must be it."

"How did you come to that conclusion?" Was that all we were going on? Thinking back, I guessed it was true. I was taking Jared's word for it, not having anything else of my own to go on. But now I did have something to go on; I had all the puzzle pieces, I just needed to figure out how they came together.

"Those Shadeland purebloods all protect each other," Jared told me, "so if the doctor says this thing didn't do it, he only wants to protect it." He rubbed his forehead, eyes still shut.

"Well...while we were getting the other ingredients some things happened..." I started, beginning to feel stupid again for thinking something was a clue. He would most likely scoff at me, just like he had the Agate. But then again, look how that had turned out.

"What sort of things?"

"They were all pregnant," I blurted, forgetting that you should never lead with the best point in an argument, "all of the five victims were in the early stages of pregnancy."

"Coincidence," he said. I saw that coming before I even considered telling anyone. I furrowed my brow and tightened my hands over the leather interior, trying to think of something to prove my point but there was nothing. Maybe that was just it though, maybe the fact that they were pregnant really was just a coincidence, and the creature was just killing for the sake of killing. Maybe I should just look at the obvious and stop overanalyzing. My head was starting to hurt from trying to figure it out.

"Do you want to talk it out?" Jared asked with a sigh as he watched me. "You look like you're about to have an aneurism."

"Talk it out how?" I glanced at him from the corner of my eye, wondering what his angle was.

"Well, let's figure out what they all had in common," he suggested and held out a hand to count on. He was suddenly being helpful and...nice?

217

"We can't though," I said, "we don't know anything about the latest victim."

"Who was the latest victim?"

"I don't know, it was a woman that lives on Eastport." Or *lived*, I should have said.

"That's not too far from here, is it?" he asked and I shook my head. It was actually only a few blocks away. "Then let's check it out."

"Why?" I asked before I could stop myself. Jared was sure that it was the Shadeland creature doing the killings, so why look into the latest victim? Why was he so willing to indulge in my curiosity *now*?

"Because I know you aren't going to leave it alone," he said, "you'll keep thinking about it until you finally do something stupid like break into the crime scene." Well…he had me there.

I was about to debate him but he was right. I had done it before, and I would most likely do it again. I signalled right and turned down a side street, heading in the direction of Eastport.

Jared instructed me to just pull up in front of the house, to not bother parking down the block or around the corner as I had the first time. I surveyed the neighbourhood and there was nobody around, nobody daring to go outside after what had happened. I didn't blame them; murder was something that never happened here. I stopped the car and turned to him.

"How do we get in?" I asked, looking around for any police but finding none. There wasn't even one posted at the door to keep people out, just more tape.

"Well I was going to walk," he said, "did you have any other ideas?" His eyes rolled and I looked away, feeling as stupid as I could possibly get. As my line of vision went out the window I saw a woman across the street quickly pull her curtains closed.

"Someone's noticed us," I said, watching as the same woman peeked through the blinds again.

"So?" he said, opened his door, "What's she going to do? Even if she calls the cops it'll be at least ten minutes before they get here."

"But what if she takes my plates down?" I was only one computer check away from being discovered. And I knew if we were caught I would be the only one in trouble. Well, me and Luke anyway.

"Relax," Jared said with a roll of his eyes, "and just look at what you want so we can leave. I'll give you about twenty minutes before anyone comes inside to question us." We walked to the front door and Jared cut the tape connecting it to the frame, not a care in the world. Stepping inside, I had expected to see something similar to Alice's murder scene, but it was normal. Nothing out of place, no blood, nothing.

"All right," I said, taking in the hallway. I didn't really know what I was looking for, I was hoping for something to jump out and say "Over here! It wasn't the Shadeland ancient, it was this guy!" But there was nothing incriminating past the doorway; nothing was screaming at me that we were wrong.

Shoes lined the wall on the side, three pairs of women's shoes and two pairs of men's boots. Past those was a decorative table, topped with a flower vase; stargazer lilies, I noted they were fake. Jared flipped through some mail that was there before tossing them back on the table.

The walls were beige but still felt warm, like a home. On them sat portraits of the family, birthday parties, Christmases and everything in between. I stopped to look at one photograph hanging at eye level of the woman I had seen in the body bag. She stood with her husband, both holding onto their son who could only be about three. They were smiling and I wondered how recent it was; it looked like you could make out a baby bump under her clothes.

I stood and stared at the photograph, remembering the smell of the morgue and the look on the man's face as he stood on his porch when I drove by earlier. He hadn't just lost his wife; he had also lost another child. I couldn't even begin to imagine what that would be like.

"C'mon," Jared said, poking his head into the hallway from another room, "this is probably where she was killed." He disappeared into the room and I began to follow him. As I passed the staircase I noticed a pattern in the carpeting.

Through all the footprints, I could make out what looked like drag marks. I brushed a small piece of the carpet back and forth, to see what it looked like facing both directions and found that the drag marks came down the stairs. Rather than find Jared I began walking up the stairs, following the supposed drag marks to the second floor. There was no way the police could have missed this and I wanted to know what they thought could cause it. I certainly had no idea.

It was clearer upstairs where the marks originated from. I walked beside them down the hallway as they jutted to the right. When they turned into a room I glanced inside; it was a child's room.

Baby blue elephants danced across the wall, a line at hip height matched with the flowers. There was a bed and a crib against the far wall, both looking used and filled with stuffed animals and other children's toys. On the floor were more toys, these ones hard, not meant for sleeping and between them was a small pathway leading to the window. The drag marks led between them, leading me to believe that either the parents opened and closed that window, or something had let itself inside.

Carefully, I stepped over the fire truck and observed the pane. The white lock was fastened from the inside. Ignoring my immediate feeling to not touch anything I unlocked it and pushed it up. Poking my head outside I couldn't see anything past the large oak tree that sat on the front lawn. If someone did come in through this window, nobody on the street would've seen them. As I leaned to come inside I noticed something in the tree.

A few feet away, perched on a branch was a window screen, tossed aside, possibly blown off by a storm. I looked at the window sill and corrected myself, ripped out by someone and thrown out of the way was more likely. Scratches tore across all sides of the window, primarily on the sides. Touching my temples, I could feel a headache growing, the world around me starting to spin just slightly.

"Who are you?" A voice said behind me. I jumped up, not recognizing it as Jared and smacked my head on the window.

"Ah!" I called out, and whipped around the see a man standing in the doorway, the husband. Holding the back of my head we stared at each other, neither of us knowing what to do.

He looked tired, really tired. The wrinkles around his eyes matched that of the man who tried to steal Charlie's diary and the man I had seen with the news reporter Cindy. A light bulb went off in my brain; they were the same man! That was why he had looked so familiar the second time; I had seen him at the café. But the man standing before me wasn't him. This man was older, much more...desperate.

"Tell me who you are," the man in front of me demanded when I didn't answer. I was still trying to connect the pieces of why the man with Cindy would try and steal Charlie's diary. The only conclusion I could come to was that he was a reporter and did it for a story, a story on the killings. But even that didn't make much sense.

"Uh," I said, looking around the room to try and think of something, "is this window always locked?" He looked bewildered and hugged an overnight bag to his chest.

"We usually keep it unlocked," he smiled to himself, empty eyes staring at the floor, "it would always get hot during the summer so we would open and close it constantly."

"I see," I said, pondering. Suddenly he snapped out of his trance and faced me when Jared appeared behind him.

"Mr. Shoemaker," he said, confident, "what are you doing here?" The man stepped inside the room, surprised.

"I was just asking the same thing," Mr. Shoemaker said, "who are you two?" Jared reached inside his jacket and pulled out an ID, flashing it at the man.

"We're with the FBI," he said, "we're just seeing the area for ourselves before heading over to the police station. And you shouldn't be here."

I scoffed at the idea of either Jared or I being with the FBI. I wasn't nearly old enough to look the part, and neither of us wore a suit, or even looked remotely professional. But the man seemed to believe us, probably too distraught to care. Mr. Shoemaker held the bag tighter to his chest.

"I just…I just wanted to get some things for my son," he glanced around the room, "he can't sleep without his Ellie…" I looked around the room until I found an elephant lying in the crib. I walked over and picked it out, handing it to the heartbroken man. As he took the toy from me I could see the tears forming in his eyes.

"I'm so sorry," I said, knowing what he was thinking. His son would never know his mother; much like my younger brother Joshua would never know his. He looked down into the eyes of the elephant, a hint of a smile on his lips.

"You know he named this after his mother," he told us, "he said he wanted to name it after her so I said we should name her Ellie. He's only two…" His thumb stroked the ear of the elephant until finally he blinked away his tears. "I should get back, I'm sorry for disturbing the…scene." He stuffed the toy into the bag and turned to leave.

"I'll escort you to your car," Jared said and I couldn't

tell if it was because he felt sorry for the man or he wanted to keep up the FBI persona. I guessed it was the latter.

"Wait," I called, reaching a hand out to stop them, "can I ask you a question?" The man nodded slowly, careful to not look directly at anything in the room. "Did you hear anything last night coming from this room? Any unusual noises?" It was a long shot, but you never knew.

Mr. Shoemaker thought for a moment before shaking his head and saying, "No, nothing out of the ordinary."

"Okay," I said, "thank you." They turned to leave and Jared shot me a look of mixed confusion and annoyance. Suddenly Mr. Shoemaker stopped and faced me.

"Although…" he started, "I did hear something but it sounded far away… sort of."

"What was it?" Jared asked, now interested.

"When Eleanor got up to check on Pierce and get her music player from downstairs…I could have sworn I had heard some kind of…clicking coming from the roof." His eyes met mine with a shrug. "I just thought it was the house but I had never heard it before. I dismissed it because it was only for a moment."

"What kind of clicking?" Jared prodded, trying to learn more. Mr. Shoemaker was at a loss for words when I chimed in, already knowing the answer before asking him the question.

"Like fingernails on a hard surface?" I said to him and tapped my nails on the windowsill, imitating the familiar sound.

"Yes," he assured me, "exactly like that!" His phone buzzed in his pocket and he flipped it out to read a text message. "I have to go…I'm sorry again…for breaking in."

"Come on," Jared said patting him gently on the back, "I'll walk down with you." They left me alone in the room, making me wonder what kinds of questions Jared would have for me when he got back. I really wasn't sure if I was going to be able to answer them, since I had no idea what I was thinking myself.

I continued looking around the room, trying to find anything else that might help. What I had deduced thus far was that someone or something did break in through the window and for some reason dragged something down the stairs. But what could they have dragged? I didn't have any idea.

I headed back downstairs, first pausing at the staircase to make sure nobody was there. When I reached the room Jared had wanted me to follow him into I didn't know what to look at - just like in the other rooms of the house and in the other crime scenes.

Everything was perfectly fine; nothing out of place except for the window, which was broken from the inside. It almost appeared as if someone had jumped through it, which didn't make any sense. Overall the room was rather inviting, the couches sitting across from each other with a coffee table in between, with a sleek black piano near the back window.

A noise caught my attention as something shuffled inside the closet on the other side of the room. I glanced back into the hallway but Jared was still with Mr. Shoemaker, taking him to his car. Everything went quiet - too quiet. I realized that someone was hiding inside the closet. With silent steps I approached the doors, holding my breath as to not make a sound. Gingerly I touched the knobs and with one last prayer I whipped them open.

"*Mrowr!*" A cat lunged at me and I yelped as it hit me in the chest, knocking me backwards to the ground. Or maybe I just jumped backwards, I couldn't really tell. I felt a sharp pain as it scratched across my collarbone and dashed away behind me. I sat up as quickly as I could and looked around; the cat was gone, already out the broken window, no other threats in the area. I touched where it had clawed me and my fingers came back with blood. *Perfect.* It didn't feel too deep at least…

Not only did I do what all the people do in the movies, I got hurt while doing it. I stood and brushed myself off when a figure stepped out of the closet.

"Are you all right?" came a hesitant voice from the darkness. I looked up as he moved further into the living room, a horrified expression on his face. He grabbed a few tissues from a nearby box and reached them out to me, as a person would when feeding an animal they don't want to touch. When I didn't take one right away he pushed it further towards me and said, "Here."

I took them from him and pressed them against the scratch. It stung quite a bit but it wasn't anything serious; I was just glad it didn't get my face.

"Who are you?" I asked after giving a nod of thanks. It was one of the major questions that had been bothering me for the past day now. This man had been talking with Cindy in the diner, and then I caught him trying to steal Charlie's diary and now he was here, standing in the latest victim's closet. Or *hiding*, I should say. It wasn't looking good for him, at least not by an outsider's perspective.

"I am not the murderer," he said quickly, eyes wide with panic as his hands shot into the air to deny it.

"I know that," I said, for some reason I had never thought he would be the killer. "Were you the one who bought the Agate?" Another long shot, but I seemed to have good luck with long shots. My hunches led me to all the right, yet dangerous places. Somehow, his eyes grew wider.

"They needed protection," he said, "they were in danger... at least I thought they were...but it did no good." He looked down, clasping at the zipper on his jacket. I heard footsteps behind me and against my better judgement I twisted my head to see Jared coming around the corner. When he saw I wasn't alone he grabbed his gun and pointed it towards the man.

"Jared, no!" I yelled, throwing my own hands in the air. "It's okay, he won't hurt us."

225

"How do you know that?" he asked, pivoting around the couch to get a clear shot of the man. I had a feeling I knew who he was, and how he was connected to the deaths. What I didn't know was why.

"Were you Heather's boyfriend?" I asked him, careful to keep my voice soft. He sniffled and nodded his head.

"Yes," he told me, "she was my true love. My name is Bayani Navarro." One of my eyebrows rose while Jared lowered his gun, content with not being in immediate danger. I knew he was ready to draw it at any sudden movement though.

"Navarro as in Rosa Navarro?" I thought aloud. Bayani nodded again. He was the "B" in the photograph I had taken from Charlie's apartment; he had to be.

"What are you—" I began but was cut off by another voice.

"Hands where I can see 'em," a man said and I moved to see Officer Harley pointing a gun at me. When he saw who I was he sighed and rolled his eyes, holstering his gun. "You again?"

"Me?" I said, pointing at myself. He didn't seem to think I was much of a threat since he had put away his weapon, but would Jared and Bayani seem dangerous? Especially Jared?

"We're with the FBI—" Jared said but Harley cut him off.

"Don't bother, boy," he said, and Jared seemed taken aback, pausing as he reached into his jacket for what I assumed was the fake ID. "I know who you two are." He clicked the radio on his shoulder and spoke into it. "False alarm, Swanson. Just a couple of kids looking to see a dead body. I'll take care of it." He lied for us? That was...unexpected.

"Thank you," I said, unsure of what else there was the say, "why did you do that?" He crossed his arms and stared me down.

"I didn't do that for you," he told me, "I just don't

want to take another one of your statements." Why was that such an issue? I thought I gave very accurate statements to him, both times. He eyed me and asked, "So what are you doing here?" I looked to Jared who gladly took over.

"Looking for any clues to find the killer," he told the officer, "we were in the neighbourhood and thought we'd pop in. What are you doing here?" He walked over to me and shoved me to the side, putting himself between me and Bayani.

"Neighbour reported seeing some people coming inside, wondered what was going on." His eyes drifted over all of us, counting. "If you're going to break into a crime scene, maybe try taking a different route other than the front door?"

"We'll remember that for next time," Jared mocked.

"Why don't you leave the work to the professionals?" Officer Harley must have known Jared was a bounty hunter and didn't seem to like him much. Then again, we were breaking and entering.

"I am a professional," Jared smirked, "and nobody else seems to be doing a very good job."

"Oh yeah?" Officer Harley said, offended. "And what have you found so far that we haven't?" It was Jared's turn to remain silent. He could tell him that we thought it was a creature from Shadeland, but that would cause too much commotion.

"Mr. Shoemaker had heard a clicking," I suggested, still feeling as if it was a clue. "Right before his wife was killed."

"A clicking?" the officer said, familiarity in his voice.

"Does that mean something to you?" Jared asked, picking up on the same thing I did.

"Well between you, me and the lamppost" – he thrust his thumb towards Jared who scowled in return – "the lady across the street had heard a clicking too," he rubbed at his newly grown beard, "she said she heard something on her roof making the noise at about midnight. We dismissed it though because of what else she claimed to have seen and considering the, ah, condition of her house."

"What else did she see?" I hoped he would tell us, and not say we weren't allowed to know. He seemed to think it over.

"She said she saw a bat," he finally said, "she said when she looked out her window to see about the noise, she saw a giant bat fly overhead and land in the tree out front."

"A bat?" both Bayani and I said it at the same time, drawing everyone's attention.

"Does that mean something to *you?*" Officer Harley pointed at us, accusation in his eyes. I didn't know what it meant to Bayani, but it sent a chill up and down my spine while squeezing at my stomach.

"No," I lied, not wanting to tell the police what I knew, or what I thought I knew, at least. I looked to Heather's boyfriend questioningly. "Bayani?"

Sweat trickled down his forehead, his pupils contracted and the grip on his coat became far too tight. Panic and despair seemed to be the only emotions visible for Bayani.

"It is not possible," he said to himself, "it is not supposed to be this far north." Jared didn't seem as interested in what Bayani had to say as Officer Harley and I were. The officer prodded Bayani further but he didn't say anything, or more likely, he *couldn't* say anything. His mouth opened and closed, trying to form words but nothing came out.

The fear in his eyes told me he knew exactly what was doing the killings. He probably knew right when Rosa died, but he denied it. That must have been why he was talking to Cindy, and why he had tried to steal Charlie's diary. He stood in front of the closet, shaking his head, still in denial.

"If you know who is committing these murders you

have to tell us," Officer Harley said, "please." His tone was controlled, calm but it was clear in his face that he didn't feel that way. He wanted to stop the killings just as much as I did. He wanted to *know* what was doing it too.

"It can't be," Bayani mumbled, "it's not supposed to be this far north." He was pleading with us, begging us to tell him it wasn't possible but we all knew it was. Well, except maybe Jared, who still wanted to kill the Shadeland ancient. Officer Harley continued asking Bayani questions, trying to get him to admit what he knew when I finally cut in.

"Does it have to do with the pregnancies?" I asked and Bayani froze, no longer shaking his head. I was on a roll with guesses today, no point letting that go to waste. His brown eyes flicked to meet mine but quickly left, to view the window. "Is that why these women are being killed?"

"I'm sorry," he said and ran for the window. Both Jared and Officer Harley reacted in seconds, rushing after the man as he dove through the broken frame. The officer called for his partner and was out the door, ignoring me as he ran past. Jared had watched Bayani escape through the window, not bothering to chase him down any further than the window.

"You're not going after him?" I questioned, coming up behind him.

"Nah," Jared said, "The cops'll find him faster, and we have more important things to do anyway."

"But he knows who the killer is," I said, "don't you think we should find him?" We began walking to the front door, no longer concerned with finding more connections. I wanted to find Bayani, but Jared really didn't want to.

"We need to do that spell," Jared said, "it's the Shadeland demon, whether Bayani thinks so or not."

"But what if he's right?" I pondered. What if whatever Bayani thought was killing these women *was* doing it, and we summoned the creature anyway? If things turned out the best they could we would kill an innocent Eidolon, if things turned out badly the creature would kill us instead. Neither option seemed very good.

"You saw the smoke, right? More than once?" Jared shut the door behind him and checked the area. The police car was parked behind mine but neither Harley nor his partner were in sight, still chasing down Bayani somewhere behind the house.

"Yes," I agreed, remembering how cold it had been both times and rubbing the chills on my arms.

"That's the creature, as far as I can tell," he shrugged and opened the passenger side door as I walked around. "It's been confirmed by you at more than one murder scene. What more proof do you need?" He had a point. This thing was present at both Charlie's and Heather's death when nothing else was.

"I suppose," I said, still not completely sure. I looked behind me to see the same woman across the street shut her curtains again. She certainly was a nosy neighbour, but that had proved to be helpful, at least with information. She had heard the same clicking noise Mr. Shoemaker had. She had also seen what I thought was the same giant bat-like figure fly overhead and into the tree in front of the baby's room. But why had she been dismissed so quickly by the police?

I sat down in the driver's seat. Maybe the bat-like creature was the same thing from Shadeland? I didn't want to rule it out completely, but it still felt off. I had seen smoke, or smog or...something hanging over two bodies so maybe that was how it got inside the places. It travelled through the air in some kind of bat form and then morphed into the smoke to get past the cracks.

But that didn't explain the broken window at this house. It had been broken from the inside, like someone had jumped through it. *Or flew through it*, said a voice in my head. But that didn't help me make sense of anything. If the creature could turn from bat into smoke, why fly through the window? Did something scare it? Throw it off guard? Plus Yamuna had said that it travelled through the Ethereal realm of Shadeland to get around. Maybe this latest death wasn't even related to the other killings; she wasn't as young as the others, or lived the same lifestyle. A throb ran between my temples trying to figure it out.

"What broke the window?" I said under my breath, hand sitting atop the keys, ready to turn them.

"Husband said it was broken when he came down," Jared said, resting his head on his hand and his elbow on the window ledge. "Cops don't know what broke it so they're assuming it was the killer escaping."

"Huh?" I said and turned the keys, the engine sputtering to a start. "When did he find her?" I said, figuring he was the one who made the grisly discovery. I couldn't imagine that happening, coming downstairs to find your wife dead, murdered in your own living room. Homes were supposed to make people feel safe, but I knew I wasn't going to feel safe in my own for a long time. Especially when I was alone at night. I told myself I would feel better once everything was finished with; when the killer was caught and put behind bars or killed and Luke was no longer a suspect. A smart voice told me I was very wrong about that.

"The victim went downstairs and a little while later the husband heard the window smashing open," Jared explained, closing his eyes, "when he got downstairs he saw what he thought was a butterfly hovering over his dead wife. He didn't see much else once he saw her."

"A butterfly?" I questioned, thinking back to Alice's scene. "What colour was it?"

"How should I know?" I pulled away from the curb, remembering it might be better that we were gone when Officer Harley came back. "He probably imagined it anyway. Too focused on the kid sitting over his mother's body." His son was there? I didn't even know that. Perhaps that was how the window had broken; the child

231

had cried out when seeing his mother get attacked and the killer had to leave before her husband arrived. I wanted to ask more questions, to find it out but Jared didn't seem to be in the mood for talking anymore. So much for the considerate guy that had appeared twenty minutes ago.

"I thought you might ask," I said, knowing I would have. It would be strange if it was the same butterfly as before, but then again it could be coincidence. Yet…nothing has been a coincidence lately. Running into Bayani twice had been by chance, but he was involved. He even seemed to go as far as to talk with Cindy, who contacted who didn't matter, maybe she knew something that we didn't; she was a reporter after all.

"Well I didn't," he said, his tone almost mocking, "I highly doubt the butterfly is the killer. It's spring, there are going to be butterflies outside and they may come inside houses." I grimaced, no argument to prove there may be more than meets the eye. He noticed my expression and matched it, "Do you have experience bounty hunting? Regular or Eidolon?"

"No…" I said slowly.

"And how much do I have?" He rubbed at his temples, a headache growing. I knew what that felt like, having my own in the works.

"At least a year of Eidolon…"

"So don't you think it would be better to do what I say, rather than gallivanting off, chasing butterflies?" I knew he was being snippy because he was in pain and had just woken up from a Cockatrice bite, so maybe it was best I didn't question him…

I stayed silent, reassuring him that he knew I wasn't going to fight anymore. I still felt bad about what had happened to him. We had gotten lucky that Dr. Wineman had known the cure, and that Violet was able to get it.

I could see Jared glancing towards me for the rest of the ride to Yamuna's house. I wanted to say something to him, anything, and I felt he wanted to say something to me too.   But instead we rode without a word, neither one of us saying what we wanted to.

Chapter 24

Driving back home I welcomed the quiet. Yamuna's house had seemed a lot darker than I remembered, and thankfully she never stepped outside to see us. I didn't know what I had expected when pulling up at the curb by Jared's car; I guessed I had imagined seeing her at the doorway, watching us. But there was nobody there, the front door closed and windows still covered.

I wondered what had become of Bayani. He dove out the window without a real explanation, and the cops chased right after him. I understood that, he was acting awfully guilty. But maybe he ran because he *felt* guilty not because he *was*; he seemed to be trying to make excuses for not knowing sooner, and he had tried to protect them. Maybe he felt guilty for not trying harder…or not warning them sooner.

I came to a stop at a red light, the street empty while Jared lagged behind me, just turning the corner. Resting my head on my hand I sighed, wishing everything would make more sense. I was doing that a lot lately. My mind focused on Bayani when I heard someone clawing at my passenger side door, trying to get it. I whipped my eyes open, not realizing I had shut them and turned to see who was trying to get to me. They began banging on the window as Bayani's desperate face appeared through the glass. Speak of the devil...

An engine roared and Bayani paused to turn and face behind us just as Jared's car raced next to mine. It came to a halt inches away from my car and mere millimeters away from hitting Bayani, who dove over the hood of my car with a bang. He toppled over to the center and cautiously peeked over at the Charger that had nearly nailed him, body shaking fiercely. Bayani pushed himself to his feet, eyes just as wide as before.

Jared pulled back and stopped the car. I looked at him through the rear view mirror, then scanned the area for anyone else who might look upon this strange scene. The street was empty, thankfully, since we were on a more residential area that only had local traffic. I was still concerned someone may look out their window; Jared's car made a lot of noise and the sound of screeching tires tended to draw attention in this kind of place.

The bounty hunter marched around to the back of the car to Bayani and grabbed him by his jacket, lifting him off his feet.

"What the hell do you think you're doing?" he demanded, fury clear in his eyes. I jumped out of the car, barely taking a moment to park it.

"Jared," I said, grabbing hold of his forearms. I noticed how strained his muscles were; there was no way Bayani would get loose, just like when Jared and I had first met and he locked me to his chest. My heart began to beat faster and the bounty hunter looked over to me, not moving his head. "Let him go."

"Let him go?" he scoffed. "He coulda been..." When he looked into my eyes he seemed to soften, calming down just a bit. He let Bayani go, narrowing his gaze on me and the man scrambled to stay standing, breathing heavy and deep. "Fine."

"What were you...Bayani?" I asked. He was hunched over now, his breath coming in short gasps. "Come here." I pulled him as fast as I could over to the passenger's seat of my car and set him down, ignoring Jared's protests. "Put your head between your knees."

"What are you doing?" Jared asked, clenching and unclenching his fist. I hoped that meant he was working out his adrenaline and not waiting for the chance to hit someone. Bayani did as I said and as he lowered his head I could see tears streaming down to the pavement.

"He's having a panic attack," I said, rubbing the poor man's shoulder, "after everything that's happened and having you attack him I'd say it was reasonable." I hadn't meant to sound mean, but I knew it came out that way. Jared had good reason to do...most of what he had done, since it probably looked like someone was trying to car jack me. It didn't help that it was Bayani doing it either.

"Hey," he said, throwing his hands in the air, "I'll let you die next time." I was going to point out that I wasn't in any real danger when Bayani grabbed my wrist, surprising me. His palms were slick with a sweat. The sudden movement made Jared flinch, and take a small step towards us.

"You are working to stop it," he asked, his words coming in between gasps, "yes?" I nodded. "Then please take this." He reached into his jacket and pulled out a silver chain, the same kind, I noticed, that had been attached to both the Agate found in Charlie's and Alex's homes. What was hanging on it wasn't a stone though, instead, dangling from his fingers was a single bullet.

"A bullet?" I asked, confused. It must've meant something, I imagined and remembered that multiple bullets had been found with Heather, in the bathroom. I pictured the detective coming out to yell at Luke, those in hand. Honestly, I had kind of forgotten about them altogether.

"Heather," his voice cracked, "Heather did not want to wear hers, she kept it in her pocket. It doesn't work then, you have to wear it!" Bayani pushed the necklace towards me and I took it, pulling it over my head. He breathed a sigh, as if his duty was complete.

"Thank you," I said, "but um...how will it help me?" My last words travelled through the air in puffs, a chilling breeze coming through my hair. I turned around to see Jared surveying the area, noticing the temperature drop as I did. But there was nothing around us as I pushed myself from the ground, not a soul. There was a siren in the distance, getting closer to us and it seemed to put Bayani on edge.

"I should leave," he said, standing, his attack over. "Be careful, please."

"Wait," I called as he brushed past us and onto the sidewalk. He glanced back at me, a strange look on his face. "What are you going to do?" He hadn't explained anything. He hadn't told us who the killer was, or what the bullets meant, or how to find anything out.

"I am trying to find out who murdered them," he said quietly, "I will make sure she does not kill again."

"Hold up," Jared said, waving his hands in front of him, "I thought you knew who the killer is." He had a point, Bayani had led us to believe he knew who was behind it. Or maybe I had just assumed he did...

"I do not know who it is," Bayani told us, "but I know what it is. As do you. The ancient creature, very old and very...evil." He nodded his head at us as a goodbye and walked off, legs wobbly on the sidewalk.

"Huh," Jared said, a sly smile on his lips. "Looks like you were wrong, *honey*." He emphasized the word he knew I had come to dislike so much. I shut the passenger door and walked back to the driver's side, ready to get in as the siren's approached us.

"What do you mean?" I asked, already knowing what he was going to say and not bothering to tell him to stop calling me "honey".

"An ancient creature," Jared repeated, "old and evil. Sounds like Shadeland to me." He shrugged his shoulders and stuck his hands in his jean pockets, strutting towards the Charger. Jared had a point. I was wrong, it was the Shadeland creature, Bayani had just proven it. He knew that we knew, and he understood that we were working towards the same goal. I sat down in my car and touched the necklace he had given me. Not all my questions were answered but maybe it was best not to focus on that.

Bayani had said he was looking for who the creature was, as if it was hiding in plain sight. But Yamuna had told me Shadeland was all around us, and that the smoke I had been seeing was actually the creature forming into our world. I held my head as it began to pound, the space around me swirling. It was still cold; I could still see my breath. I opened my eyes as I heard a siren and saw a blurry fire truck rushing through the intersection in front of me. But not only that, I also saw a small insect land on my windshield wipers and flutter its wings.

Everything began to move again and I heard Jared honk behind me, telling me to get going. I was finding it hard to breathe, my head hurt and I couldn't see straight. I tried telling myself that I was just tired, sleep deprived but I knew that was wrong; Luke and Richard had seen to it that I slept, even if it was only for a few hours. I held my head, feeling the temperature around me return to normal.

"What's wrong?" Jared was beside me now, my door open. When had he gotten there? Kneeling beside me he touched my forehead; his hands felt cold, but it was rather soothing. He swore, but not at me, it seemed to be at himself. "You have a fever."

"No," I said, meekly trying to push him away and failing, "I'm fine." Now was not the time to be sick, there was no way I could have a fever. We were so close to figuring out the puzzle, I wasn't about to lose out on that, to not help Luke when he most needed it.

"Yes, you do." Jared pulled me out of the car and led me over to his, sitting me down on the passenger seat. I leaned my head against it and closed my eyes; just leaving them open was making me feel worse. And now that I knew I had a fever it seemed to make it escalate. Jared used a firm hand to push me into the seat and ordered, "Wait here."

Jared shut the door and disappeared. It felt like a matter of seconds before he was back but it must've been longer than that. He sat down next to me and buckled my seat belt beneath my arms.

"Where's my car?" I asked, confused. I opened my eyes to see it parked on the side of the street. That was awfully fast.

"We'll leave it there for now," Jared said driving past it, "your boyfriend can pick it up later." I laughed, a little out of it.

"He isn't my boyfriend," I said, "I wish people would stop saying that." I had never wished that before, so why did I now?

"Really?" Jared asked, disbelief clear in his voice. Nobody ever believed me; not my dad, not my brothers, even our coworkers thought we were dating. Why couldn't a guy and a girl be friends without people thinking there was more?

"Really," I assured him.

"Well, try and get some sleep," he said as I closed my eyes, "you look like you're getting worse."

"I'm not sick," I said. "I can't be sick." He didn't say anything back. It was true, I did get sick easily, but now was not the time. I didn't care if it killed me, I would help prove Luke's innocence, and I would help stop the killer.

I had strange fever dreams then. It didn't make sense to me, but I was at a tea party, sitting at the same table set I had as a child. My guests were a light brown rabbit, a barn owl and a wolf; a beautiful, white wolf. As I drank my tea all I could think about was that I didn't want any of

239

them to kill each other. I looked around the room and saw we were at my father's house, in the backyard where I used to play with Luke.

"What happened?" the owl asked the wolf. But he didn't speak in English, he hooted it, yet I still understood. I was trying to wrap my brain around the idea of being able to understand owls when the wolf replied.

"She's got a fever," he said in his wolf language. He set one paw onto my hand, quickly taking it away when the rabbit squealed.

"She should rest then," the owl said, "we can do the spell without her. It'll be better that way."

"No you can't!" I yelled, shooting my hand out to grab him and spilling my tea over the plastic table.

"It's dangerous," the owl told me, "too dangerous for a young girl like yourself."

"What do you know?" I asked, trying to clean up the tea. "You're just an owl."

"Yeah, you're just an owl," the wolf barked a laugh. As I patted the pink plastic I heard a whisper calling to me, drawing my attention to the window of my father's house. The wind grew cold as I stared at the familiar blurred yellow butterfly, sitting atop the windowsill.

"What are you looking at?" the rabbit squeaked.

"I'm being stalked by a butterfly," I giggled, "it's been following me everywhere." Why could I not stop laughing?

"Why didn't you tell anyone?" asked the owl and I shrugged, sitting back down.

"Jared always ridiculed my ideas," I explained, feeling a little guilty. "I thought I did tell someone...didn't I? I did...I don't think they believed me." It was warm again, a little too warm. I moaned, trying to take off my sweater but finding I couldn't figure out how to get my arms out of the sleeves. "It's too hot out here."

"Calm down," the wolf told me and I felt something cool touch my cheek, "go to sleep."

Chapter 25

It felt hot inside my room, too hot for anyone to be able to stand. Rolling over in bed I kicked my covers off, hearing them hit the ground beside me.

"Would you stop that?" someone asked and I opened my eyes to see Jared set down a glass of water on my nightstand, the condensation dripping down to the wood, ice clinking in the glass.

"What?" I asked, still groggy and trying to remember what had happened. Images of owls and butterflies danced in my mind but I couldn't make sense of them. Finally, I remembered the spell; someone had said they were going to do it without me. I shot up and grabbed Jared's arm as he bent over to pick up the blankets. "The spell!"

"Relax," he said with a roll of his eyes, "we haven't done it yet."

"Really?" I asked, hearing the glee in my voice.

"Really." Jared threw my blankets on me and sat down on the bed. "How do you feel?"

"I'm fine." I told him, and it was a half-truth. My

throat felt sore, and my head had a slight throbbing to it with every pump from my heart, but the room wasn't moving on its own, and I felt all right to sit up without falling over.

"Really?" he questioned, eyeing me.

"Really." I played with my hands in my lap after moving aside the blankets. "What happened? I don't remember much."

"I drove you back here, carried you up and Luke gave you some medicine after he sent Violet home. That's it." Jared looked away, an odd habit of his but understandable when it came to his cousin. Checking the time I saw that I hadn't been asleep that long, only a few hours; the sun was only just starting to set. I was surprised I wasn't out longer.

"Um…thanks," I said, my voice so small I was embarrassed. He *carried* me up? "Where's Luke now?"

"He went to get your car," Jared inched closer towards me on the bed, eliminating the distance between us. "Can I ask you a question?"

"Uh…okay."

"Why are you trying so hard?" I could feel his eyes on me, boring into me but I kept my gaze down, trying not to look at him. I had been expecting that question for a long time, and had somehow managed to dodge it.

"I don't know," I lied, thinking back to when Luke asked something similar. "For Luke I guess." It was easy to tell him, he already knew everything about me, but Jared? Jared was…different. He put two fingers under my chin and lifted my face, his own only inches away. I flinched and hoped he didn't catch it. How could I tell him the truth?

"Luke isn't a suspect anymore," he whispered, "so what's the real reason?"

I tried to look him in his eyes but it was hard. I almost felt like I was going to cry, but over what? The fact that I was probably projecting my feelings over my mother onto Charlie? Because some stupid, naïve part of me thought that if I solved this, I would somehow solve my mother's death? Or maybe it was because I knew that once this was all over, and the creature was dead, that Jared would be gone. Everyone I had met would probably never be seen again; not Violet, not Richard, not Charlie and not…Jared.

"Well?" he prodded.

I just stared at him, thinking. His eyes glanced down then back up quickly to meet mine. I couldn't think in a straight line, my feelings were getting in the way…along with the fever. Before all this happened I wouldn't have cared about people leaving, but now…something was seriously wrong with me. I barely knew him and for some reason the thought of never seeing him again made me sad, and what made it worse was the fact that he wouldn't—

"Ahem," Richard cleared his throat behind Jared. "Am I interrupting?" He stood in the doorway, holding a bottle of aspirin. Jared almost leapt off the bed and me out of my skin. How long had he been standing there? Or more importantly, how long had Jared and I been sitting there with not an inch between us?

"No," I said, swinging my legs over the side. Dr. Wineman eyed us, more Jared than me.

"Here," he said, walking over and handing me the bottle, "Take two and go back to sleep."

"I'm fine," I said, taking two pills out as ordered, "I can be there for the spell." Richard sighed, no fight left in him. If I was anything right now it was determined.

"I see," he said, shaking his head, "so you still want to do that." The doctor paced back and forth between my dresser and the door.

"Look doc," Jared said, "we know it's Shadeland doing the killings, so let's just do the spell before sunset so we can kill this thing, 'kay?"

"But you're wrong," Richard thrust his hands before

him, frustrated. No matter how much he told us we weren't going to believe him. I guess I understood how he felt, he was determined to prove to us that we were wrong, but I just didn't think that anymore. Though, it didn't take much to change my mind lately. Whenever I was pointed in one direction someone began pointing to another and I stupidly tried to go both ways at the same time.

"And how do you know we're wrong?" Jared didn't seem to be in the mood to listen to anything the doctor had to say. "You won't even tell us how you know it's not this thing."

"Well how do you know it is?" the doctor stared Jared down, both of their gaze's unwavering. I remained silent, shrinking onto my bed by lifting my knees for something to hug. Something told me I wasn't allowed to take part in this.

"You told us exactly what it was back at the college," Jared explained, hands on his hips. "And to top it off that Bayani guy told us it was too. We don't need any other proof."

"Excuse me…" I said, my voice almost inaudible.

"He told you it was the Shadeland ancient?" Richard questioned.

"Uh…excuse me…"

"He told us enough for me to know we're on the right path."

"Guys…" my head still hurt and their voices were getting louder with each sentence. I had something to say, but I just couldn't find a way to get it out, to make them hear me.

"So you—" the doctor was near shouting now when Luke cut in on him. He jumped around the corner into my room, fury on his face.

"What's going on in here?" Luke yelled and rushed to my side. He stuck an arm around me and looked up at the two men. "If you're going to fight do it somewhere else!"

"It's okay…" I said, "but I just…I had a question." I

shrugged, wondering if that had even noticed me during their argument.

"I'm so sorry Liv," Richard said and Jared just watched me, waiting. "What did you want to ask?"

"I was just wondering," I started, the doctor's guilt clear in his eyes over his behaviour. "Is it really so dangerous to summon this thing?"

"It is extremely dangerous," he told me. "That is why—"

"I thought you said it was only dangerous if there wasn't a pureblood there," Luke interrupted. "But you'll be there and so will I." Caught. Richard obviously didn't want me or Jared to know about this.

"Yes…but it is still dangerous for those of an impure blood line," the doctor glanced at Jared, "and more so for humans. Do you even have a plan as to what you're going to do when we summon it?"

Jared took out his gun and waved it in the air. "This'll do it," he said with confidence.

"A gun will not simply kill—"

"But cursed bullets will." Richard's eyes widened but quickly narrowed towards me. What was it about cursed bullets that frightened so many people? How were they so much worse than regular ones?

"All right," he said, "we will do the spell. But you won't like the outcome." The doctor walked out of my room, leaving me alone with the bounty hunter and my defender.

"Do you think it'll work?" Luke asked us, heading for the door as well. He stopped to face me, wanting me to answer and not Jared.

"I hope so," was all I said, since I really wasn't sure what I believed anymore.

My apartment felt very open now that all the furniture had been moved. The couch had been pushed against the back wall while the coffee table rested on top of it, crooked. The single chair sat beside the window, making a clear spot in the center of the living room; perfect for summoning spells. At least, that was what I kept telling myself.

No matter how much anyone said it, I still had a strong feeling that we were wrong; that the spell wouldn't really get us anywhere. I tried to dismiss it along with the waves of dizziness. I hoped these feelings were only a result of my fever. Clenching my phone in my pocket I watched as the doctor ground the pixie's dust together with the mermaid's scale in what would never again be my cereal bowl.

He mumbled something under his breath but I couldn't understand it, most likely because he didn't want any of us to hear it. Jared stood by the television, watching the doctor work his magic while Luke sat next to me, cross-legged, his arms holding up his knees.

Richard picked up the dragon's venom and dripped it into the bowl. Something about the purple liquid made me feel uneasy, remembering how it had dripped onto my hand. Thinking about it made the back of my hand feel warm. I shifted my position, giving away how uncomfortable I was.

"You don't have to be here," Dr. Wineman told me, "it's all right if you want to wait in your room." Why? So I could listen in and then hear the gunshots? No thanks. Not knowing what was going on was worse than knowing.

"I'm fine," I said, ignoring another dizzy spell. The doctor eyed me and I hoped I hadn't wavered. He went back to mumbling to himself and added more venom.

"This is the final ingredient," Richard said as he lifted the victim's blood from the carpet. Behind him Jared cocked his gun, ready to shoot anything that moved. The sound made me reconsider where I was sitting; if the creature appeared between the doctor and myself, I would be in the line of fire. The doctor looked at the gun over his shoulder, "You won't need that."

"Says you," Jared growled, shifting his feet to prepare

for an attack. I saw the doctor actually roll his eyes and I knew he was thinking something along the lines of "typical human". The mermaid had a similar expression when we had first attacked her. It was a glimpse under the doctor's mask for me, showing his arrogance towards the human race. I had been told more than once that that was how I often appeared to those around me.

The doctor poured all the blood into the bowl before reaching into his pocket to pull out a single match. He flicked his wrist and flame rushed up, making me jump. Luke touched my shoulder and for once it actually made me feel better. Richard dropped the lighter into the bowl and it exploded in pink and yellow flames.

"I summon thee," he whispered and the fire rushed upwards, scarcely missing the doctor's face. Neither he nor Jared flinched, unlike me and Luke. He set the bowl down on the carpet and folded his hands in his lap, eyes shut.

After a few moments the fire died down to pink embers and I risked a glance at Jared, limbs as rigid as they could get.

"Nothing happened," Luke whispered to me and I agreed. Besides the light show, nothing had changed. The doctor kept his eyes closed, so I remained silent and waited. I wasn't about to interrupt whatever was happening, not now. Not after everything we had done to get the ingredients.

A breeze ruffled my hair from the window and I looked over to find it shut. Everything was locked tight, I had made sure of that, so where was the breeze coming from? The doctor opened his eyes, revealing them to be a deep fuchsia. I wondered if my surprise showed on my face as he stared at me...no...he wasn't staring at *me*.

I refocused my eyes to see a slight smoke between us, only a foot away from where I sat. It swirled in the air, not nearly as big as when I had seen it before hanging over Charlie, hanging over Heather. The thought of it being smaller didn't make me feel any better about its presence.

Another breeze flew past me and around the room, releasing a low humming as it went by. The temperature dropped low enough for us to see our breath and it set Jared on high alert. He slid his feet till he was opposite the window, giving him a clear shot when the creature was fully formed. Richard never signalled him to lower his weapon.

After a long minute, the smoke began to change again, trying to take form in our world. It struggled as it changed, like it was having difficulty. Eventually it lowered itself onto the ground and hovered until finally, it formed…into a small, yellow butterfly.

The creature fluttered its wings and puffed away the excess smoke in the air. Wiggling its legs it faced me before turning around to see the doctor, his eyes still that deep pink.

"What is that?" Jared asked, sounding more annoyed than anything. I was still stunned in disbelief; the same butterfly I had seen at Alex's house, and then with Heather and even at the mermaid's river was now sitting in front of me, declaring itself a demon. I just didn't know how I was supposed to react. Jared smirked, "This'll be easier than I thought."

He holstered his gun and made his way to the bookshelf. Picking out the largest one he could find he came back and lifted it high over his head.

"Not the book!" Luke jumped to his feet and ripped the novel right out of Jared's hands.

"Hey!" The bounty hunter protested but Luke was already putting the book back where it belonged. If I was able to concentrate clearly I would have laughed, knowing how Luke was when he had a book; they had to remain pristine, not a crack in the spine, not a dent in the pages. In a weird way, I understood what how he felt.

Drawing my gaze back to the creature I saw it was carefully balanced on the doctor's fingers, flapping its wings to stay up. As its wings moved I felt the cold air brush against my face; it was the same cold I had felt so many times before, usually with death in the room, but this coldness actually felt kind of nice against my overheated skin.

"Don't touch the books," Luke ordered, giving Jared a stern look. It was very out of place on his features but sent the appropriate message. He and the doctor were rather alike, I thought, they both looked harmless, despite how menacing they tried to appear. Maybe that was why Luke liked him so much.

"Fine," Jared said, pulling out his gun again, "I'll just shoot some holes in your floor."

"That won't be necessary," Richard said as the butterfly hopped off his knuckle, "he won't hurt you."

"He?" I questioned, noticing how he had given it a gender. It approached me in the air, softly floating on the air, too slow for it to be natural.

"Yes," the doctor said, motioning me to put out my hand. As I put my fingers in the air the creature landed on them, tickling me as it had before. "Meet Azazel."

"Azazel as in...?" I trailed my sentence off and the doctor nodded.

"Yes," he assured me, "there is a demon in your lore named Azazel, but they are not the same. He's quite nice, he doesn't hurt people." *Oh. I was going to say* X-Men... I decided to keep that to myself, feeling silly.

"Tell that to all the women he killed," Jared said with a huff. He remained in a battle stance, still not convinced we were safe. For some reason I felt we were; all the fear and uncertainty I felt before was gone now that I could see the creature. Maybe it was just the knowing that eased my mind.

"Why is he a butterfly?" I asked, watching as the ancient danced back and forth between my fingers. I could feel a smile on my face, enjoying his simple beauty. "And why does it get so cold when he's nearby?"

"I'm not sure," Richard confessed, "this isn't his true form. It may have been too hard for him to become whole in this world so he chose…this. " He gestured to Azazel, as if that would explain everything. "But when he tries to come into this world he's unintentionally bringing the ether with him; making it cold. It's quite common when purebloods come through."

"You really didn't do it," I whispered to him, "did you?" Azazel shifted his feet left to right then back again, as if to convey a shake of the head.

"If he didn't do it then who did?" Jared asked, setting his gun away and kneeling down next to me, getting closer to look at Azazel. Luke remained at the bookshelf, taking small, wary steps towards us.

"And who was Bayani talking about?" I asked, feeling that question was more important than Jared's, even though they were essentially the same. Rosa's brother had said it was an ancient creature, a creature not normally found here. Azazel and the killer both fit that description well.

With a frozen gust, the creature jumped from my hand and towards the side table by the couch. Slowly, he landed on the remote, a familiar feeling of curiosity growing inside me. Jared and I both followed him, wanting to know what he was doing.

He sat on the television remote, right on top of the number five. Circling around on the white number he finally flew over to the television. What did he want?

"I think he wants us to turn the TV on," Luke suggested, now next to the doctor. I saw that Richard's eyes were back to their normal colour as he stood up, brushing invisible pieces of lint off himself.

"Great," Jared said sighing, "we brought an ancient demon from Shadeland so he could catch up on the Kardashian's."

I raised my eyebrows, wondering if Jared really knew who they were and why he would know. I couldn't imagine being a bounty hunter allowed him to watch too much reality TV.

I picked up the remote and turned on the television, watching as Azazel returned to the doctor's side, landing on his shoulder. Rubbing my arms for warmth I saw Cindy come onto the screen, reporting on a car accident that had happened earlier that day.

"Could you mute that, please?" Richard requested and I did so. "What did you say?" He held one finger in the air and stared upwards, listening to something.

"What are you—" Jared began but was shushed.

"He's trying to tell me something," the doctor explained, "it's hard to understand."

"What?" Jared mocked. "You don't speak butterfly?"

"Most of Azazel's essence is still in Shadeland," Richard explained with a remarkable amount of patience, "it's hard to hear him through the Ether." Luke and I exchanged a glance, wondering what "Ether" was. I had read the term before and all I imagined was it was what made up Shadeland; a pink dust or smog coming to mind.

"What does it…sound like he's trying to say?" Luke leaned closer to the doctor, as if that would help him hear it as well. He grimaced when he found nothing.

"He's trying to tell us something about the blonde woman," Richard's brow furrowed, frustrated, "something about the creature is there?" Azazel flapped his wings hard, breathing cold air all around the room. "Yes, he's sure the killer is involved there."

"Cindy is the killer?" Luke asked, scared. He actually liked her, after she had apologized for spreading his picture around he seemed to feel better about what had happened, knowing *someone* actually felt guilty. I was still on the fence as to whether I liked her or not.

"Not necessarily," Richard said, "it's not clear. He's trying to tell me who but…his connection with this world is weak. It sounds like he keeps saying… 'man'?" Suddenly the temperature rose to its appropriate degree as

Azazel disappeared into a puff of smoke, his message undelivered. The glowing embers in my cereal bowl died out, leaving nothing but ash behind with the muted television.

"What happened?" I asked, wanting to learn more from the ancient.

"He's gone," the doctor stated the obvious, "even with the extra power from the mermaid's scale he is not strong enough to keep a connection for so long. The blood only supplied a limited connection for him."

"But he's come through before, a few times," I said. How could he leave so fast?

"When you saw him it was probably only a short time, correct?" I nodded, knowing it was only a matter of minutes at most. "Then when he showed himself to you, that was most likely all he was able to sustain. Which reminds me...when did you see him? Azazel is a very shy man, he doesn't show himself easily to others; especially..." Richard shrugged, open palms.

"I saw him at the...Alex's house," I said, avoiding the "you-shouldn't-have-done-that" look from Luke, "and then with the mermaid and then with Jared, at Heather's house."

"You saw him at the siren's place?" Jared questioned, surprised. "Why didn't you say something sooner?" Was he really asking that? He had mocked my ideas at every turn, he even mocked the butterfly at the Shoemaker house!

I didn't say anything to him and instead looked away, angry. He was not allowed to question my decisions now.

"Focus," Richard said, "we need to figure out who Azazel was talking about."

"All right," Jared sighed and turned to pick up the coffee table, I moved out of the way as he set it onto the ground and planted himself on the couch. Begrudgingly, I sat next to him, arms crossed. "What we know so far is that it's a man." Jared rolled his eyes, knowing nothing was narrowed down.

"And the killer works for the channel five news," Luke added, sitting on my other side.

"Great," Jared muttered, "just great." I thought about it, considering the meaning of Azazel's message.

"Maybe he didn't mean 'man' as in male," I thought aloud, "maybe he meant 'man' as a race. Like he was trying to tell us the killer is actually human?" I looked at the men around me, watching as they contemplated the idea.

"It's possible," Dr. Wineman said touching his lips. "We shouldn't rule it out."

"Do you think we should talk to Bayani again?" I asked, since he was the best lead we had at the moment; the only other one being the giant bat seen outside Heather's home, and high above the trees of the northern woods. If all else failed, I would mention it again, just in case.

"I'll do that on my own," Jared said as he pushed himself off the couch, "I'll get more out of him that way." As he walked to the door I followed him, putting on my shoes as fast as I could.

"I'll go with you," I said, not wanting to stay home.

"Hell no," Jared pushed me back with one hand as he opened the door, "you've still got a fever, you need to stay here."

"I'm not letting you do this alone," I grabbed his hand and threw it away, hoping that would help me assert myself. "I'm going!" Jared ground his teeth, staring at me before he looked away, as always. He walked out the door and I followed after him, steps determined to keep up.

As I shut the door behind me I swore I heard Luke say, "I've never seen her do that before."

Well, I thought, *I've never had a good enough reason before.*

Chapter 26

Going out with Jared was probably not the best idea I had ever had; in fact, it may have been worse than deciding to break into a crime scene for the second time. I sat in his car and leaned my head on the window, hoping to feel better but finding my headache wasn't quite going away. It honestly wasn't that bad, but it was still a hindrance.

"I should have left you there," Jared said as he turned a corner.

"I would just have followed you," I laughed, wondering why I would say that out loud. I was surprised nobody had tried harder to stop me. Jared caving and letting me come I had anticipated, but why did Dr. Wineman and Luke let me leave? It wasn't like either of them. "So where are we going?"

"We're going to track where Bayani went and hopefully find him." Straightening in my seat I turned my head to face him.

"How are we going to do that?" I tried to think like Bayani had. He knew the creature was ancient, and the fact that the woman saw a bat fly towards Heather's house seemed to mean something to him. At least…I thought it mean something.

"I'm thinking," Jared said, at a loss for ideas.

"Maybe we should talk to the neighbour?" I suggested. If I was Bayani, I would talk to her in hopes of confirming my suspicions. It wasn't so farfetched; he had broken into Charlie's apartment to steal her diary after all.

"Neighbour?" Jared questioned. "The crazy woman who saw the giant bat?"

"She might not be crazy," I said, wondering why everyone said she was. It didn't make me feel any better about myself for seeing the same thing. Eidolon's were all over the world now, out in the open, was it really so hard to contemplate one being a bat? I didn't think so, but it was apparent that others did. "Maybe she did see something, and maybe Bayani went to talk to her about it."

"What about your theory that the killer is human?" Jared asked, but he seemed to be mulling over the suggestion of talking to the woman.

"It was just a theory," I sighed, closing my eyes, "I really don't know what Azazel could have been trying to say.

I was about to suggest trying to summon him again but knew there was no point. There was no way Jared and I could collect all the ingredients again, especially since the siren was dead now and there probably wasn't another one around. I wondered if there were any other areas nearby that women had killed themselves after an unfaithful lover…did they all become Lorelei's? Or did there have to be very specific circumstances? Could anyone become an Eidolon so easily? That thought kind of scared me.

"Here," Jared said reaching into the glove compartment in front of me, "drink this." He passed me a lukewarm bottle of water. Graciously I took it and clicked off the cap. As I drank it I couldn't believe how cold it felt going down my throat, nothing had ever tasted as good.

"Thanks," I said, setting the plastic cap back on it to

realize I drank the whole bottle. Jared eyed me and then the bottle before continuing.

"We'll talk to the woman," Jared said, making a U-turn, "but just to find Bayani. No talking about bats. Understood?"

"Understood." Just because I understood he didn't want to talk about it, didn't mean I wasn't going to. Jared really needed to be specific with his words.

Jared stopped the Charger across the street from the Shoemaker house, the purring engine filling the street. No one was outside, no kids playing before dinner, nobody walking their dog; it was a ghost town. The sleepy city of Ellengale had become a nightmare since the killings began.

Just as Jared went to open his door I stopped him, grabbing his forearm but quickly released it when he looked back at me.

"What?"

"What are we going to tell her?" I asked, having the thought suddenly occur to me. We couldn't just knock on her door and start asking questions, not without getting some back at least.

"Just act official," he said and stepped out of the car. I followed him up to the doorway, watching the windows for any sign of the woman. I caught a glimpse of movement behind the curtains and when Jared lifted his fist to knock the door was already opened, locked with a chain to make sure nobody could get inside.

"Who are you?" an older woman asked as she peeked through the crack.

"We're with the FBI, ma'am," Jared said, flashing a small leather wallet, "mind if we come in and ask you some questions?"

"You don't look like cops," she said, looking us up and down and then stared at me, "especially you." I understood why she would be suspicious; Jared was wearing a leather jacket and jeans while I sported a hoodie and moccasins. Not exactly FBI material.

"Yet we are," Jared said, putting away the wallet. I wondered what he had there; it couldn't possibly be an actual badge, could it? "We won't take much of your time."

"Hm." The woman closed her door, the chain clanking telling me she was actually going to let us inside. I was amazed that she would, but if she believed Jared's story then she would feel she had no choice. The door opened with caution, the woman standing in a bath robe eyeing us down. "Hurry or you'll let them out."

Jared stepped inside first and I after him. The second we were in she slammed the door, just as two black cats tried to escape. I assumed they were the 'them' that weren't allowed outside.

"Thank you," Jared said, fake smile in place. With a bony hand the woman motioned us into the closest room, the living room. I peered around her home and wondered if the fever was getting to me because what I saw didn't seem real.

The walls were coated with clocks, some old, some new, some looked badly hand made even. All of them were set to the same time exactly, right down to the second. The ticking was so loud I didn't know how I couldn't have heard it from outside, with the door open or shut.

"Watch your step, girl," the woman said just as I tripped over a cat rubbing against my shins, "they like new people."

I could see Jared trying not to say anything, careful to breathe through his mouth. When I finally tore my eyes away from the incessant ticking clocks, I noticed the smell. It was the overpowering, sour stench of cat urine and as I looked around the living room I counted at least twelve of them, sitting all over. They decorated the furniture, dangling over the tables and the fireplace mantle, some were stretched out on the couches as well. I was about to classify this woman as a hoarder, but she didn't have nearly

257

enough stuff, though she was in the beginning stages. Maybe she was only a cat hoarder right now. Various papers and magazines lay strewn about amongst the cats, a couple of dishes sat on the table between the couches and more clocks beside them.

"We won't be long," Jared said, staying standing as the woman sat down, "Miss…?"

"You can call me Mrs. Weston," she said, "now sit or I don't say another word."

Jared gave a wary look to the couch but reluctantly did as he was told. I followed suit and sat next to him, an orange tabby jumping into my lap as I did. It's fur was soft, and well groomed unlike the couch; that was as solid as a rock. The woman said, "That's Marmalade."

"Could you tell us if anyone has been around, asking you about what you saw before Heather Shoemaker's body was found, Mrs. Weston?" Jared asked, getting right down to business. She huffed and began petting a white-haired cat next to her. I stroked Marmalade, trying to focus on her purring but finding it difficult with the woman's unkempt appearance.

"Why would you want to know that?" she questioned. "I'm just a crazy old lady living alone." The more she talked the more I found I stared at her teeth. I just couldn't look away from her. Mrs. Weston's teeth were crooked and yellow, some decaying and some not even there. Her grey hair was scraggly atop her head, hanging loosely over her face, matted and unwashed. The blue bathrobe she wore was covered in cat hair, but otherwise clean of stains as it hid her nightgown. If people called her crazy, I understood why. Somehow, I tore my gaze from her and looked around the room for photographs, curious to see if there was any of her when she was younger. There was nothing, not a single frame containing a memory, no pictures freezing time in its place. No evidence of family or loved ones whatsoever.

"We're looking for a man," Jared explained, ignoring

his obvious thoughts of how he agreed with her, "he's about 5'7", tan skin and black hair. Narrow eyes, looks exhausted and about as jumpy as a…kitten." He glanced down at Marmalade, still purring in my lap.

"Hm," Mrs. Weston looked down her nose at us, possibly debating if we were worth talking to, "I've seen him."

"Did you talk to him about anything? What did he ask you?"

Jared was getting pushy and I could see that the old woman wasn't about to give him any information. Her stare tightened on us, crow's feet darkening. How she ever got laugh lines was beyond me.

"He asked you about what you saw, didn't he?" I asked, playing with Marmalade's paw, doing anything to avoid looking at Mrs. Weston.

"He did," she agreed, "he actually made me look sane." Her laugh came out as a bark, emotion getting the best of her. I felt a little sorry for her, but wondered why she would consider herself insane. Was she going solely on what others said?

"What did he say?" Jared questioned again, leaning his forearms on his knees with anticipation. I thought it was odd for him, but…I thought a lot of things he did were out of character. Whenever I thought he would go one way he ended up going another.

"He wanted to know about the bat I saw," she said, getting haughty, "he didn't think I was imagining things or 'high on cat-nip'." She huffed again. Had someone actually said that to her?

"Did he say anything else?" Jared was prodding now and I was actually getting impatient with him. I wanted to hear more about the bat. "Mention anything about where he was going?"

Mrs. Weston shrugged and stroked the cat. "He did say something about needing to talk with someone."

"Did he say who?" Jared asked and Marmalade rolled

over onto her back, exposing her stomach. I began poking her paws to tease her and she twitched with each one but never left my lap. Jared seemed disturbed that I was so comfortable around cats but I didn't understand why. They were just cats…though there were a lot of them.

"No," she told us, "nothing like that."

"What can you tell us about the bat?" I asked, trying not to smile as Marmalade meowed at me. "What did it sound like?" I already had a hunch at what she was going to say, but I still wanted to hear her version of it.

"Well," she started, "I had just put out fresh water for my girls when they started hissing at the window. When I looked outside there was nothing there but then they all ran away and hid! When I went to draw them out they only hissed at me more."

"And then?" I prodded, waiting with little patience.

"The cops said I was hearing things," she said, "but I know what I heard."

"What did you hear?"

"A clicking," her eyes grew distant with the memory, "like someone was crawling over my roof with their fingernails but it was getting quieter the more I listened. When I looked outside again that was when I saw it; a giant bat flew right over my house and onto the Shoemaker's property, landed in that big tree out front." I was curious to know how she heard anything over the clocks. As it was I couldn't make out the sound of Marmalade purring in my lap with them ticking away.

"Did the wings seem to be about four feet each?" That was what I had guessed I had seen, though it was rather far away. "And did the body not look like the body of a bat?"

Jared stared at me, mouth agape but Mrs. Weston had a big smile. My body felt too hot to care, I needed to know this, even though Jared had instructed me not to ask. He should have expected it anyway.

"Yes," Mrs. Weston eventually agreed, "exactly like that. You saw it too?" There was so much hope in her eyes, and I realized it was because she was beginning the think she was crazy. I supposed that if enough people told her she was nuts, she would believe it eventually. That was hard though, knowing you couldn't trust your own senses; at least I thought it would be.

"I think I did," I admitted, not really wanting to admit anything with Jared staring at me. He looked mad now, and I knew I was going to suffer for keeping a secret from him later. Maybe he would go easy on me though, because of the fever? It was possible. Kind of. "Over the forest."

"All right," Jared said standing and pulling me to my feet. Marmalade dropped from my lap and skittered under the couch, scared by the sudden movement. "Thank you for your time Mrs. Weston but we need to be going."

The bounty hunter dragged me to the front door with Mrs. Weston trailing behind. Did he not have any other questions for her? We didn't really get any information, at least not any *new* information. Jared gripped my wrist, it was firm but I could tell he was resisting the urge to hold tighter, not wanting to hurt me.

"Wait," Mrs. Weston called as we stepped into the cool evening air, "there is one thing." Jared and I turned to face her but he never let me go; why did he have such a habit of jerking me around everywhere?

"What is it?" I asked, trying to sound polite and professional but I thought it came out sounding exhausted. Although, it actually sounded like I cared; that didn't usually happen unless Luke was around.

"When he said he was going to meet someone," she said, stopped at her doorway, "he said he was going to meet 'her again'. Is that what you wanted to know?" Her eyes gazed into mine, as if asking me not to leave, asking me to confirm her sanity. I listened to the clocks behind her, finding the rhythmic ticking irritating and knowing there was nothing I could say to make her feel better.

"Yes," Jared answered for me, "thank you very much, that's helpful. Goodbye now." He pulled me back to the car but didn't unlock it, instead we stood beside it. "What the hell was that?"

"What was what?" I asked, feeling a little groggy. My mouth felt dry again and seeing a full water bottle on the passenger seat wasn't making it any better.

"You saw it?" he asked me, I almost thought I heard disgust in his voice. "Why didn't you say anything?"

"Would it have mattered if I had?" Honestly, I didn't think it would have. Not at first anyway. Until Officer Harley mentioned it with Bayani there, I hadn't given it much thought; most of my focus was on Jared and the spell. I had tried to tell myself that it didn't matter, but clearly it did.

Jared pointed his finger at me, comeback ready but he stalled. He took his hand out of the air and unlocked my door, even going as far as to open it for me. So maybe the fever did make him hold back, just a bit. I sat down in the Charger and drank a second bottle of water, finding the more I drank the more I wanted. My throat was burning now, but I didn't want to say anything; it would only get me sent back to bed when we needed to find Bayani. Jared sat down next to me, setting his hands on the steering wheel but he had never started the car.

When he finally turned it on and drove away from the Weston house I asked, "Where are we going?"

"We're going to talk with the person Bayani went to find," Jared said, as if I should already know.

"Who's that?" I knew it was a woman, which he had already spoken to, but my fever was keeping me from thinking easily. I couldn't think of a person that we would know in connection to Bayani.

"Cindy," Jared explained, "he was with her at the diner, so she's our best lead to find him." I smiled and looked out the window. I wasn't happy because he wasn't sending me back home, and I wasn't happy because he knew where to go next; I was happy because he said "our best lead". He was finally including me.

Chapter 27

I had considered calling Luke, to tell him what was going on and what we had found out so far, but in reality, we hadn't found out anything. All I would say was that while he and I had been hunting pixie's I had seen what could have been an Eidolon on a killing spree fly over our heads. I decided it would be best to not tell him, especially after seeing Jared's reaction.

I watched as Jared walked up to the front desk, completely fine with what we were doing. I, on the other hand, was extremely anxious. We were about to ask Cindy if she knew anything about Bayani, and if he had told her anything. What if she decided to follow up on our questions, try and find out what we knew and report on it? We couldn't let that happen, it would lead the cops to us, and then they would start asking questions. Different scenarios played in my head, all leading us to the police and nation-wide infamy; something which Luke already had. I peeked around Jared's shoulder to see a small and very young girl sitting at the receptionist's desk. A girl I recognized from school; not my grade, but I could tell she knew who I was.

"Hi," Jared said, giving the girl a killer smile, "I was wondering if Cindy was around?" The nameless intern behind the desk squeaked and blushed hard enough for me to feel embarrassed for her. She gazed up at Jared before quickly picking up the phone and dialling an extension with shaky hands.

"H-Hello Ms. Hart," the girl said, "there's a man here to see you." The person on the other end said something and the girl blushed even harder. "Who is it? Um...it's..."

"Jared." He smiled again and I saw the girl resist another squeak. There was no way she wasn't going to be telling her friends about this; the girl that always hung around Luke Harroway was now hanging around a tall, dark and handsome older man who looked to be in his mid twenties. At least I didn't have to face it at school anymore. Wait...did I just call Jared...? Damn.

"What is it referring to?" she asked into the phone again and cautiously looked up at the bounty hunter.

"Bayani Navarro." I was surprised he was being so honest, wasn't this something we should lie about? When I asked him he just chuckled under his breath.

"There's no point," he said, "she'll find out somehow. Just let me do the talking." I pursed my lips, wondering if he was going to blatantly flirt with Cindy as well. I remembered when she had apologized to me in the diner he had been looking at her a little too much. It made me feel...uneasy.

The intern looked at the phone and then hung up, turning to face us...or I should say, turning to face Jared.

"She said she'd be right down," the girl looked down at her restless hands before pointing to some chairs across the lobby, "you can wait over there."

"Thanks," he said with a wink and walked away. That was too much for the intern, and the second Jared turned his back her hands held her cheeks, trying to hide the red.

As I walked behind Jared I heard the familiar clicks and saw her texting away furiously. I just hoped she wasn't going to try and take a picture.

The bounty hunter and I sat down on the cushioned chairs, Jared placed his feet on top of the round table filled with magazines.

"I think she's a little young for you," I said, feeling bitter. I don't know why I even bothered saying anything, it was none of my business who he teased but for some reason I couldn't help myself.

"Sorry," he said, placing his hands behind his head, "are you jealous? Because she doesn't look much younger than you."

"No, I'm not jealous. Besides, I'm almost eighteen...just a few months away." I was silently cursing my late birthday, not only was it late, it was as late as they came; December thirty-first.

"You sound jealous," he laughed, "do you want me to wink at you more, honey?" He blinked an eye shut and I looked away, feeling my face warm. It was just the fever, nothing more. Jared smiled, knowing he had beaten me. I had nothing to say back to him, if I told him to be quiet it would be like I was jealous when in reality I wasn't. I just felt bad for the girl, that was it. Though it made me begin to contemplate how old Jared was; he couldn't be much older than Luke, could he?

My phone rang in my pocket and I clicked "Ignore" immediately, striking Jared's curiosity as we waited for Cindy to arrive.

"Not going to answer?" he questioned. "What if it's Luke?"

"It isn't," I told him, knowing I was right.

"And how do you know that?"

"Because Luke would text me," I set my phone back into my pocket, "it was probably my dad or my brother."

"You have a brother?" Jared's eyebrows raised. Was it so surprising I had siblings? Whenever someone found out, they had to same look. I didn't understand it.

"I have four."

"Four?" he repeated, probably trying to imagine what they looked like. Most people thought they would look like me, average height and build but they weren't that at all. All of them were over six feet and all of them liked to play sports. My oldest brother played a lot of football while the others played hockey; they had a thing for contact sports where they could tackle anything that moved near them. Most people didn't dare move near them, though.

Ever since Luke's face had been plastered across the nation they'd been calling a lot. I had spoken with my dad once, telling him that it was a mistake but he was still worried. Luke had called him too, when I was out with Jared but they kept calling and I really didn't want them to know anything more than they did.

Yanking me out of my guilty feelings about my family I heard a thick clacking coming down the stairs behind us. Cindy breezed by to meet the intern who pointed towards Jared and me. The reporter immediately came over to greet us, wearing what one would call a smart yet feminine beige pant suit. It was nice, for a reporter I guessed.

"Good evening," she said and only then did I realize that it was possible she wouldn't be available. She could have been live on the air, or at home even. She sat down at the chair perpendicular and leaned forward asking, "What can I do for you?"

Cindy had a glimmer in her eye that I imagined she got only when she was excited about a story. She gave me a sympathetic head nod, reminding me she knew who I was before drawing her attention back to Jared. I couldn't help but wonder if it was for the same reason as the intern.

"I'm looking for Bayani," Jared said. He planted his feet on the tiles below and leaned towards her. "Have you seen him around?" Cindy's lips pinched together in thought, debating on what to tell us.

"Why are you looking for him?" she rested back in her chair, determined to get something out of us.

"We're just wondering where he is, he's a friend," Jared shrugged innocently but I knew Cindy wasn't buying it.

"A friend, huh?" she said slowly, peering at me from the corner of her eyes. I didn't have much energy to do anything, not that I knew what I was supposed to do anyway. "He might've come by to see me earlier."

"About what?" Jared kept his stare at her, attempting to break her down. She was a news reporter; I doubted he would be able to crack her, since usually she was the one trying to get information from people. Cindy eyed us both for a long time before she finally answered.

"He wanted to talk," she said, "but he wasn't making any sense. We'd become friends over the past couple of weeks after his sister died, and I was trying to help him through it." Her eyes grew dark, thinking of the past. "But he kept saying it was all wrong, everything was wrong. He said something about the killer being too far north." That sounded familiar.

"So what did you do?" Jared asked.

"I called the police," Cindy sighed. "I heard they were looking for him for something so I contacted them while getting him a drink. I didn't want to...but he seemed to have..." She opened her palms to us, trying to think of an appropriate word.

"Lost it?" I suggested, raising my eyebrows and leaving all tact behind. Reluctantly, the reporter nodded.

"What was he saying that wasn't making any sense?"

"He kept talking about needing to find out who the killer was, that only fire could purify it. That's what scared me the most, I wasn't sure if he was going to hurt someone. Otherwise he was just mumbling to himself." She shrugged when someone called her name as they ran around the corner of the stairs.

"They need you back up there," a woman said to her,

"you're back on."

Cindy excused herself, knowing we weren't going to give her any information and walked off with the other woman. She stopped at the bottom of the stairs and turned to us picking a card out of her pocket. After the other woman left I remembered she was the weather girl, the very same one that had apologized to Luke. She and Cindy looked strikingly similar and I wondered if they were related somehow.

"Could you call me?" she asked, handing Jared the card. "I just want to know if he's okay. He's been through a lot, I think the stress just got to him."

"Sure," Jared said and tucked the card away in his pants pocket. We stood and separated, Cindy going back work and us heading out the door. It felt like Cindy was hiding something from us, like she knew something we didn't and had no intention of telling us. It didn't matter anymore though, we were almost out the door and she would never talk, at least not without getting something in return.

I noticed the intern watch us as we left, most likely wondering how we were connected. Little did she know he was a bounty hunter and I was merely his...assistant? Well, until we found the killer that's what I seemed to be, but not by his choice.

"How are we going to get in to see Bayani?" I asked as we walked back to the Charger. I couldn't imagine they would just let us waltz right in and question him; he might even be a suspect now, after being caught in the last victim's house.

"I'll go in and talk to him," Jared said, "you'll have to wait in the car."

"Why?" I whined. That wasn't fair, why did I have to wait in the car while he got to find everything out? He might not even ask the same questions I wanted to.

"Because the cops don't seem to like you much," Jared said, stating the obvious. "You've been all over the place and causing a commotion."

No, I haven't. I wasn't even caught the first time I broke into a place, nor was I caught with Violet. How had I caused a commotion?

"Look," Jared sighed, "they know what you look like because of Luke. Let me get in and out, it'll go faster because most of them haven't seen me." He had a point there.

"All right," I agreed, reluctantly. We climbed into the car and drove away, giving me the feeling of being watched. As I looked up to the second story windows of the glass building we had just been in I noticed a blonde turning away from the window, dressed in a pant suit. Had Cindy been watching us leave? Okay, that settled it, she knew something. But what could it be?

Did she know something about Bayani? Or did she know something about the murders? Maybe she was just worried about her friend who she had just sent to jail…no, that didn't seem right. I felt a sharp pain through my temples and rubbed them as I thought.

"Do you want me to drop you off?" Jared asked, noticing my actions.

"No!" I said too quickly. "I'm fine…I'm just kind of thirsty." I felt parched but it made sense; I still had a fever and the only thing I'd had to drink in the past two days was…well two bottles of water Jared had given me. I was dehydrated and it was messing with my head.

"Are you sure?" he checked, his hand about to reach to check the temperature by my forehead but quickly withdrew back to the steering wheel.

"Yeah," I told him, "I'll just close my eyes while you talk with Bayani." Jared never said anything after that, settling with the fact that I wasn't fighting to go with him as I usually had. But he did surprise me by going into the trunk and getting another bottle of water for me. After that he just went inside to see what he could find out.

Hopefully Bayani would tell us something useful,

something that would lead us to the killer. I shut my eyes and rested my head on the window, resisting the urge to fall asleep to the purring of the Charger.

Chapter 28

It felt like only a matter of seconds before we arrived at the police station, and only a few blocks away from home. I checked the clock quickly, noticing the sun was setting fast, filling the world with a purple haze; it was just past seven. If we didn't hurry, there would most likely be another body in the morning.

Without a word Jared left the car and opened the trunk, leaving me in the passenger seat. When he returned he handed me two more bottles of water which I gladly took.

"Thanks," I said again, feeling as if it was all I said to him lately. He was being really nice to me, considering. I wondered what had changed.

"Just try not to get yourself shot," he ordered, "or attacked by something, or caught by the police."

Jared listed off my past aggressions easily but I could say the same to him. He had been shot at too, and attacked by the siren and bitten by a Cockatrice and caught by the police while breaking into an active crime scene. But, he was technically paid to do it, if he managed to kill this creature. He locked the car and walked into the police station, not bothering to order me to stay. I think I wore him down.

As I waited for him to return my mind began to wander. What if Bayani did tell us what the creature was, and what if he was right? How were we...well, how was Jared going to kill it? A thought occurred to me then, what if it *was* a human? Sure, the cause of death for the victim's was blood loss, and the why and the how were still out there, but Azazel had said "man" to the doctor, more than once by the sounds of it. If the killer was human, were we going to kill him? I shoved that thought away— no, we would tell the police and the man would be arrested.

But then I started thinking about more ethical problems. Why would I be so ready to kill an Eidolon murderer but not a human one? I thought of Luke, knowing he was Eidolon and wondered if that applied to him. I felt it didn't, but would a stranger feel the same way? If Luke had killed someone, would a stranger just order to put him down because he wasn't human?

What about the mermaid? She had been human once, and after her heart was metaphorically torn from her chest she had killed herself, and somehow turned into a siren, beginning to kill others. Jared had shot her, more than once. Did she deserve a chance at redemption or was death the only way of stopping her? This was confusing, I didn't understand how I felt. I had always considered the death penalty harsh, since the people could live in confinement, a fate some considered worse than death. Yet, here I was, ready to hunt down and take out an Eidolon. If the killer was human, would I be as willing? Something inside me whispered "no" and I felt sick to the point of crying.

Now was not the time to have a moral debate with myself, I needed to stay focused. Once we discovered who the killer was, I would deal with my issues then. But maybe…maybe I could ask Jared his thoughts when he got back? Just one question, since he had more experience in the area than I did. One question couldn't hurt…could it?

I leaned forward, covering my eyes with my hand as my elbows rested on my legs. Between my feet sat the water bottles Jared had given me, completely forgotten while I sat and fought with my inner voice. Picking one up I took a large gulp from it, feeling it soothe my throat temporarily. It was better than nothing, I thought.

I stared out the window and watched as the lower the sun got the emptier the streets became. Contemplating, I considered what Dr. Wineman had said in his last class about certain Etheric's being truly evil, no chance of changing. One he mentioned was the mermaid.

For some reason, that made me feel less guilty over killing the siren. Evil was evil, and evil had to be stopped. A weight lifted from my shoulders, thinking with such simplicity. But I knew it wouldn't last forever, soon enough I would start thinking about who was evil and who wasn't; why the Eidolon's were treated so differently than the humans. I wasn't innocent in my thinking about them, despite what I liked to believe.

The Charger's locks clicked open and Jared opened the door, climbing into his seat.

"Okay," he said, "that actually went better than expected." Hope filled my chest and I looked up at him.

"It did? He told you who it is?" As the words left my mouth I knew it was too much to ask, but Jared seemed so positive then, and he was never positive.

"No," he said, pulling out a map from the glove compartment. He had a lot of things in there; a gun, water, a map and more. I wondered how it all fit. "But I think I know where to find it."

"How?" I asked as he stretched the map across the dashboard. Ellengale was displayed in front of me, some tiny side alleys not listed, too small to matter. My street was one of them.

"Bayani was still a little...out of it," he explained, "but he did say something useful. He said it's actually feeding on the women, I couldn't get what it was feeding on, but that's why it's killing." I remained silent, trying not to think of Charlie being a meal to some unholy creature and Jared gave me a sympathetic look, knowing what was on my mind. "So I thought that creatures tend to not stray too far from their nest to feed." Jared pulled out a marker from his pocket and marked down where all the victims were killed.

An "X" over where my street should have been drawn, an "X" over Alex's house, another "X" down Eastport Drive, an "X" on where Rosa had lived and one final "X" over the college. All of them were on the north side of the map, bunched together, except for the college which, remained further to the East.

"Rosa had been taken from The Corner," I mentioned and Jared marked it down. That screwed up the pattern I had noticed; while all the other marks were in the north, the club was towards the south.

"You said you and Luke were in the northern woods when you saw this bat thing, right?" he pointed to the area and I nodded. "Well I asked that disturbingly perky Officer Bunny if there were any houses up there and she said there were a few right about...there." He circled a small clearing on the map in the woods, and finalized it with a triumphant dot.

"Those used to be a camp until it shut down and were sold as cottages," I mentioned, remembering my first and last dreadful summer there. "What exactly does that mean?"

"Those houses are only a twenty minute drive to here," he gestured to the clumped X's by my house, "and the same to here."

Jared pointed at the college with the pen. It wouldn't explain the club, but I kind of got his point.

Rosa had been knocked unconscious and taken back

to her house by a man, John Walker, where she was then killed. If whatever was killing these women had Walker as a partner, then she would still fit the pattern of staying in the north. Something about Jared's theory seemed right.

"Did he tell you anything else?" I asked, just to be sure. If we went into the woods, at night when this thing came out the most, we should at least know what we're up against.

"No," Jared said, "he just kept saying fire would be the only way. Whatever's up there, fire's gonna kill it."

"So should we go there now?" I asked, noting that the streetlights had turned on. I wasn't sure what the protocol was in this kind of situation. Were we supposed to go and get Luke and Richard to help or go at it alone?

"There is no 'we' now," Jared said, reminding me of our last conversation when he said it, "this is way too dangerous. I'm taking you home."

"But I want to go with you," I said. I wanted to find out who it was, who had killed all these women. A part of me understood that it would be dangerous, but I still wanted to go, I had to go.

"You're sick," he told me, "what do you think you're going to do? You look like you're about to pass out." I wasn't sure if he was lying or not, but maybe it was true. I didn't dare check the mirror to see my appearance but just as I was about to start arguing something caught my eye; something in the sky.

High over the town I could make out the familiar figure of a large bat, flying south, just over my apartment. I stared at it, unable to think of what to say when Jared asked, "What?"

To answer I pointed at the figure. It was too dark to see clearly, the moon hidden behind the clouds, but I could see the wings stretch across the sky. As Jared leaned forward to see what I was pointing at the clouds shifted and revealed the moon, just as the creature flew past it, allowing us only a glimpse of what appeared to be a human torso.

"Is that...?" I trailed my sentence off, not sure if I should say "killer" or not. I wanted to though; I could feel the words ready to jump from my tongue.

"Hold on," Jared tore out of the parking lot and headed for the creature in the sky. He didn't seem bothered that we were surrounded by police officers as he broke the speed limit leaving; luckily, they didn't seem to care.

Jared raced down the streets, chasing the flying creature as best he could. I didn't know how he was watching it and the road so well, I could barely focus on finding the creature. As we drove down the darkening roads the thing disappeared, diving suddenly into a residential area.

"Where did it go?" I asked, no trace of it left behind. My heart was thumping loudly in my chest, but it did take my attention away from my fever.

"Somewhere around here," Jared said, scanning the area. Our pace was slow as we travelled down the empty street, looking for any sign of the thing. Jared pulled the car over and clicked his lights off, waiting. I rolled the window down half way, hoping that might help us and it actually did.

Not too far away, I could hear the same clicking I had heard before, the same clicking that Mrs. Weston heard; like fingernails on a hard surface. Being able to focus on it now, it sounded different. I just didn't know *why* it sounded different.

"Where is it coming from?" I questioned, not seeing anything around us. Remembering that Mrs. Weston had said it was on her roof I began to scan the tops of houses. Jared told me to wait in the car as he stepped outside, gun drawn. I followed after him, only to lecture. "You can't shoot it here!"

"Why not?" he asked, narrowing his vision to one house. He took careful steps across the street and I looked up to see what he was looking at. Crawling along the slanted rooftop was what appeared to be a person, with large, bat-like wings extending from their back, ripping through their jacket. Or at least, it was most of a person; it was merely a woman's torso, no legs, nothing from the waist down that I could see at least. I was glad at that moment that it was too dark to see clearly. Whatever it was, it didn't see Jared or me watching it as it climbed over the ledge and peered into a window.

"Someone will hear," I explained, looking around at the black windows, "they'll call for help."

"We'll be gone by then," Jared raised his weapon, aiming at the thing. I rushed to him and grabbed at his wrist, yanking it upwards as he pulled the trigger. The shot echoed through the air and I had to cover my ears again, not able to stand the sound. He shouted at me, the sound muffled, "What the hell are you doing?"

"You can't—" I wanted to tell him that here was not the place to kill this thing but was cut off by a horrifying shriek. The creature's wing had been clipped and it saw us now as it fell towards the ground, only to catch its claws on the bricks. It hung above the front door and all around us lights were coming on. The thing noticed this too and quickly opened its damaged wings and took off over the house, diving back down into the yard behind.

"Get in the car!" Jared yelled at me and took off after the creature on foot. For a brief second I had considered doing as I was told but instead chased after him, only ten feet behind. We ran past the minivan sitting in the driveway and burst through the unlocked fence to the backyard.

All around us were children's toys and play sets. On the far end, sitting against the wooden fence sat a small plastic house, complete with fake flowers sitting atop the fake window ledge. Jared stood in the middle of the yard, careful to not keep his back to anything for too long. Next to him was a large dog house, hopefully without a dog inside and beside it was a swing set and a variety of balls but the creature was nowhere in sight.

"Where is it?" I asked and Jared didn't seem surprised that I had followed him.

"Shh," he said, turning his back to me. He was watching the playhouse, the plastic door open to reveal a blackened interior.

Something shuffled forward inside and I saw blue eyes shimmer in the pale moonlight until the clouds moved again, cloaking the figure in darkness. Whatever it was, it was letting out a laboured breathing, it's long, thin fingers reaching out and clutching either side of the plastic doorway. With a scream, it launched itself at Jared, teeth bared like the siren.

Jared cursed at it and fired his gun, only grazing its arm as the bullet ripped past and lodged into the playhouse. It tackled Jared but he never went down, he lifted the creature under its arms and threw it towards the dog house. It landed face down with a thud at my feet. The bounty hunter's gun had been thrown to me during the brief confrontation and I raced to pick it up just as the back door of the house flung open.

My hand floated over the weapon as I turned to see a man standing there, arm out to keep his wife back. She was pregnant, I could just make out the large bump under her nightgown. When I heard the creature hiss at Jared I whipped my head to around see it.

It lifted itself up with its arms, setting its half body gently on the grass. Blonde hair washed over its shoulders and a business jacket thankfully hid most of its body. Whatever it was, it was female, with skin as grey as stone. If I didn't know any better, I would say she looked a lot like Cindy but the features were too contorted to be certain.

"What the hell is that thing?" the man called out, not really to anyone in particular. "Get in the house!" He pushed his wife back inside and slammed the door, not

279

worried about anyone else. I didn't blame him; he was only protecting his family.

"Get me the gun!" Jared yelled and I looked down at my shaking hand, already holding the weapon. Jared's hand was held out to me, a few meters away and I rushed to him, shoving the gun into his hand.

As he raised it towards the creature she flapped her wings and rose a foot into the air when I heard a deep growling. *What now?*

The creature turned its head, listening to the noise as well when suddenly a Boxer jumped out of the dog house and onto it, tearing into its shoulder. She shrieked again as she clawed at the dog's head, trying to get it off but failing. After a long while she managed to get it off and the dog whimpered, retreating back into its home, its face clawed and bloody. Before Jared could shoot again she flew into the air with another terrifying scream, heading north towards what we had guessed was her nest.

Both Jared and I stared as she flew off until finally the darkness took over her figure and she was gone.

"Did that look like—"

"Yeah," I agreed before he could finish his sentence. Sirens sang in the distance, predicting the coming wave of police and ambulances. "We should go."

We ran back to the car and drove off as quickly as possible. Maybe we would get lucky and nobody had seen us? The husband and wife that lived in the house may have, but I had a feeling they were too focused on the flying torso with wings to look at us. I understood that; ask me what they looked like and the only thing I could say was that she was pregnant.

"Do not do anything like that again!" Jared said, voice raising. "You could have gotten killed."

"Yell at me later," I said, annoyed that he was actually going to lecture me. "We have bigger problems right now. Like that...thing...what was it?"

"I don't know," he admitted and pulled over as three

cop cars raced by, followed by a fire truck. At least they weren't chasing us down, I thought. "But at least we know who it is. Call the doc and make sure he's still at your place, he might know what it is."

I pulled my phone from my pocket and dialled, having a little difficulty with my hand shaking so much. When I found out that he was still in my apartment with Luke we were already pulling into the parking lot below. I didn't tell him what had just happened, but I did tell him we saw the creature and explained what it looked like, briefly mentioning that the woman in the house looked pregnant.

"Oh no," he said and I pictured him covering his eyes, "I know what it is. How could I have not..." Richard grunted in frustration, feeling blind for not realizing sooner. Jared opened the lobby door, allowing me inside first. He kept a hand on my shoulder and I found it comforting, my own hands beginning to calm down.

"We'll be up in a few minutes," I told him when he stopped me. I touched Jared's hand to tell him to stop and he released his grip.

"Don't come up," the doctor instructed, "we'll be coming down." Just as I was about to hang up the phone I heard him ask Luke, "Do you have any salt?"

And with a click the line went dead.

Chapter 29

"We need to hurry," Dr. Wineman said, four bags of salt in his hand. "It may already be too late." He hurried over to Jared's car and we all followed after him when the bounty hunter held my arm.

"She needs to stay here," Jared said, yanking me backwards.

"No, I don't," I argued, knowing he was still right. Richard was at the passenger side door and opened it, causing Jared to be confused. He held up his keys, wondering how the doctor had gotten the door open.

"Yes, you do. How many times will I—"

"We don't have time to argue!" the doctor smacked his hand down on the roof of the Charger, surprising everyone. "We need to go now, I'll explain on the way, just get in the car!" Luke and I headed for the back seat while Jared grumbled to himself, knowing he wasn't going to win this battle.

We drove out at a nerve-racking speed heading towards the forest.

"So what is this thing?" Jared asked, taking the

subject off of me.

"Each of you take one of these," Dr. Wineman handed Luke and I a small bag of salt which we curiously took. I exchanged a look with Luke but he just shrugged his shoulders, not knowing any more than I did. "Take this as well." The doctor handed us each a lighter. I didn't know Luke had any in the apartment; I got the BBQ lighter, easily lit with a switch. Did he know I couldn't use the dollar-store kind? I flicked it on to see if it still worked, having not used it in a while; the orange flame popped out the end with ease and I turned it off.

"What is this for?" I questioned. Bayani had been mentioning fire a lot, to both Cindy and Jared and now the doctor was handing us lighters. Connected? I thought so and it was no wonder the reporter had had him locked up.

"And what the hell is this thing?" Jared looked at the salt bag, skeptical before tossing it back to me. "Hold that." I caught it and set it on the seat next to me.

"This creature is very dangerous," Dr. Wineman said and Jared cut him off.

"No shi—"

"It is called a Manananggal," the doctor interrupted. "It is a vampire-like creature from Philippine folklore which appears as a woman by day but...well you saw the form it hunts in at night."

"A Manananangal?" Luke asked, getting the name wrong.

"A Manananggal," Richard corrected and looked at the bullet necklace around my neck that Bayani had given me, "it means 'one who detaches'. At night it detaches its upper body from its lower once it feels it has found a suitable hiding spot. Where did you get that?"

"I got it from Bayani," I said and looked at everyone around me. "Wait...at night? Charlie was killed during the day."

"I'm aware," Richard said, "it is very unusual for a Manananggal to hunt during the day because it's very dangerous for them. Not only could they be seen they could easily be killed, at least by humans."

"Finally, we're getting to the part I like." Jared pushed harder on the gas pedal as we sped past the downtown shops. Please, let there be no police around. "How can it die?"

"When she separates her torso from her legs," the doctor explained, "she is the most vulnerable; it's the only way she can be killed. Though there are many ways stated in the lore, the best way to kill one is by salting the lower half of the body and lighting it aflame, that way at daybreak she cannot return to human form, killing her. You say Bayani gave that to you?"

"That doesn't sound too difficult," Jared said with a nod of his head.

"Yes," I answered the doctor, ignoring Jared's thoughts, "why?"

"Some areas believed that wearing a bullet necklace would help protect them from the Manananggal." So Bayani had given me the necklace in hopes of protecting me? I thought of him in jail, feeling guilty that I couldn't help him when he was trying to keep me safe; just like he had tried to keep the other's safe. The bullets found at Heather's crime scene must have been there to protect her but they didn't seem to have done any good.

"So we just have to put salt on her legs and...light her on fire? Then it's done?" Luke changed the subject, sensing what I was thinking. I was grateful for that.

"Well," the doctor dashed all our hopes of a solving this quickly with a single word, "normally if one knows where the creature has left its lower half it would not be, but not only do we not know where she is residing, she knows we are coming. Did you shoot her, Jared?"

"Maybe," Jared answered, looking at Richard from the corner of his eye, "why? Is that bad?"

"Possibly," Richard straightened in his seat and looked out the front window, "I was just wondering how upset she will be when we find her."

We made it to the northern woods in just less than ten minutes, which under normal circumstances would be good. Too bad these weren't normal circumstances.

Jared had managed to find the hidden dirt road which led to a row of wooden cabins. Four of them sat against the tree line, facing across a small lake I had never paid much attention to. I had never come this far into the woods in a long time and I had a feeling I never would again. The Charger ground to a halt next to a black SUV in the designated parking area by the cabins. Jared let the car idle for a moment before turning it off, watching the houses.

"You believe her to be in one of these?" Dr. Wineman asked, peering out the front window.

"Yup," Jared said, hands folded over the steering wheel. "These are the only houses around for miles that aren't in town."

"Just because these are the only houses in the area," Richard chided, "doesn't mean she is here. Manananggal's are very clever in hiding their lowers halves."

"No," Jared said, opening his door, "it's here." He stepped out of the vehicle and I did the same. Luke and the doctor soon followed after us. I passed Jared a bag of salt and he slipped it inside his jacket. As we stood the doctor faced away from us and I thought I heard him sniff at the air; my fever was beginning to play tricks on me.

"Which one do we check?" I asked, when suddenly a clicking resonated through the air. It sounded as if the creature was directly behind us. I spun around quickly and got a major head rush, expecting to see her flying down from the trees, claws and teeth ready to tear out our throats. Jared pushed me behind him and drew his gun, preparing to fire but there was nothing there.

"Calm down," Richard said as he turned to us, "it is not close by."

"Are you kidding me?" Jared laughed. "It sounds like

it's right beside us."

"It is a trick," the doctor informed, "the closer it sounds the further away it is; the quieter the *tick-tick* the closer it is. You wounding her must have slowed her down, otherwise she would be here by now." Jared set his gun in its holster, still watching the trees.

"Then let's find her better half before she gets back," Jared turned and headed for the first house, pulling me along at his heels. "We'll check here, you two check that side."

"Wait," Luke stopped us and we turned to face him, the temperature lowering fast, "I'll stay with Liv."

"She'll stay with me," Jared started us walking, "she tends to attract these things so I'd like to be nearby when it happens."

"When what happens?" I asked as we made it to the door of the first cabin.

"I don't know, but something always happens when you're around." Jared pushed me to the right and swung the wooden door open, quickly drawing his gun. As I kept my back to the cabin I watched Luke reluctantly follow Dr. Wineman to the house opposite us, his eyes refusing to leave me alone. All of the houses were black so we had no way of telling which one would hold the creatures legs. He gave me a gentle shove and said, "C'mon."

I stepped inside the darkened house after Jared, scarcely able to make out the rustic furniture in the front room. As I reached to turn on a light for better visibility Jared grabbed my wrist. I apologized, realizing my mistake. It wouldn't be very smart to turn a light on, if they were all supposed to be off.

Jared took the lead, hopping around corners with weapon at the ready. As I trailed behind him I kept my finger on the trigger of the lighter, bag of salt clutched in my other hand. We made our way through the cabin; living room, kitchen, bathroom and finally the bedroom. All of them were empty, no lower bodies hiding anywhere.

"Not here," Jared said as I walked past the bedroom window. The clicking sounded far away now, at least further than it had been. Was the creature near us then? Was she waiting just outside? Suddenly the clicking stopped and a light flicked on in the cabin next to us.

"Jared," I said, just as he was about to leave the room. He came towards me and pulled me to the floorboards, allowing us to peer over the ledge into the other house.

We were looking into the living room of the other cabin just as Cindy Hart walked across to the bookshelf. I gave Jared a knowing look and found he was giving me the same; so the Manananggal was Cindy. She looked normal now, completely human, not even hinting at the stone-skinned creature she had been twenty minutes ago. She picked a book from the shelf and began to leaf through it when Jared tapped my shoulder, telling me we were leaving. What bothered me though was that she didn't seem upset, was she not expecting us to find her? She didn't even have any wounds on her; her clothes perfectly intact. Maybe it was best that Cindy believed herself to be safe, that way we could take her by surprise…

"She's attached," I whisper to Jared through the black, "how are we supposed to…" My voice trailed off; I didn't want to say it. I didn't even want to think about how Luke would react.

"Let's find the doc and figure it out," Jared led me out the front door and into the evening air. As my foot touched the earth below I saw Luke and Dr. Wineman leave the cabin kitty corner to us. While we had searched one place, they had already finished with two. Was I slowing Jared down? I pursed my lips and looked around, noticing a different light was on the cabin next to us.

"We didn't find anything," Luke declared as they met us outside the last house. "It's in there then?" I could still hear the clicking, but it now sounded as far away as it could be. Cindy was just inside the house and the constant clicking was just a reminder.

"She's...reattached herself," Jared told them, "what now?"

"We'll need her to detach again then," Richard touched stroked his chin, "perhaps if we confront her she'll detach in desperation."

"Good enough for me," Jared suddenly turned and walked up to the cabin door. In one swift movement he had his gun out and kicked down the wooden door, splintering the frame by the handle. He dashed inside, leaving the rest of us outside, mouths agape.

We made it inside in time to see him pointing his gun at Cindy, whose eyes were wide with fear, hands in the air.

"L-Luke?" she asked when we walked into the living room. "What are you doing here?"

"Cindy?" Luke asked, eyes growing just as wide. He looked hurt to see her. "You're the killer?"

"Me?" she pointed at herself, leaving her hands in the air as Jared's arm stiffened. I could see his fingers growing tense by the trigger, anticipating the shot when Dr. Wineman cut in.

"Don't Jared!" he yelled, being smart enough to not swat at Jared's hands. "She's human."

"How do you know that?" he said back, keeping aim on Cindy.

"I'm not the killer," Cindy pleaded but Jared wasn't about to listen to her.

"That's what they all say."

"Please," the doctor said, waving his hands for Jared to put the gun away, "trust me, she's human. But this is where the creature resides, I can s—I can tell." The bounty hunter eyed Richard, debating on whether he should believe him. Eventually he put his gun away and Cindy lowered her arms, releasing the breath she had been holding. I did the same, not realizing I had stopped.

"What are you doing here?" I asked her, curious. If she wasn't the killer, then why would she be inside the cabin? Cindy leaned over, hands on her knees as she tried to calm down. I guessed she had never had a gun pointed at her. Did I react like that after first meeting Jared?

"I was,"—she straightened her back, able to breathe again—"I was going to have a drink with a friend, but she said she'd be late so I should just let myself in."

"Who's your friend?" Richard asked before I could. Cindy gave us a confused look, as if we should know whose house we had broken into. Well, we had thought it was her but now...

"It's—" Cindy flew forward, the boards beneath her feet lifting with a great force to reveal a hidden stairway. Jared caught her before she fell as a man lunged out from the opening. The reporter spun backwards beside me when Jared threw her aside and pulled his gun again.

"Who's that?" he asked but none of us spoke. The man in front of us was John Walker; middle aged but still quite muscular, he could clearly hold his own in a fight. He was the very same man that had assaulted Rosa in the parking lot of The Corner and taken her home to die. As he watched us in silence his eyes seemed distant, as if he was sleepwalking.

"Oh, right," the doctor said with a nervous laugh, "I forgot to mention something."

"Which is?"

"Manananggal's tend to collect men," he explained, "they are put into a trance and used as...slaves of sorts, to protect the lower half of the creature while she hunts." Then that was why he had kidnapped Rosa; he delivered her to the Manananggal to be killed.

"You couldn't have said something sooner Doctor?" Luke asked, staying on his toes should Walker lunge at us. I agreed, this was something that should've been mentioned. But we had left in a hurry...

Richard apologized and said, "Her other half must be down there. Quickly, before she returns." Surprisingly, Jared put down his gun.

"Now I don't want to hurt you," he said to the man, "but we need to get down there."

"I won't let you through," the man told us, "I won't let you hurt her." There was look of love in his eye that disturbed me. He was compelled to protect her and I wondered how long he had been in the cellar. Was someone missing him? If we managed to kill the creature, would he be okay? Even if he came to his senses he was wanted for kidnapping and as a possible partner for the murders.

"Okay," Jared turned to us, "I'll deal with this guy, you find the legs." He passed me his bag of salt from his jacket and began stretching his arms. Lunging forward, Jared tackled the man to the ground. As I looked over to Cindy I could see she still didn't understand what was going on. Jared yelled, "Get going!"

The battle between Jared and John covered the distant clicking I heard as they fought their way into the other room and out of sight. I saw Luke walk over to the window, picking up a picture frame but I couldn't see what he was looking at. What I saw behind him, through the glare of the yellow lights, was the face of the Manananggal. She was surrounded by black as she pressed against the glass, her grey skin illuminated and eyes glaring at us.

"Luke!" I called out but it was too late, the creature broke through the window and they fell to the ground with inhuman screeching, wings beating the air. The frame Luke had been holding flew across the room and crashed near the battling men.

"What is that?" Cindy screamed, her usual calm voice gone. She was now looking at what was most likely her friend, or...half of her friend attacking a man; the same man she had once accused of being a killer.

"Hurry down to the cellar," the doctor turned to me, eyes changing to a deep fuchsia, his bones sharpening, "find the legs and burn them. Now go!" He removed his glasses and handed them to the reporter, she took them, eyes never leaving the creature.

"Oh my God," she whispered as the doctor approached the creature. I didn't stay to watch, knowing that if I continued to look at Luke I would try to help him. I spun around and headed for the cellar, choosing to trust the doctor, despite everything.

When I reached to the top of the stairs I caught a glimpse of Richard, kindly doctor and professor, throwing the Manananggal off of Luke and into the kitchen. I glanced down into the darkness below, not wanting to go down without any visibility or go alone for that matter.

"I think it's time you fought someone stronger than you," Richard said to the creature, slowly walking towards it. He moved swiftly, his footsteps making no noise; a predator preparing for the kill. Behind me Jared touched my shoulder and I almost screamed.

"C'mon," he said, covered in blood and quickly forming bruises. He walked down the stairs first, pulling me by the wrist. "Watch your step." As I walked down everything was gone, no light at all to give me sight. I touched my foot down hard on the earthen floor, expecting another step.

The fight upstairs was quiet, barely any sound getting down to us. I felt Jared turn to me.

"Got that lighter? You might want to turn it on," he reached into his pocket and pulled out his own, trying to flick it on.

I did the same with my long one until the familiar *fwoosh* yielded flame. I looked up at Jared and froze.

"What?" Jared breathed.

My eyes fell behind him, the fire not only illuminating us, but also another face behind him. Another of the creatures slaves watched us, silent with a deadly glare.

"Um..." I said, not sure how to tell him. Jared caught on as he created another fire in his hands. Eyelids low he sighed, blowing out his lighter.

"There's someone behind me, isn't there?" I nodded,

trying to stay calm. Jared whipped away some of the blood on his face and whipped around, attacking the man. I could tell he was tired, his movements slower now. "Find the legs!"

Squinting around the cellar I couldn't see anything. Finding the legs was easier said than done, especially when I kept thinking about whether or not there was someone else down here. Jared led the man to my left so I went right, sticking the flame in front of me to light my way. It was a cellar, so it couldn't be that big, could it? But then again, cabins didn't normally come with cellars, did they?

I found my way to the wall, touching it for support. The grey masonry was cool to the touch and caked with dirt as I ran my hand along it. I heard Jared cry out in pain and I remained motionless.

"Jared?" I called out after hearing someone hit the ground, my chest feeling like a drum set.

"I'm fine," he groaned, "he's down. Find the legs yet?"

"No," my heart calmed down knowing he was safe. I continued following the wall when I saw Jared light another fire and begin searching. We each wandered down opposite walls when my foot caught on something on the ground. The lighter dropped from my hand, going out as it hit the floor. "Ah."

I kneeled down the find it and as my hand searched the earth I bumped into something solid. Wrenching backwards I touched the lighter and quickly flicked it on to see what I was near. I lit up a pair of feet, dressed in conservative black pumps; the legs.

"You found them I see," Jared said as I stood. My eyes followed the light upwards till finally it showed me the purple cloth which covered the creature's lower half. Jared pointed me to the stairs. "Look that way."

"What?" He grabbed my shoulders and forced me to look the other way.

"You probably don't want to see what's under this," I

heard him remove the cloth and listened as it crumpled to the ground. Unzipping the bag of salt he poured it over the legs. A shriek erupted from upstairs, and something came crashing down; the Manananggal.

"No!" she screamed, springing towards us. Jared pulled me out of the way in time, the creature attacking her own body with another scream. My lighter stayed on as my eyes watched her skin sizzle and smoke. The salt was burning her!

"Liv!" Luke called to me from atop the stairs.

"Come back up here!" Richard cut in. "Now!" Jared ripped the lighter from my hand and set the creatures skirt on fire. The flame engulfed her lower half in an instant as she cried out, her wings catching fire. He pushed me towards the stairs, the light pouring over them like halo.

We ran for it and I made it halfway up them when I turned to find Jared wasn't behind me. He was a few feet away, pulling the second slave to safety. I hadn't even thought about him.

The Manananggal hissed, her tongue shooting out; it was like a needle as it cut through the air and I didn't want to think of its purpose. She dove for Jared, slashing at his chest. She hit him down and he drew his gun, firing one shot. I didn't even cover my ears as the sound rang through the cellar, growing louder with each echo; I was too busy staring at the blood on Jared's chest.

"Liv!" Luke grabbed my arm and heaved me the up the rest of the stairs. He gave me a hug and I actually pushed him away, trying to return to the darkness below. I stopped and moved out of the way when I saw Jared dragging the unconscious slave out.

"Are you okay?" I asked, looking at his wound. He was coated in blood and dirt, the Manananggal had clawed right through his jacket.

"Just a scratch," he breathed and brought the man away from the doorway downstairs; I somehow doubted his words. Richard slammed the wooden slab shut and ordered us to move. He walked over to the bookcase, eyes still glowing pink, and threw it down. Seconds before it hit, the hidden door came up, giving me a glance of the creature, desperate to escape, and brightly lit with flames. It slammed down, books shooting away in all directions.

"I thought you said she would die after the salt and burning," Luke questioned, careful to watch the bookshelf as it jumped up a bit; the creature was still trying to get out but her cries were muffled by the floor. The shelf was too heavy for her to move and she eventually gave up. At least, I was hoping the fact that she was on fire distracted her.

"She will die at sunup," Richard said, his eyes returning to their normal colour, "she will not be able to reattach now." He patted Luke on the shoulder to reassure him. Across the room Cindy fell backwards onto the couch, eyes lost and mouth open.

"Wh…what? She…she was the killer?" she asked. She couldn't comprehend what her friend had done. Richard sat down next to her and I caught her flinch. "Why? Why would she kill them?"

I wanted to know that too.

"She fed off of them," the doctor said, putting a hand on her shoulder, "she was a monster doing what was in her nature. She was the predator and they were her prey." I didn't like how simple he made it seem.

"But…what was she feeding on? They didn't even release the cause of death!"

"She fed on the hearts of their unborn children," Richard sounded as if he wasn't sure if he should say it or not, "and their blood."

"She was my friend," Cindy sniffed. I understood her pain, but at least I was able to feel the relief of knowing my friend was innocent while hers was a killer. Seeing her reaction now though…it made me feel as if something was wrong with me. While she was horrified and frozen…I broke into crime scenes and teamed up with bounty hunters. Yet I still felt what I did was what I was supposed to do. Cindy whimpered, "She was my friend."

Cindy covered her face as the doctor continued to try and calm her down. Nothing would work though, not after what had just happened. I faced Jared and stepped forward, hearing glass crunch beneath my foot. Kneeling down I picked up the picture Luke had been looking at seconds before he was attacked; I remembered who the killer was, seeing her again in the photograph.

"The weather girl?" I asked aloud. Jared came closer to me and peered at the picture. Luke nodded at me, confirming my theory but what he didn't know was how I was finally able to put the puzzle together. My knees weakened with my realization and Jared was the first to catch me, helping me sit down on the leather chair against the wall.

I didn't recognize her solely from the news; I had seen her in real life. When we had gone to the club with Charlie and her friends I had seen her there, I had stolen a seat from her. I had seen her after Charlie was murdered too, bumping into her in the parking lot while trying to escape Jared. That was how she had found the women so easily and that was who Charlie mentioned in her diary. Not only did she kill these women, she had stalked them, waiting for the perfect time to strike.

That was it, the mystery solved and she would never hurt anyone again.

I glanced at the clock on the wall; there was still a lot of time until the sun rose.

"Do you hear that?" Luke asked, cocking his head to one side. Jared and I listened when suddenly there were sirens in the distance, coming closer with each passing second. "What are they doing here?"

Somebody shuffled behind us and I heard Jared curse. Turning I saw a man run out the back door, cell phone in hand. There was a third man in the house and he did the only thing he knew how to when he was in danger;

he called the police. Nobody chased after him.

"We need to go, now." Jared snatched me from the chair and began to take me to the Charger, Luke in tow.

"No," Richard said, raising a hand to stop Jared but withdrawing, remembering the gash he had on his chest, "I'll go, but you need to stay."

"Why would we stay?" Jared barked and kept moving, out the front door. The air felt so good on my face as it burned under the moonlight.

"Jared," the doctor grabbed his shoulder and spun him around as he let go of my arm. "You need to stay here with the others and speak with the police."

"I need to stay here with the others," Jared repeated, his voice distant. What just happened? Before I could ask the doctor was gone, vanished into the ether. Luke and I searched the area but there was no sign of Richard; he had left us, just as the first police car rushed up and halted.

The officers jumped out and drew their guns, aimed at us while Jared stood, still staring at where the doctor had been.

Chapter 30

Officer Harley sat down next to me on the steps of the police station with a very obvious sigh. He rubbed the stubble coming in on his chin, neither of us saying anything. I played with my hands in my lap, never making eye contact with him, too worried to think straight.

"Could you just tell us what happened?" he finally asked, not looking at me. "You aren't in any trouble but we need to know what happened."

So what had happened exactly? Should I mention how Dr. Wineman had left us in the woods, leaving Jared and Luke to take the blame? Was I supposed to say how Cindy was a wreck and unable to speak after what she had seen, her state nearly catatonic? Or maybe I should just tell them how we had hunted down a Manananggal and killed her? The sun was beginning to rise over the trees and the Manananggal was officially dead, the cops having found her body cut in half and almost in ashes in the cellar. Her body looked human, and nothing I could say would make this look like anything other than a grisly murder.

"I want to talk to them," I said, still staring down at my hands.

"You know that can't happen," Harley said with another sigh. This wasn't the first time he had tried talking to me; when I had been placed in the back of his cruiser he had tried getting information from me. I didn't say anything, not knowing what I was supposed to do. I wanted to ask Jared what I was supposed to do…

Hugging my arms to my chest I shifted away from the officer. I was told how lucky I was to not be dead, since they had mistaken me for a victim. As of right now they believed Luke and Jared to be the killers, well, along with the two slaves. Most of the cops seemed to think that anyway. After I had been "saved" and taken to the hospital Det. Young had come to talk to me, and tell me everything would be all right. Somehow, I doubted it would be. His kind manner disturbed me then.

"They found the woman's body," Harley told me, "and they have a witness saying your friends killed her. If you don't tell them what happened, they'll go to jail." Interesting, I thought, he wasn't saying "we".

"You know they didn't do it," I said, the sun coming over the rooftops just enough to blind me. I took my cell phone out and dialled for the doctor; it was my thirteenth time that night. It went right to voice mail and I immediately hung up. How could he leave us, just like that?

"Liv," came a voice in front of me. I looked up to find Richard standing there, four men in black overcoats behind him. "Please come with me."

"Doctor," Officer Harley said as he stood, a strange respect in his voice, "it's good to see you again." Dr. Wineman gave us both a sympathetic smile. He held his hand out to me but I remained motionless, watching as three of the mysterious men walk into the police station.

"Who are they?" I asked, trying to make sense of everything.

"They are here to retrieve Luke and Jared," Richard stepped towards me, hand still outstretched. I pushed myself up from the stairs, ignoring his offer.

"What do you mean?" Harley asked before I could. My eyes kept on the fourth man behind the doctor. With the rising sun behind him I couldn't see his features, he wore a hat low over his eyes but I felt like he was looking back at me. Something about him seemed rather...menacing.

"Leave," he said, his voice deep with...something. Something otherworldly, something...old. Without another word the officer left.

"Was that necessary?" Richard asked him, concerned.

"This has gotten too far out of hand," the man said, "you and Azazel should not have gotten involved." He came forward and it took most of what little strength I had left to remain where I was. He didn't seem to like that I didn't back down. "You are a pest."

I furrowed my brow, unable to respond. What had I done to make him so upset? What had I done to deserve such attitude?

"Please," the doctor said, trying to calm the situation down, "it is not her fault."

"What isn't my fault?"

"Nothing," the man said, his tone dark. "Now leave." I didn't move, but I felt the urge to as the cloaked person walked by. He was shrouded in...something. Something that made me think he was an Eidolon. Once he was out of earshot the doctor's eyes met with mine.

"I'm very sorry," he said, "members of the council do not like humans very much. Especially when they get involved with purebloods. Could you come with me?"

"Why? Who was that?" I didn't want to go anywhere with him, not now. I wanted to see Luke. I wanted to see Jared.

"Please, I understand that you're upset with me," Dr. Wineman pleaded, "but it was necessary if you wanted them to be released. And they will be, but it will take some time for the council to free them."

"Then I'll be right here when they get out," I sat myself back down on the concrete steps, determined to win. I couldn't leave now; I wasn't even going to think about how high my fever was, or how thirsty I was. The only thing I would think about now was Luke and Jared. The doctor sat down next to me with a sigh, just as Officer Harley had. I asked, "What's the council?"

"Those were some of the junior members of the Shadeland Council," Richard said without much prodding, "they're here to get Luke out of jail and are including Jared in that, as a favour to me." He didn't sound happy that they were doing him a favour; maybe because it was something similar to Yamuna and her "deals"?

But those were members of the council? The very same council members that went to the world leaders to expose themselves? No wonder there were riots. Seeing them now, feeling their presence...was that how the other humans felt around all Eidolon's?

"Why? What do they care about Luke?" I thought I knew the answer but wanted to make sure.

"He's a pureblood," the doctor rested his arms on his knees, "and purebloods protect their own kind."

So that was it, then? After everything that had happened in the past two weeks, they were just going to swoop in and save the day? No, that wasn't right. That wasn't *fair*.

"Why didn't they help sooner?" I laughed bitterly, thinking about how simple everything would have been if they had. Jared wouldn't have turned to stone, Luke would have never been reported as the killer and Violet never would have made a deal with Yamuna. It wasn't right, how they were only just coming into the picture. A lot of lives could have been saved, or at least salvaged if they had come sooner.

"Because they don't care about humans," Richard

said, "until now the only victims were human. Now with Luke about to be convicted for murder they decided to step in. An Eidolon pureblood on trial for such publicized murders wouldn't *reflect* well on them."

"So that's it then?" I asked. "The Manananggal is dead now and Luke will walk free because it might make the council look bad?"

"Yes." We sat there, thinking and watched as the sun continued to rise. People began to come out of their houses, walking their dogs and heading to work. Nobody paid any attention to us, not even the cops walking in and out of the station.

"What are you?" I asked, breaking down. That was something else I couldn't figure out; I didn't even have an inkling as to what kind of Eidolon he was.

"I'm a pureblood," Richard answered, avoiding the true answer.

"I know, but *what* are you?" He turned to me.

"Does it matter?" I considered it.

"I suppose not."

An hour passed by before the four council members walked back out of the police station, Luke and Jared behind them. I jumped to my feet and grabbed hold of Luke, wrapping my arms around his slender frame.

"Are you okay?" I asked and he said he was fine. When I finally let him go I turned to Jared, busy glaring at the men who had just released him. "Jared?"

"I'm fine," he answered. Dried blood covered him head to toe, a black eye freshly formed. Some bandages were visible beneath his torn shirt and he quickly zipped up his jacket to cover them; it just barely did the job, being torn as well. "If you'll excuse me, I need to get paid."

As he walked off down the street I opened my mouth to say something, anything. But my voice was gone, no words coming to me. I wanted to ask if I would ever see him again but I knew I didn't want the answer. Luke and Richard watched me struggle but never said anything themselves. I stared down the street until Jared was out of view, just like that. No goodbye, nothing. Violet was right; I was just another girl in another town that he would forget about. Why did I care so much?

My head began to throb and my bones ached, the night finally catching up with me. The edges of my vision began to darken and I heard someone calling my name, faintly, as if it echoing through a cave. Everything went black.

Chapter 31

I awoke to find myself in my room, Luke sitting next to me on the bed, reading a book. When I shuffled to face him he turned to me with a smile.

"Hey," he said, pushing the hair out of my eyes, "how're you feeling?"

"Sick," I said, my voice was hoarse, causing a burning sensation to ignite in my throat. "What happened?"

"You fainted," Luke explained as he marked where he was in his book.

"Have you talked to Jared?" I asked, not able to avoid the question. He had just left, without even saying he would be back. I wanted to see him again, even if it was just to say "thanks". Somehow, I knew even that would be asking too much.

"He's gone, Liv," Luke said, his eyes dimmed. "He called and said something about a job in Florida."

Something inside me broke and I looked away from my lifelong friend, knowing he could read my mind without using his abilities. He touched my hand and I pulled away, guilty and lost over my feelings. Maybe if I found Violet I could find a way to contact him…

"Can you get me some water?" I asked, needing him to leave the room.

"Sure," he said and reached down to feel my forehead, "and maybe a couple more aspirin."

"Thanks," I said and he walked out of my room. I listened to his footsteps down the hall and I quickly picked my phone from the nightstand. Scrolling down my contacts I found Jared's name was still in there. I opened a text box and typed a simple "Thanks" inside. Staring down at the letters, I wanted to add more but found I didn't know what words to use. If I asked him to stay for just a little longer would he? But what did it matter to me if he stayed or left? I clicked *send* and began to think what I might do should he reply. My eyes stared at his name until I couldn't do it anymore; choosing to look at the positive.

I leaned back in bed and basked in my temporary peace of mind that everything was okay. Luke was out and that was all that mattered. My phone suddenly beeped and it made my heart skip two beats. I checked it and saw that it was from Jared, my heart couldn't handle what I read: *I'll be in touch.*

That meant Jared would be coming back; that meant I would get to see him again. I thought that was what other girls must've felt like when they had a crush on someone; it was an amazing feeling. But that bliss only lasted for a second when I heard a dusky voice next to me.

"You are weak," said the councilman from my window. I shot up to see him leaning against the ledge, arms crossed with his fedora covering most of his face. "Human's hearts are so fragile, just like the Fae." He sounded disgusted.

"Why are you here?" was all I could think to ask. He glanced at the open door and with a flick of his wrist it shut, locking Luke outside, or more likely, me inside.

"To give you this," he reached into his jacket and I

flinched, making him smirk. When his hand came out he revealed a small grey kitten, frantically swinging its legs for freedom. The councilman tossed it at me; I barely managed to catch it.

"A cat?" I asked, confused.

"That is Azazel," he explained, with an expression that made me feel as if he was talking down to me, as if to say "stupid human". "We bound him to this form, as punishment."

"Why?" I held Azazel in my hands as he hissed at the pureblood, tiny claws slashing at the air. A white collar dangled around his neck with a strange charm attached. I couldn't make out what it was, not with the councilman standing there.

"He loves humans so much, he can stay with them. And now he can never leave." The councilman smiled and straightened his back, hearing Luke coming back down the hallway.

"What—" I began, listening as Luke searched the bathroom cabinet for the aspirin.

"You are weak," the councilman said again. He disappeared into the Ether but I heard his voice resonate through the room, the hair on my arms rising from the sinister echo. "The Clan will make quick work of you."

Fenridge: Book Two of The Ethereal Crossings

Send to: Jared
From: Liv
Message: Liv needs help. Something's wrong with her, and she might not survive. - Luke

ABOUT THE AUTHOR

D.L. Miles graduated from Sheridan College and currently resides in Southern Ontario. She loves playing World of Warcraft and Halo, and is far too attached to fictional characters. You can find her online and discover her other novels at...

dlmilesbooks.wordpress.com
@somethingofdev
facebook.com/somethingofdev

21002871R00169

Made in the USA
Charleston, SC
02 August 2013